ISAAC UNKNOWN

Book 1

By

James McFadden

ISAAC UNKNOWN
BOOK 1

Copyright © 2023 James McFadden

ISBN (print): 979-8-88993-022-8
ISBN (e-book): 979-8-88993-021-1
Library of Congress Control Number (print): 2025931339

Written by James McFadden
Edited by Joi Massat

Published 2025 by MoonQuill
Arlington, VA
www.moonquill.com

TABLE OF CONTENTS

The Ebola Cowboy 1

Instinctual Remnants 17

The Demon and the King 27

The Pony and the Twins 36

Arrangement 47

The Head Librarian 52

Sixteen-Point Elder Tick 56

The Great Vampire Hunt 66

The Bubba 77

Mabahazi the Magnificent 88

The Belial Fly 92

The Automaton 101

The Iron Ambassador 108

The New Voice 118

The Gleamstress and the Cat 122

Scissors and Scarves 129

The Witch Hunters 134

With Teeth 141

The Shanty of Madness 150

The Dipshit in the Pit 159

At Home with the Cannibal Clan 165

Momma Unleashed 174

The Jug Plan 182

The Slow and the Curious..188

Fire and Ice 196

Reflective Reunion 204

The Hall of Chains 210

The Reliquary 218

The Fine Art of Skinning...227

The Journal of Ublesh 234

B-Movie Mania...244

The Faux Apprentice 252

Pandemonium 261

The Gorgon...271

Boiling Blood...284

The Red Wastes 290

Chapter 1
THE EBOLA COWBOY

The dogs would have been ideal travel companions if not for the stench of decay. They didn't pant. They didn't bark. Except for the occasional twitch, they barely even moved.

Two were Rottweilers, brutish and scarred from lives of guarding fields of junk and scrap. The pair had been deemed unfit for adoption when their owner shut down his business and abandoned them. The third was a mastiff, a former family pet who committed the crime of aging; the canine was so large that it had to lie prone in the station wagon's cargo bed. The same veterinarian euthanized all three and made a profitable side venture of selling such carcasses when people like Isaac came calling.

Isaac adjusted the rearview mirror and glanced back at the animals. He wasn't sure why they moved, but they did—a turn of the head, a subtle shift of weight. The life-force-sharing spell he used to reanimate them should have rendered them incapable of independence. Every motion from them was like an IV drip from his vitality, and he didn't need them to waste it. He checked on them often, ready to scold. Isaac couldn't afford to grow more fatigued because one of them suddenly remembered how to lick its own balls.

He grew anxious under the gaze of their dead eyes. When he turned the mirror away, Isaac caught a glimpse of his reflection. While he wasn't the most robust-looking individual on his best day, the spell had taken a toll on him. His fair skin was pale, and his wavy hair lay flat and lifeless against his scalp. Even his beard seemed thin, like it lacked the strength to keep growing. He looked like a man coming off a week-long bender.

It was clear that he had overextended himself, which was why his original plan had only called for the two Rottweilers. Even after the vet had offered up the mastiff, Isaac had been resistant to the idea until he read the ID tag on the dog's collar. *General.* It seemed too fortuitous. He couldn't pass up the chance to have a pony-sized beast with such a fitting name lead his undead pack. Now he was paying the price.

The Sonoran Desert sped by outside the car's windows. The setting sun cast a red glow across the sand and the towering saguaro cacti. Only a few minutes from his destination, he pulled off onto the next dirt road.

On the passenger seat lay a weathered leather satchel. He undid the clasp and removed a small paintbrush and a sealed glass jar. He held the jar up, allowing the dying sunlight to reflect through it. The contents resembled cereal soaking in a yellowish liquid. He shook the jar, opened it, dipped the brush, turned to the animals in the back, and said, "Smile."

The dogs curled their lips back in a silent snarl.

* * *

The sun had set when Isaac pulled into the rocky parking lot. He stared in dismay at the ramshackle bar with its boarded-up windows. Most people would assume the place was abandoned if not for the flickering fluorescent over the battered front door. Someone had painted *The Devil's Hole* in sloppy red letters next to the entrance in lieu of a sign.

"Yeesh, I wonder which hole. Maybe an unholy combo of them all," Isaac joked to his undead audience, and then he sighed at their predictable response. He supposed he could command them to bark happily at his quips, but that would be too self-indulging.

A rusty jeep and five motorcycles occupied the lot. Isaac didn't know much about bikes, but he recognized that these were serious machines. Not the Japanese racers that college kids rode. No. These were Harleys, covered in dust from traversing the desert roads.

He stepped out of the car, and the cool air washed across his face. It stirred him up a little and made him forget his weakness for a moment. The stars glittered, and the full moon shone, but neither did much to alleviate the absolute darkness of the desert night.

Isaac glanced up and down the road. No headlights. Even so, lingering didn't seem an intelligent option. Following his command, each dog lumbered out of the car and sat down to face him. They sat in a row, staring silently, with the Rottweilers on either side of the mastiff—two soldiers flanking the general. For a moment, Isaac felt a little guilty using them in such a manner. Despite reanimated corpses being boring traveling companions, he had become oddly attached to them. Didn't say much about his social skills, he supposed.

He whispered, and they responded by disappearing into the desert.

Feeling strangely alone, Isaac hefted his satchel over his shoulder and headed for The Devil's Hole. As he passed the first motorcycle, he noticed the colorful design printed on its leather saddlebag. It was the devil—the old-school bright-red man with horns, a forked tail, and a black pointy beard—riding a motorcycle with flaming wheels. A pitchfork lay across the handlebars, aimed like a jouster's lance. The words *Asphalt Devils* were stitched above the design, and *The Highway to Hell is Anywhere We Ride* scripted below. Isaac looked from the emblem to the spray-painted sign.

"Shit," he whispered. The last thing he needed to contend with was a biker gang. He naturally assumed he'd stand out in this craphole, but it seemed definitive now. He'd never heard of the Asphalt Devils, but their lack of notoriety probably signaled inferiority complexes. At least the motorcycles gave him an adequate headcount. He pushed open the door and wrinkled his nose as a wave of body odor washed over him.

Isaac had seen movies where a stranger walked into a bar and the locals all stopped what they were doing to stare, but it had never actually happened to him. He'd spent days without a shower, crossing the country with three dead dogs, and he *still* wasn't scuzzy enough for this place.

There were five bikers and a bartender—all froze and eyeballed him. Had this been an Old West saloon, the piano player would have stopped, and the ensuing silence would have made this even more uncomfortable. At least the jukebox remained mindless enough to keep playing.

He nodded at them. It was the lowest-key, manliest greeting he could think of, and completely for naught, as no one acknowledged it.

Isaac took a seat on one of the rickety barstools, wondering briefly if it would even support his weight. The bartender, a portly man with a terrible comb-over, stared at him while repeatedly wiping the same glass but not making it any cleaner. Finally, seeing that Isaac was just going to sit there and smile politely, he asked, "Yeah?"

"A beer and a whiskey chaser."

The bartender poured a shot from a bottle Isaac had never heard of and pulled a semi-chilled beer from the cooler. He carelessly plunked them down, whiskey sloshing out of the glass. "You sure you want to drink here? You look a little... *clean* for this place."

"You think? Even with my stubble?" Isaac rubbed his chin. "Actually, I come in here all the time. Well, I used to. Not too long ago, I was a regular."

"That so? I've run this place for ten years and don't remember you. And I'm really good with faces."

Isaac nearly said something about him not being really good with his own face, but choked it down with a sip of watery whiskey. "You got me. Never been here before. But you got such good online reviews." Isaac held the shot glass up. "I had to check it out."

This should have forced a smile onto the bartender's face, but he didn't seem capable of any emotion other than irritation. "Fine. Whatever. I'm not going to complain about people spending money here. Just watch yourself and mind your own business. But don't be surprised if I'm mopping up your blood at the end of the night."

"Oh, I'll help you with that. After all, it'd be my mess, right?"

The bartender snorted and, having had enough of their banter, walked away. For a few moments, Isaac sat in silence. The crack of the billiards blended into the country music, which melded into the loud jabbering of the bikers, creating a cacophony of redneck clamoring. He managed to stifle it all in his head by focusing on the drinks in front of him, hoping to wait thoughtlessly until his associate arrived. And he had just about managed it until someone tapped him on the shoulder. It was a rough poke, one that said, "Give me your attention now," as opposed to "Excuse me, good sir."

One of the bikers stood there, a drunken grin on his face. He wore a blood-red bandana, which held back his long stringy hair, and a dark pair of sunglasses. Isaac wondered how the man saw anything in the dim place. An Asphalt Devil patch was on the right breast of his leather jacket.

"You're not from around here."

Isaac—not sure how to respond—shook his head, then nodded, then did a combo shake-nod.

"We figured you weren't."

"I bet there's a lot of figuring going on in here." Isaac looked over the man's shoulder at his seated comrades.

One biker looked like a skid-row Santa Claus, with a long gray beard and a body so wide he must have needed two motorcycles strapped together. The second was an intimidating fellow. Even seated, he was a giant of a man. His beard and hair were trimmed short and neat, probably so no one could grab them in a fight. Whereas the other Devils all wore smug grins, he simply had a cold, hard stare like there was nothing in this world worth smiling about. Isaac glanced over his other shoulder at the pool players. Their game had slowed, and in between turns, they watched Isaac's interaction with the same smirk Bandana Man wore.

"What's that you said?"

"I was just saying good guess. I'm not from around here."

"Just like we figured," he said again, and Isaac nearly rolled his eyes. "We don't get a lot of strangers out here. It's part of the point of having a bar in the middle of nowhere. Now, we sometimes extend an invite to other bikers, even truckers, but you don't look much like either."

Isaac feigned surprise. "Really? Well, my bike's in the shop. But I'm a trucker. No. Wait. Biker. I'm a biker."

"That so? What're your colors?" the biker asked, clearly wondering how far Isaac would take this lie.

"Huh? I'm a White guy."

"No, asshole. Who do you ride with?"

"The Flying Wombats. Out of Pittsburgh."

"The Wombats?"

"Yep."

"What the fuck is a wombat?"

Isaac thought about telling the truth but opted for something cooler. "A breed of giant vampire bat."

The bartender, positioned at the other end of the bar with his index finger second-knuckle-deep in his left nostril, chimed in. "A wombat is an Australian marsupial. Looks kind of like a groundhog." He kept digging around in his nose.

"Thanks, Ed," the biker said.

"Yeah, thanks, Ed," Isaac mimicked.

"A vampire bat, eh…" Bandana Man said sternly. "So, either you think you're funny, or you think we're stupid."

Tired and cranky, Isaac realized he needed to curb his sardonic tendencies before things went sour. There were a dozen ways this evening could blow up in his face, and he didn't need to start with a bar fight that he would probably lose.

"I tell you what. I'd like to donate to your colors. Maybe something like two bottles. That should be enough to rent space for a few hours. Then I'll be on my way."

Pleased with Isaac's offer, Bandana Man turned to his seated comrades and shouted, "Hey, Panzer, two bottles?" The giant called

Panzer nodded. Bandana Man turned back to Isaac. "Fine. Two bottles of bourbon. But mind your step. Stay out of our way, don't mess with the jukebox, and we'll get along just fine." He slapped Isaac on the shoulder as if they were now buddies.

Ed set two bottles of bourbon on the bar. Bandana Man picked up one in each hand and, with a mocking sneer on his face said, "Oh, and the shitter is ours. You need to piss, you go outside. Watch out for the rattlers." He walked off, holding the bottles up like a pirate with freshly acquired booty.

Isaac turned back to his own drink and noted, with revulsion, Ed's grimy hand palm-up in front of his face. With a sigh, he dug in his pocket and handed over wadded-up bills. He didn't bother asking for change.

"A word of advice," Ed offered. "That was a smart move with the bottles. If I were you, I'd clear out before they got too drunk. Things can get rowdy, especially if they don't know or trust you."

"I can't. I'm meeting a business partner. Believe me, I wouldn't be here otherwise."

"A business partner? Here?" Ed looked incredulous. "He must be a stupid son of a bitch."

"You're at least partly right." Isaac chuckled, and for a moment, he debated trying to warn off the lot of them, but he knew it would achieve nothing. It would probably just aggravate them. Troublemakers never shied away from trouble.

Ed shook his head. "Something tells me that before this night is over, I'm going to be really glad I ain't you."

So Isaac, already exhausted, settled onto the uncomfortable stool with his cheap booze and ruminated on the fact that this sleazy dive-bar bartender was happy to not be him. It wasn't the best start to the evening, and he had a hunch it was only going to get worse.

* * *

For the next hour, Isaac quietly sat there. The Devils drank, talked boorishly, selected awful songs on the jukebox, and generally made him wish he were someplace else. He resisted the urge to look around, knowing that eye contact could be a sign of aggression and there was no need to give the Devils any excuses. They seemed to have forgotten him, and that suited him fine. So he traced lines through the condensation on his bottle until the door to the bar swung open with a bang.

The new arrival towered over six feet but bore a markedly thin frame. He was dressed *cowboy* to the hilt—leather boots, a black Stetson, a long brown duster over a once-white T-shirt, and tattered jeans. Dark gloves and a filthy saddlebag on his shoulder finished the look. He walked slowly, his head down so that the brim of his hat cast his face in shadow. Isaac guessed that the newcomer would have enjoyed having a pair of spurs so that the jingle-jangle emphasized each step.

The pool game paused. Bandana Man snickered and elbowed Panzer and Skid-Row Santa. Ed raised an eyebrow. Isaac rolled his eyes.

Maloc the demon. So fucking dramatic.

He paused near the bar, all eyes on him, and raised his head so the light crept slowly up his face, like a curtain rising on a theater set. By the time he was fully pulled from the shadow, his face was angled towards the ceiling, and he stood there as if posing for a sculptor.

Once the bikers got a good look, a wave of uneasiness swept through. The dry skin of the demon's face hugged too tight around his head, like leather that had been pulled taut and left to bake in the sun, hardening until it took on the shape of the skull beneath. It had an unhealthy tinge to it, yellow or green, depending on how the light struck it. His wide, bloodshot eyes sported yellow-and-brown irises, accompanied by cracked, splotchy lips. It appeared that a man suffering from a variety of diseases had crawled from his deathbed to go and fetch a drink.

Isaac scanned the bar, gauging reactions. Ed had resumed his "looking busy" routine—wiping dirty glasses and eyeing Maloc like he might need to be thrown out before the evening was over. The Devils appeared conflicted—amused by his outfit, irritated by his cocky entrance, and disgusted by his appearance.

Maloc laughed when he saw Isaac, revealing teeth yellower than his skin. It was boisterous and overdone, the way someone laughed at a joke they didn't understand to avoid looking stupid. "Isaac!" he called out, not because of the distance, but so that everyone in attendance had to listen. He strode to the bar, pausing to say "Howdy, boys," to the Asphalt Devils, who narrowed their eyes at him, and plopped down heavily on the stool next to Isaac. "If I had known this place was four-star, I would have worn my T-shirt with the caviar stains. What're you drinking?"

Isaac held up his shot of whiskey, swirled it around, and then brought it to his lips. With a swiftness that could scarcely be followed, Maloc snatched the drink, downed it, and handed the glass back, all before Isaac could close his anticipating mouth.

"Like I said, what are you drinking?" Maloc repeated with a smug smile.

"I suppose I need another."

Maloc roughly patted him on the back, knocking the magician forwards into the bar. "Don't worry about it. I'll order. You can just pay." Despite Ed being only three feet away, Maloc shouted, "Hey, barkeep!"

Ed glowered. "Yeah?"

"We're going to need another round. Right here." He tapped his index fingers on the countertop as if Ed needed guidance on where to place them. As Ed went about his work, Maloc turned to Isaac and said, "As soon as we have our libations, we'll get down to our dirty dealings. You look like crap."

Isaac simply shrugged as he bit back a counter-remark about Maloc's general appearance.

"Now, Ed, I gotta tell you, you look like a real bartender," Maloc said as the proprietor plunked their drinks down.

"What's that mean?"

"I was just out in Los Angeles, and it seemed that every place I went to had these really handsome guys working all the bars. Struggling male models and actors. Just too pretty."

"So, you're saying I ain't good-looking?"

"What I'm saying is those guys can't be bartenders. They don't know about life in the gutter. And that's what you want when you go to a shithole bar. You want to be surrounded by miserable bastards who are clinging to a lower rung on the universal ladder. Scumbags who wallow in the mud, eat from the trough and go back for seconds with eager piggy faces. You want cheap, watered-down booze, bad lighting, and dirty bathrooms, which I haven't checked out yet, but I have a good feeling. And finally, you want a bartender who carries the mantle of King of the Miserable Shits. A man who looks like life beat the hell out of him, and he just doesn't care. A bartender who will scream out to God, 'Fine, God. If you only give me shit to eat, then I will eat shit with a smile on my face.' In short, what I'm saying, Ed, is that this is my kind of place." Maloc lifted a beer in salute, then turned and walked to the most secluded empty table.

It took Ed a moment to process the rant. "Did he just say that I was the King of Shit?"

"I'm not sure what he just said," Isaac lied.

"How'd he know my name?"

Again, Isaac lied. "He must have heard me say it."

Ed leaned forward, lowering his voice. "He crazy?"

Wincing at the man's breath, Isaac whispered back, "No, he's just an asshole."

"I reckon. Your friend has 'troublemaker' written all over him. Me, I don't mind some harassment from the drunks. But he best watch his step as long as the Devils are here. They go looking for trouble, just like he does."

"I'll try and make it quick." Isaac grabbed his beer and joined the demon.

Maloc leaned back in his chair, balancing it perfectly on the rear legs. "Y'know, Isaac, I like this hee-haw, howdy-doody cowboy shit. I never bathe, and I still fit right in."

As Isaac sat down at the table, the demon's gaze fell onto the satchel, and didn't veer from it until the magician removed it, set it on the floor, and finally nudged it under his chair. Only then did those jaundiced eyes float upwards to meet Isaac's stare.

"I've got what you wanted."

Maloc took a swig of his beer. "Don't be in such a rush. This is my last night on this mortal plane. I think that we'll take this slow. I'll enjoy my beer, then probably your beer. Then you'll buy me some more beers."

"Can you even get drunk?"

"Not even close. But I just have this feeling that once I'm back in Hell, I'll start wishing I had a beer. This world does have its delights."

Despite his revulsion at sitting with a Hellspawn, Isaac felt a twinge of curiosity. He had never assumed that Maloc would be so chatty. "Why do you want to be here, then? It's still bad, right? Even Hell might be better."

Maloc thought hard for a time, which was a disturbing sight—a death-mask face with furrowed brow as a hateful mind searched for warm memories. "I love the randomness of this world," he finally said, and seeing Isaac bemused, he elaborated. "When I reclaim my position in the torture pits, those chained souls will know exactly what is going to happen. There's no spontaneity to the whole ordeal. Not like here. There's a certain gratification that you get grabbing someone off the street. Smuggling them away to a secluded spot. Going to work on them. And through the whole process, they never give up hope. Up until their dying breath, they think they'll escape, or Prince Charming will rush in and save them. That false hope adds such spice to my work. In Hell, hope is an impossible thing."

Isaac managed to hide his sour face by taking a swig of beer and pretending the taste disgusted him. "So, you'll miss all that and beer. Well, if we could continue with the task at hand."

His curiosity had been replaced with revulsion. He reached for his satchel, but the demon resumed his soliloquy, and Isaac reluctantly went back to the role of interested listener.

"On the flip side, I have to admit that I've become bored with mortal flesh and bone. So bored. I'll get my hands on a fine specimen, and they're good for maybe a few hours before ruination. You only get one chance to do everything. In my pit, I could torture someone forever. Cut them all up, grind up the pieces, put them back together, and start over. That way you get to know the poor soul. It's some real bonding."

"And I bet they appreciate that quality time," Isaac said a little too sharply, but the demon didn't seem to care.

Maloc tilted his head back, a dreamy look crossing his face as he savored dark thoughts. "And the tools, Isaac. I miss my tools. I had such a collection there." He opened his coat and took a large Bowie knife from a sheath on his belt. "This is the best I can do here." He twirled the knife with phenomenal grace, flipping it back and forth from hand to hand. "Don't get me wrong, mortals have made staggering strides in pain infliction over the centuries, and I always had a decent variety of weapons and bondage devices. But they pale in comparison to my collection in Hell." He slid the blade smoothly back into its sheath. "It's time to go home."

Isaac glanced around the bar as casually as he could, hoping Maloc's knifeplay had gone unobserved. *Nope.* The pool players had simply returned to their game, the cracking of the billiard balls serving to break the silence, but the seated bikers eyed them, starting to talk. Finally, Isaac looked back at Maloc, who smiled so wide his head might crack.

"Can we get back to business here?" Isaac said. "Before trouble starts."

"From who? These hicks? Screw 'em. What are you afraid of? Aren't you a powerful wizard?" The demon wiggled his fingers at Isaac, mock-casting a spell. "You magicians are all the same."

"You've known a lot of magicians?" he asked, his curiosity again overriding his desire to be away from the beast. Curiosity—killer of cats and magicians.

Maloc's upper lip curled in disgust. "It was a magician who brought me into this world. He had more aspiration than talent and was unable to pull me through the void in my true form. Instead, he stuck my spirit in this dead mortal shell." The demon pulled off a glove and rotated his hand around for examination. "He didn't do a terrible job. He worked some incantations on the skin, making me strong and resistant to magic and mortal weapons. But he didn't seal it very well, and, as you can see, some of my true essence has leaked out over the centuries."

Isaac kept a blank face. "You can't even notice."

"Eventually, this magician attempted some powerful summoning. An archdemon that I may have suggested he try to convene with. And that was that. He was never seen again."

"So, you set him up. You gave him a name he couldn't control. You knew he'd die."

"Of course. I may be in mortal skin, but I'm still a demon where it counts. That's why people shouldn't deal with my kind."

"Funny you say that to me while I'm in cahoots with you."

Maloc held up his hands and attempted what Isaac assumed was a "*Who me?*" smile of innocence. The demon was incapable of this expression and, in the end, only resembled a deranged mugshot.

"So, then I was free. I traveled the world. Met a lot of beautiful people. Killed them. Enjoyed myself." He stood. "Get us another round of drinks. I'm going to go check out the stench in the shitter."

Isaac winced. "That's just nasty."

Maloc walked to the rear of the building, passed the pool players without even looking at them, and disappeared into the restroom. Remembering Bandana Man's warning about the bathroom being off-limits, Isaac casually scanned the table of bikers. They hadn't budged but definitely looked unhappy. He guessed that Maloc's unhealthy appearance forced them to keep their distance. It made sense that even the bravest would avoid someone who looked like the Ebola virus in a cowboy costume.

"How's your date going?" Ed asked as he took Isaac's money.

"Wonderfully," he replied. "But I owe that to the ambiance of this place."

Ed just scowled. He and Maloc returned to the table at the same time. The demon immediately downed the two shots and both beers.

Unsurprised by this, Isaac took the opportunity to smack his satchel down on the table. "You finally ready?"

In his first serious tone of the night, Maloc replied, "Let's deal."

Chapter 2
INSTINCTUAL REMNANTS

From his bag, Isaac removed a broken wooden crucifix and a bundle of papers tied with string. Maloc, tight-lipped, looked over the objects curiously.

"This cross was used in the exorcism of a kinsman of yours named Rumael in 1809. The diagrams and spells are designed so you can do this on your own. You can head home whenever you want."

Maloc tentatively placed a fingertip on the top piece, eyes squinted as if expecting to be shocked. When nothing occurred, he grew bolder and picked it up, feeling its weight in his palm. "Rumael," he repeated. "The name means nothing. I had recommended the crucifix used to exorcize Lord Asmodeus. Earning his favor would have been a boon."

"Asmodeus is an archdemon. Hence, that cross is a major relic. It's currently under armed guard in the Vatican."

"I know that," Maloc hissed. "That's why I wanted it. I could've gated back to Hell in style with that. This"—he jabbed his finger down on the broken cross—"is like riding the bus."

"You needed a cross used in an exorcism. You got one."

Maloc ran a tongue the color of boiled liver over his front teeth while eyeing Isaac suspiciously. "I suppose it should do well enough," he conceded. "My turn?"

Isaac nodded, and the demon opened his coat and removed a folded cloth secured with string. Inside rested a single black card. The borders of it were adorned with strange red markings that shimmered and shifted as if being constantly redesigned. In the center was a man dressed in white robes standing atop a rocky hill. He lifted a gleaming silver trumpet to his mouth, and a black crown adorned his head. Isaac reached for it, but a hiss from Maloc stopped him.

"No touching."

"I need to see the other side to verify its authenticity."

"You'll have to figure out how to do that without me removing your hands at the wrist."

Isaac nodded in resignation. Maloc smiled, proud of his bullying, then watched in surprise as the card flipped, overturned by an unseen hand.

He narrowed his eyes. "What magic is that?"

"Telekinesis," Isaac answered casually, without taking his eyes from the card. "So, I didn't touch it."

The inverted side depicted a similar picture, except with the majesty destroyed. The man's robes hung in tatters. The crown hung from slack fingers, and the trumpet lay, snapped in half, at his feet. The red runes that shimmered around the border now went in reverse.

"Well, there you have it. The Emperor. One of the original Black Tarot. Even a single card would still fetch a fortune. You could sell it for a king's ransom and never have a care in the world again. Or you could use it and be damned," Maloc said. "But I think you're damned already."

"Maybe so." Isaac patted the rolled papers. "Here are the diagrams and chants needed to open your gate back home. I assume that we can conclude things here?"

Something across the bar caught Maloc's attention. The big biker stood in front of the jukebox, scrolling through the selections. Bandana Man shouted out, "Hey, Panzer, pick something decent this time!"

"Panzer. Panzer," Maloc said with a dreamy sway as if remembering a long-lost love. "That's a good biker nickname. Hey, Isaac, did you know that that was the word for the German tanks in World War II?"

"Yeah, I know," Isaac sighed as the deal went off track again with another Maloc tangent.

"The Panzer Tiger was a fearsome machine. It would have won the war for Hitler if he hadn't run out of gasoline. Lucifer has one in his private collection. Now, that is a collection of art to be admired. When you finally get to Hell, you should check it out. It's open to the public on Tuesdays and Thurs..." Panzer's selection began to play, and the acoustic twang of country music filled the bar. "Oh, we can't have this," Maloc said, his voice becoming menacingly low. "Not on my last night on the earthly plane. I won't go out to country."

"It's not so bad," Isaac lied. Country music had been playing all night, and it bothered him that suddenly the demon was offended. Trying to redirect back to their conversation, he asked, "You were saying something endearing about the Nazis?" But Maloc didn't respond. He had turned to stare at the jukebox as if it were a living thing that had affronted him. "I thought you liked the whole country-western scene?"

"Only the hygiene part," Maloc said, heading to the jukebox. He studied it for a moment, as if searching for the weak spot, before smacking his open palm against its side with such force that the machine scraped several inches across the floor. The country song ended abruptly and was swiftly replaced with a more mournful electric guitar. Isaac recognized the song as "House of the Rising Sun" by The Animals.

Maloc turned back to the magician, a large smile on his face. "Now, this is music to arrange infernal machinations by!" he exclaimed before clapping and singing along as he returned to the table.

"You mind not beating on my property like that?" Ed shouted. But the bartender's frustration changed to curious confusion as he listened. "I didn't know this song was on there."

"It isn't." Maloc laughed.

Ed looked from the jukebox to Maloc and back again. Appearing uneasy, he moved to the other end of the bar.

Maloc sat back down at the table. "That trick always spooks 'em. Now then, where were we?"

Isaac leaned across the table and held up a piece of the cross in each hand, but before he could say anything, a gruff voice boomed.

"Hey, I was listening to that!"

The voice belonged to Panzer, who glared menacingly at Maloc. Once again, the smile vanished from the demon's face, and Isaac slouched back in his chair.

Maloc winked at Isaac before shouting back. "That's right. You *were* listening to it. Now you're not."

The sharp retort seemed to confuse the biker for a moment. A man of his dimensions was probably not used to back talk. He paused, his gears grinding, before one of his companions muttered something to egg him on.

Then Panzer said, "I'm going to give you to the count of three to switch it back." He crossed his arms across his barrel chest.

"By the time you count to three, this song will be over. And it's a really long song."

Isaac winced at the last statement as he scooped the cross and tarot card into his satchel. Maloc watched from the corner of his eye but seemed unconcerned. The demon had his dander up and seemed bent on doing his professional best to heat the situation to a boil. The Devils surrounded the table.

"What did you just say?"

Maloc tipped his cowboy hat back and looked up at the giant. "I said I don't give a fuck about who you are or how high you can count."

At this, Isaac held up his empty beer bottle. "Hey, I'm getting another. Does anyone want anything? My treat." No one responded, so Isaac hefted his satchel, slinked out of his chair, and walked hunched over, like a man exiting a running helicopter, to the bar.

"Don't go too far, Isaac," Maloc called out, and the threat in the statement was clear.

"That's it. Get this punk up," Panzer said.

The two bikers who had been playing pool each grabbed one of Maloc's arms and lifted, but they may as well have been trying to uproot a tree. Maloc didn't resist or retaliate. He simply sat with a smile and let the men jerk on his arms. Panzer stared incredulously.

"Oh, stop. I can't take it. Please have mercy," Maloc fake-begged, his voice high and whiny.

"Get him up," Panzer ordered.

"He weighs a ton," one said, and as they tugged and yanked at the grinning demon, one of them knocked his hat from his head. Suddenly, Maloc was on his feet. Both bikers fell back in surprise. He caught the hat before it hit the floor and cradled it lovingly. Isaac noted that Maloc was even more disturbing with a bare head. His hairless scalp was covered in dark blotches and scabs. Eye to eye with Panzer, he calmly put his hat back on and straightened out the brim.

Isaac sat down at the bar. Ed watched the scene with a smug *I-told-you-so* look. "Your boyfriend has it coming. King of Shit, huh?"

Isaac found that he couldn't disagree, ignored the "boyfriend" comment, and turned back to the confrontation.

"Look, man," Panzer said. "You're really sick or crazy. I'll cut you some slack. Just get out of our bar."

"But my song's not done." Maloc waved his hand at the jukebox, and the song ended abruptly. "There, it's done. I bet your song is next, and then we can all be friends again." He put a finger to his ear and cocked his head towards the jukebox. The familiar strumming of "House of the Rising Sun" began for a second time. "Oh, wait, it's my song again." He burst into laughter at this, and the bikers exchanged confused glances.

"Look, mister, I'm getting really tired of you. This is your last warning," Panzer ordered, but his tone had weakened.

Maloc sighed and folded his hands behind his back. "Panzer," he said sternly, like a teacher about to lecture an unruly student. "I want you to know how disappointing this is for me. I've been expecting this situation to savage up into violence much quicker. You and your stooges are professional assholes. On any other occasion, if someone talked as much shit to you as I have, you would have beaten them to death by now, right?" The biker gave an almost imperceptible nod. "Then why am I still standing?"

Panzer seemed to regain some of his bravado under Maloc's bullying questions. "Maybe it's your lucky day."

"No. I'll tell you what it is. Right now, there's a little voice inside your head. It's whispering a warning to you, but you can barely hear it."

The biker snorted in contempt.

"You know I'm right, Panzer, and I'll tell you what that voice is. It's *instinct*. A very minor form of sixth sense. Every mortal creature on Earth possesses it to some extent. Only humans have learned to ignore it. At this moment, your inner voice is warning you, but it doesn't scream as it did a few thousand years ago. It's atrophied to a whisper that you've forgotten how to listen to. But you're hearing it now, just a little, and it's trying to save your life." Maloc smiled, smugly impressed with his speech. "That's why I'm still standing here."

Panzer looked utterly perplexed. He thought, long and hard, which appeared to Isaac to be a futile process, and glanced at his companions, who could give no intellectual assistance other than shrugs. Finally, he turned back to Maloc and said, "Huh?"

Maloc gritted his teeth, and for a second, Isaac thought this was it—the killing spree was about to begin. But the demon shook off the anger, apparently only so that he could launch into another self-righteous soliloquy. "Okay, let's go about this another way," Maloc said. "You know what a tiger is?"

Panzer nodded slowly.

"If there was a tiger right here, right now, it would tear all of you to pieces. But it would never fuck with me. Do you know why?" No one answered, so Maloc just continued. "Instinct. Such animals, despite being powerful and vicious, still listen to their instincts. Humans are the only things on this earth that would be stupid enough to fuck with me."

Panzer again missed the point. He laughed, if not wholeheartedly, and addressed his biker brethren. "So now he's not even human."

Seeing their captain laugh encouraged them, and soon they were all chuckling at Maloc.

At the bar, Isaac shook his head. A demon telling the truth was an ominous sign. Pride was indeed going to get the Devils killed.

Maloc waited patiently for the laughter to subside. "I see that reason avoids you. So, let's be more direct. I'm not leaving. I'm going to continue to do things to piss you off. Don't you think we should just settle this now? I tell you what," Maloc said, removing his hat and gently setting it on the table. "I'll give you the first hit. You can even use these." Maloc pulled a set of brass knuckles from his pocket and tossed them onto the table.

This bold move stunned Panzer. It was probably the first time in his gigantic existence that someone had ever challenged him so directly. He narrowed his eyes, searching for Maloc's angle.

Santa chimed in. "First hit? Damn, Panzer, with those knuckles it'll take his head clean off."

The goading was all it took to override Panzer's momentary good sense. He rolled his shoulders, threw a few air jabs to loosen up, and then slipped on the knuckles.

"Panzer," Isaac called out from the bar. "You'd be better off using your bare fists."

The giant biker snorted and pointed at Isaac. "You better be gone by the time I finish with him or you're next." He turned back to Maloc. "You asked for it, asshole."

"You could even say I was begging for it. Which side would you prefer?" Maloc waved his hand at his face, as a salesman would at a new car on display.

"I'm right-handed. So, I'll need..." Panzer paused.

"You'll need my left side, then. Idiot." Maloc stuck his chin out.

That was the breaking point.

Panzer put all of his strength into a right-handed haymaker, which landed flush on Maloc's cheek and sent him stumbling backward, hands cupping his face. The bikers let out victorious cheers and congratulated Panzer, each pat on his back raising a cloud of road dust from his jacket. Panzer smiled as well, gratified that he had finally belted the asshole, but seemed disappointed that Maloc still stood.

"Did that hurt, old man? It looked really painful," Bandana Man mocked.

Maloc still had his hands over his face and made weird moaning noises. To the bikers, it was the pain of a man who had just gotten his comeuppance. To Isaac, it was horrendous overacting.

"Take this asshole outside," Panzer ordered. The rest of the Devils stepped towards Maloc, who suddenly held his arms out straight to his sides as if to say, *"TA-DA!"* His rotten teeth were outlined with a thick, black fluid, which dripped from his lip with the consistency of honey.

"That actually hurt more than I thought it would," Maloc said, raising his fists in a boxing stance. "My turn."

Panzer fell back, bumping into two of his cronies, who stumbled back in turn feeling not so confident in their champion anymore. "Get away from me, you freak!"

"C'mon, Panzer. It's my turn. Put your chin out."

"You ain't touching me!"

"We had an agreement. You took your turn and now you want to renege on our deal?" Maloc's voice became low and threatening.

The air became hot and stale, and the room itself seemed to shrink, drawing all of its occupants closer together. At the same time, Maloc looked somehow bigger. He stood up straighter. His shoulders appeared broader. A wave of fear swept through the room, and every man shivered. Every man but Isaac, who could only shake his head in resignation at what was about to occur. Maloc's demonic aura expanded, leaking from his body and filling the room. Which meant the demon was angry.

And playtime was over.

Chapter 3
THE DEMON AND THE KING

"Well, Panzer, if you're not going to let me hit you, then I'll just hit him." Maloc gave Bandana Man a sudden backhand that sent him spinning to the floor.

All of Maloc's warnings about instincts, all the fear spread by his aura, and all the hesitation in the Asphalt Devils evaporated. Panzer charged with a bellow, expecting to bowl the demon over, but instead he slammed into an immovable object. The other three bikers leaped in, grasping for his limbs, trying to restrain him. Bandana Man crawled to his feet, mouth bloody, long hair dangling from his now-bandanaless head, and lunged into the fray.

The superior numbers did not help, and it became obvious that Maloc was toying with them. He easily slapped aside or absorbed their punches, and when one attempted to grapple, Maloc slithered out of their grasp or simply tossed the man aside. But the demon refused to land any serious blows. As frustration set in, the Asphalt Devils escalated things by pulling knives but discovered that they couldn't cut Maloc any more than they could punch him.

Maloc's rotten smile never left his face, and it spurred the Devils on. In the background, the jukebox played "House of the Rising Sun" for the third time.

"Shit!" Ed bellowed. "They're destroying my bar!"

Isaac hopped from his barstool an instant before a Devil smashed into it. "Ed!" he shouted over the din as he leaned into the bar. The bartender turned to him, a wild mix of panic and anger on his pudgy face. "Get out of here, Ed."

"What?" Ed scrunched his face up as Panzer threw a chair that missed its mark and broke to pieces against the wall.

"Get out while you're still able."

This got Ed's attention. "What do you mean 'still able'? You two up to something? You're in this together?" Ed's eyes grew wide as if he had uncovered a plot. "This is some kind of setup, isn't it?"

Isaac chewed back a remark about the obvious dollar value of the establishment. "No. I'm trying to save you."

"Listen, punk." Ed aimed a sausage-link finger at him. "Nobody comes into my place, starts trouble, and then throws me out! Not without answering to Wilma!" He ducked behind the bar and emerged with a sawn-off 12-gauge pump-action shotgun. Engraved on the stock, in fancy script letters, were the words *Wilma Wagon Fixer*. The short, unkempt bartender had transformed into the tough owner of a Dodge City saloon.

Isaac froze, not wanting to give the man an excuse to blast him by making any sudden moves. "Ed, this is not a robbery or a setup. That guy is just crazy."

"This is a permanent cure for crazy," Ed said. He fired the gun into the air. The deafening blast brought a halt to the battle. The bikers stood exhausted and battered. Maloc grinned like a kid on Christmas.

"Enough!" Ed shouted, aiming Wilma at Maloc.

"Ed, I love it!" Maloc exclaimed. "You broke up the bar fight with a shotgun blast. That is *so* Western. You want to wear my cowboy hat?"

"Shut up, freak! I've had enough of you. I should put you down and do the world a favor. Now, take your last chance and your boyfriend"—Ed tilted his head at Isaac—"and get out."

"You're just throwing us out? These clowns get to stay?" Maloc waved his hand at the panting bikers, mock incredulity on his face. "Well, that's just not fair, Ed." Maloc turned to face Panzer and made an exaggerated shrug. "I guess we'll just have to wrap this up."

Shit. Isaac resisted the urge to shut his eyes. He'd known from the start how this would end.

Maloc threw a punch that caved in Panzer's face. The demon's fist, embedded up to the wrist inside the man's head, made a wet slurping sound as he pulled it free. Blood flecked with bits of flesh, nose cartilage, and skull fragments dripped from his fingers. Panzer toppled over, his arms and legs twitching with futile resistance to death.

Panzer's companions froze, eyes wide in shock as they stared at their knight, their champion, lying faceless on the roadhouse floor. But they recovered quickly. They were, after all, seasoned men of violence.

The demon went with a new strategy for this round. Instead of playing defense, he did absolutely nothing at all. Like a cooperative Caesar, Maloc gave himself up for sacrifice, and the remaining Devils surrounded him with plunging knives. While the steel cut skin as well as they'd hoped, all other expectations were dashed. He didn't fall or cry out. He didn't bleed—just more of that slow molasses oozed from the wounds. He didn't even stop smiling. All the Devils accomplished was bringing themselves into his orbit.

After weathering a dozen attacks, Maloc snatched Santa by the beard and hauled him nose-to-nose. "I offered myself up like a canvas and all you could do is hack away like I'm a side of beef." He shook his head in disappointment. "Art is truly dead." With that, he effortlessly pulled Santa into a headlock that ended with a twist and a crack.

As Santa's lifeless body thumped to the floor, the Bowie knife whistled from its sheath. Maloc was indeed an artist with the weapon, and two precision strikes dropped both the pool players, leaving only No-Bandana Man, who bolted for the exit. Not wanting to throw his Bowie, Maloc scooped up a dropped Devil blade and hurled it. It caught the biker in the back of the neck. He managed two more gasping, gurgling steps before he collapsed.

In the time it took to draw a deep breath, it was over. Ed stood stupidly behind the bar, Wilma hanging loosely in his hands. While Isaac was not surprised at the outcome, he was still shocked at the speed and savagery. Silence reigned for several moments before the jukebox started with a click, and "House of the Rising Sun" once again filled the air. Maloc faced the bar, pivoting slowly and deliberately, making the movement as dramatic as possible, bloody Bowie dripping. "There is a house in New Orleans," the demon sang along.

Isaac stepped away from the bar when the demon's eyes turned to Ed.

"Hey, King," Maloc called out. "They're playing my song again."

Ed snapped out of his stupor and successfully fired the shotgun despite his trembling hands. The buckshot peppered Maloc from waist to sternum, sending him stumbling backwards into the table, and knocking him flat on his back, where he lay motionless. As his hat meandered to the ground with him, Ed let out a heavy breath.

Isaac could only sigh. "Run now, while he's down."

Pumping another shell into the rifle, Ed whirled and put the barrel in his face. "Get out," he growled, emboldened.

Hands held high, Isaac made one last entreaty. "He's not dead. He's of a demonic stock that is impervious to human-made weapons. You knocked him down. You messed up his clothes. But all you really did was piss him off," Isaac rambled, not pausing to take a breath. After all, *he* wasn't immune to buckshot.

"You're crazy. And I got the cure for crazy. Just like I told you." Ed raised the weapon to his shoulder, and for a second, Isaac thought he actually intended to shoot. But when Maloc stood up, the bartender completely forgot about him.

"Look at that," Maloc said, holding out his shirt to examine the buckshot holes. "What a mess." The demon gave Isaac an admonishing look. "You spoiled my surprise. I was going to leap up when he came over to my corpse. Just like the serial killers in movies. It would have been a hoot."

"Maloc, you've had your fun. Let Ed go. You said he was a good bartender."

"Hell needs better bartenders." Maloc was apparently in no mood to let Isaac spoil his good time. The demon turned to Ed. "You see, Ed, I'm going back to Hell tonight—and not alone. All these Devils will meet me there. And so will you."

Ed brought the shotgun to bear on the demon and took a step back, only to bump into the rack of booze, bottles rattling. He gasped, gulping for air like a drowning man. Wilma shook violently in his hands. Maloc angled the Bowie just right to reflect the light into Ed's face. The bartender fired, but his aim had faded with his confidence, and the blast went wide, shattered the glass top of the jukebox, and permanently ended Maloc's theme song.

"Oh, you bastard," Maloc hissed. He flicked the knife underhand like a softball pitch and impaled the bartender squarely in the forehead. Ed somehow stayed on his feet. A thin string of blood dripped from the wound and ran down his nose. His eyes rolled back, and Isaac wondered whether it was a natural reaction, or the man tried to get a look at the knife handle protruding from his forehead. In either case, Ed stood still like that for several heartbeats, the shotgun still aimed at Maloc with hands as steady as stone.

"You're dead, King. Now, fall over," Maloc ordered.

The bartender let out a final breath, which sounded like an "oh" responding to the teasing. Then he followed the directions and slumped over. Wilma fell to the floor with a *thunk*.

"All hail the King of Shit." Maloc bowed reverently. He picked his hat up from the debris and placed it lovingly on his head. "I have to admit, you seem pretty composed for a man that just saw a cemetery's worth of death. Most magicians do very badly with violence."

"I played a lot of violent video games as a child."

Maloc snorted. "Why don't you hop over the bar and grab my knife." He pulled up a barstool and sat down.

Isaac did as ordered, hoping to placate the demon now that his bloodlust appeared momentarily sated. He knelt over Ed's body. Sightless eyes stared up at him. He tugged on the handle and barely suppressed rising bile when Ed's head lifted with it. Placing a foot against the bartender's scalp, he yanked it free and set it on the bar. "You know you still have a knife stuck in your back?"

"Oh, so I do." Maloc took a deep breath and scrunched up his face, like someone pushing out an uncooperative bowel movement. The weapon popped out of his back and clattered across the floor.

"Neat trick."

Maloc cleaned his blade on Ed's dirty bar rag. "Now then, how about giving me back my property."

Isaac obliged and removed the crucifix pieces and the bundled scrolls from his satchel. "Well, good luck to you, Maloc. I hope they have a giant banner that says 'welcome home' when you get back to Hell."

Maloc studied the objects. "Something's missing."

"What? Everything's there."

"Nope. I'm positive something's missing."

Isaac frowned. He should have known he wouldn't get out of here so easily. Just as he had with the Asphalt Devils, Maloc set the situation to simmer. "So, what's missing?" As he asked, he reached out with his telekinesis and wrapped it around Wilma Wagon Fixer. It was a bit heavy for Isaac's telekinetic might to lift, but he could drag it, and Ed's pooling blood aided a silent slide across the floor.

"Well, I had a fancy tarot card before those goons started that fight."

Isaac fought back a curse. "The card is mine, fair and square."

"Isaac, Isaac, Isaac," he said. "You, of all people, should know that a demon's definition of fair and square is quite different from that of a mortal. I used you to get the job done. You were like a flesh puppet." Maloc smiled, impressed with his creative insult. "So, hand over the card."

"This is a shitty thing to do."

"Oh, quit whining. I'm a demon. Consider it that whole 'teach a mortal the folly of dealing with demons' shtick. Besides, you can't stop me from taking it. Do you really want to continue arguing?" Maloc's jaundiced eyes twinkled.

"Fine. Be a jerk." Isaac tossed the satchel onto the bar.

Maloc smirked like a bully who had just taken lunch money until he opened the bag. He shoved an angry hand around the interior. "Where is it?" he growled.

"It's in there." Isaac took back the bag, reached in, pulled out the card, waved it around, and then replaced it before handing the satchel over once again.

The demon opened it. Still empty. "Parlor tricks now, Isaac? It'll be hard to do sleight-of-hand after I chop them both off."

"Actually, the bag is an opening to a dimensional pocket that only I can access. So, there's nothing you can do to get them out. I call it an everbag."

The demon let out a snort that sounded mildly impressed. "What you're saying is that I have to torture you until you agree to pull the card out?"

Isaac frowned. "Yeah... I suppose that was the only outcome of this strategy, wasn't it?"

Maloc leaned forwards. "I'll be honest, Isaac. I always planned on killing you, but just like I did for King Shit there, I was going to make it quick in appreciation of your work. But now, with all these silly games you've been playing"—he held up his Bowie knife—"I think I have time for one last artistic endeavor. I wish we had some music, but King shot up the jukebox."

"So, you can play a song on a jukebox even though the song isn't on the jukebox, but you can't play a broken jukebox?"

Maloc shrugged. "It's just the physics of that spell. You know how it is." He waved the knife. "You ready?"

Isaac snapped his fingers, and Maloc's favorite song began to play. Not from the jukebox, but from the air itself. As Maloc looked around in surprise, Isaac telekinetically pulled Wilma up into his hands, chambered a shell, and shot the demon in the face. The blast knocked him off the stool and sent him sprawling to the floor.

With Wilma tucked under one arm, Isaac snatched up his everbag and rushed out the front door.

Chapter 4
THE PONY AND THE TWINS

Maloc hated getting shot. It wasn't painful as much as just disorienting. He wiped buckshot from his eyes and spit some from his mouth. The shrapnel in his cheeks and forehead would simply dissolve like a mortal's body breaks down splinters. He stood up and casually dusted himself off, not concerned in the least that Isaac had made away with his property.

Imagining how panicked Isaac would be when he discovered that the tires of his vehicle were slashed brought a smile to Maloc's face. The magician was in way over his head. Even now, he could picture Isaac fleeing on foot through the desert. Not that it mattered. Maloc could trail him by scent. Demons had a spectacular sense of smell for all the foul things in the world: blood, rot, excrement, and fear.

That thought made him pause. *The smell of fear.* He hadn't gotten a whiff of it from the magician. Isaac had seemed oddly composed all night, even during the murder spree. The room remained thick with the residual scent of fear only now fading.

None of it had emanated from Isaac.

Uneasiness crept into his dark spirit, and a ghost of a shiver rode down his spine. For an instant, he thought of the feeling as an instinct, which was not only implausible but also insulting.

With a snarl he hurled a bottle, his anger rightfully replacing his anxiety. This was why he wanted to go home. He'd been on this mortal plane too long. It was getting into his head. He'd just compared himself to a mortal. A plaything. A flesh puppet. Concern was for lesser beings. Here he was immortal, almost a deity. Certainly a god to the corpses around him. Certainly death to the fleeing magician.

Maybe he would let Isaac get a little further away. Let him run until he dropped. Let him hope for escape. He stooped over to get his hat, which had fallen off his head when Isaac had blasted him. The demon's prized Stetson was riddled with holes—the result of being shot point-blank with a 12-gauge. In a fit of rage, he tore it to bits.

"All right, Isaac. You're going to be my last bloody masterpiece." He threw open the door to the parking lot and stepped out into the cool Arizona night.

He froze.

The magician hadn't run. He sat on the hood of the station wagon, drumming his feet on a flattened tire. That feeling that wasn't an instinct crept back into Maloc's head. *What is this*? He scanned the desert and listened to the wind. Something was there, but he couldn't pinpoint it. He sniffed the air. Rotting meat came to his nose—delicious but unexpected.

"I thought you'd be running."

Isaac looked surprised. "Through the desert? In the dark? With all the prickly plants everywhere?"

Maloc bristled. "What are you up to, Isaac? There's something here. What is it?"

"Just us. Not afraid, are you? A little voice in your head saying things that you don't understand?"

That blow hit home. Maloc flared, the anger pushing the uneasiness out of his head. He could wade through tougher magic than a lightweight like Isaac could bring. He'd killed more powerful magicians with his bare hands, laughing as they tried to voice out spells from under his choking grip. *Enough of this.*

Maloc started across the parking lot, taking ponderous steps that raised clouds of dust. He tossed the knife into the air, so high it disappeared momentarily into the night, and caught it by the handle when it fell. Isaac golf clapped. Maloc tossed it again, higher this time. During its descent, Isaac lifted his hand and pointed at it. The blade froze in midair, about ten feet above Maloc's head. He looked at the magically suspended knife, then at Isaac, then at the knife again. With a flick of his hand, Isaac sent it spinning away. The sound of it clattering across rocks echoed through the desert.

"Oh, you little prick." Maloc stared along the knife's path. "That is fucking it! That blade would have made your death so much easier. Cuts are less painful than broken bones." He breathed hard, the rage consuming him, his aura radiating from his body in waves of foul heat.

"You've talked a lot of shit. I think you just have a big mouth."

Maloc lost it. He opened his mouth and screamed; the loathsome sound mixed the shriek of an injured cat and the roar of a tornado. A hatred that Maloc had not felt since he was painfully pulled to this plane three hundred years ago enveloped him, and he stomped across the dirt lot.

Isaac whistled. This action struck Maloc as odd, but he was beyond thinking about anything other than bloodletting. That was until he saw what looked to be a pony emerge from behind a screen of desert scrub. It trotted across the road and stood next to Isaac.

Maloc stopped, his surprise once again quelling the rage. It was a dog. The biggest dog he'd ever seen. He wasn't sure what breed. He had never learned much about animals, as he couldn't get near them. They'd always sense his infernal origins and scramble away.

"This is my bodyguard."

Despite his anger, Maloc laughed. "A dog? This was your big plan? Lure me out here so your dog can eat me? How pathetic. As soon as your *bodyguard* gets a whiff of me, he'll bolt with his tail between his legs."

"But he's a good boy."

Maloc shook his head in disbelief. The guy had balls but was not too bright. He walked forward, hand extended to the animal, the way one would approach a strange dog. Nothing happened. Maloc's smile shortened a bit. It must not have his scent. He knelt, clapped his hands together, and called out, "Here, doggy." The dog just stood there. Finally, he waved his hands in the air and shouted, "Boo!"

The dog didn't move. No flinch or flicker. It didn't even blink.

Then the wind shifted, and Maloc ceased smiling altogether.

The dog was what he had sensed when he left the bar, strongly emanating the smells of death. But this was wrong. The odors seemed off, as if laced with something. Magic, he realized. His eyes opened wide. The dog had no life of its own.

Isaac affirmed this. "Yep. This is General, and, as I bet you just realized, he gave up the ghost a while ago. And you know those instincts you've been blathering on about all night? The ghost took those with it."

Maloc took a step back. "You couldn't have done this. You don't have the skill."

Isaac pointed. "Meet the twins. One and Two."

Maloc looked over his shoulder. Stocky, black-and-brown dogs emerged from either side of the roadhouse. They stood at each corner, silent guardians—as dead, he realized, as the first dog. He tensed. Man-made blades and bullets were one thing. Earth-born fearless fangs and claws were another matter entirely.

Isaac snapped his fingers, and the dogs charged. No barking. No snarling. The only sounds were the pads of their feet on the ground.

Maloc assumed a fighting stance. General reached him first, jumping with jaws agape. The demon caught the dog in mid-leap, one hand around its throat, the other under its belly. Using its own momentum, Maloc hurled General past him. It landed headfirst with a loud crack. Maloc spun, barely avoiding the snapping jaws of Twin Two. He grabbed the dog by its head, pushed it into the dirt, and raised a fist to crush its skull.

Their state of life didn't matter, the demon thought. It didn't matter that they weren't afraid of him, didn't matter that their natural teeth could rend him. He was still faster. Still stronger. Still a better killer.

Then Twin One sank its jaws into his cocked-back arm.

Living without pain makes one forget just how awful it is. It had been a hundred years since he had screamed from it. But he did so now.

Releasing Twin Two, he began to beat on One's head with his left hand, raining blows that should have knocked it senseless. Instead, the dog shook its head to and fro, teeth serrating demonic flesh.

Wisps of smoke wafted out from between One's jaws as the bites began to burn. A searing pain spread to his hand and shoulder like acid poured into his veins.

40

Isaac had done something to these beasts other than raise them from the dead.

Twin Two rolled to its feet and bit deeply into the distracted demon's left leg, directly below the knee. Again, the wound smoldered like hot ash. He grabbed at Twin One's head, tearing off one ear, then the other. Finally, Maloc wedged his fingers into its mouth, pried up its upper jaw, and shoved the beast aside. His right hand now free, he brought his fist down hard onto Two's head but found that he couldn't swing the arm at full force. The steaming bites had sapped his strength.

General slammed into him from behind, knocking him to the dirt. The dog's massive mouth came for his neck. He twisted, and General tore into his left shoulder instead. Again, Maloc howled in agony. Twin One dove back into the fray, tearing into Maloc's right thigh. General released his shoulder, going for the neck once again. Maloc thrust his right arm into its mouth, sacrificing the limb to save himself.

Panicked, infuriated, and hurting, Maloc thrashed back and forth, desperation aiding his failing strength. With his free left hand, he punched General's flank, landing sledgehammer blows that shattered ribs and destroyed organs, but achieved nothing. He pulled his leg free of Twin Two and then kicked the dog in the head, his bootheel shattering the Rottweiler's skull but leaving intact its jaws, which went to work on his ankle.

Isaac whistled. The dogs halted their attack and backed up, keeping Maloc at the center of their triangle. The magician still sat on the hood, drumming his heels like a bored child in a waiting room. When Maloc made eye contact, the magician smiled and waved. "Can I get you a beer?"

Maloc pushed himself to his feet using his undamaged left arm, standing wobbly on shredded legs. His right arm hung uselessly. "What... did you do to me?" he croaked.

"I coated their teeth with a paste made from communion wafers, holy water, and snake venom. All-natural poison mixed with all-holy poison. Pretty good idea, eh?"

"That's deceitful."

"And you're tougher than I thought." Isaac whistled.

All three dogs crashed into him, and the demon went down in a flurry of fur and snapping jaws. He fought back as best he could, but the battle was over. The dogs knew no pain or fatigue. They were beyond everything but their vicious orders. As strong as Maloc was, he could not slow their grisly attacks and grew weaker and weaker until he was little more than a giant chew toy.

* * *

Isaac called off the attack. The dogs stopped shredding Maloc but held him pinned, undead jaws clamped like locked manacles. Isaac hopped off the car, strolled over, and knelt next to him.

"This isn't possible," Maloc hissed. He could barely speak with the General's jaws around his neck. Thick black ichor oozed like sap from his countless wounds.

"I guess you're just not a good judge of talent."

"You planned this from the start." Maloc sounded emotionally injured by Isaac's betrayal, but that was typical of demons. They always expected everyone else to play by the rules.

"Oh, stop with the sob story. You're just mad that I outsmarted you." From his everbag, Isaac removed a glass jar. When he pulled out a pocketknife, Maloc's eyes widened. "Relax." Using the flat of the blade, Isaac scraped Maloc's blood into the jar. "Demon ichor has a lot of uses. Used in potions. Made into poisons. Spread on toast."

"I will see you dead for this."

"Yes, yes, of course you will."

"Why did you wait for me? If you're such a powerful magician, then why didn't you just escape?"

"I had a job to do."

The demon's discolored eyes went wide. "Someone hired you to do this? Who? I demand to know!" Anger made him struggle, but it was brief, as it caused the canine teeth to shift painfully in his flesh.

"Exactly who they are, I really can't say. Just a voice on the phone to me."

Somehow, the defeated demon managed to look even more dejected as he said one word. "Arrangement."

"Yeah. I work for Arrangement. But it's just a title. I have no idea who they really are, other than a paycheck. When you started looking for a magician to help you get home, I guess you drew their attention. I know most of the rules about this crap are unwritten, but crossing back to Hell in a mortal body is a no-no. On top of that, they certainly didn't want the tarot card going with you." He leaned an elbow on General's massive head, which elicited a hiss of pain from the demon as the jaws shifted. "They even ordered me to not destroy you utterly, which is fine, because that would have been a lot more work. I guess they want you to suffer."

"You're going to pay for this. I won't forget this betrayal."

"You're right about that. You won't forget this at all. These wounds won't heal. Sure, the snake venom will run its course, but since your demonic insides are particularly averse to anything holy, well, you get the idea."

"You've crippled me," Maloc said softly, with the realization of someone informed they have a terminal disease.

"Yep." Isaac held his hand out, and Maloc's Bowie knife lifted from the gravel and floated to him. He tucked it into the everbag, and then, as a final dig, he opened the bag wide so that Maloc could see it was still empty.

Isaac patted the demon's coat and dug his truck keys from a pocket. As he did, he felt something else and removed another folded cloth tied with string. He unwrapped just enough to take a peek.

Another card from the Black Tarot.

The illustration showed a mass of snakes undulating, like a holographic image, in small spasms. Their eyes shone red, and tongues flicked. He quickly looked away and covered it back up. The reputation of these cards held that they shouldn't even be idly looked upon.

"You sneaky bastard," Isaac said as he tucked it into his bag. "You were gonna trade one card for passage and cash in the other back in Hell. Not a bad plan."

Maloc snarled. "You're a dead man, Isaac. You're not the only magician out there. I'll find someone to heal me. Then I'll find you."

"Oh, there's a spell to cure you, but the key ingredient will be the dog teeth. I'm going to hide them in a very secret place. So, you better pray that nothing happens to me, because then you'll never find them."

Isaac whistled again and pointed at Maloc's pickup truck. The dogs released him and trotted to the vehicle as fast as their multiple broken bones allowed. Maloc struggled to move but only flopped over in the dirt.

"See you around, Maloc."

"Isaac," Maloc called out. "You'll regret this."

* * *

Isaac drove as far as he could before exhaustion forced him to pull off on a gravel side road. Now that the job was done, the fatigue rushed back with no nervous energy to offset it. He hopped into the bed of the truck amongst his pack.

Despite their horrific wounds and rotting stench, he sat with them until dawn. Listening to the desert sounds, he watched the stars fade and the eastern horizon turn red. When the sun provided sufficient light, he set to his final task.

He ordered the dogs out of the truck so that when the spell was broken, he wouldn't be forced to haul their massive weight out. *No need to take any further dignity from them.* He pulled down his collar, fingered the leather pouch secured around his neck with string and plastered to his chest with duct tape.

As he peeled the pouch away from the beating of his heart, the dogs fell to earth, their bodies finally joining their spirits at rest. Isaac felt a wave of refreshment as the shared life force rushed back. Despite the drain lifted from his soul, he was still dead on his feet, but the sun warmed his face, and that helped.

He opened the pouch and sifted through the contents. Teeth, one from each dog, meticulously scrimshawed with runes and then colored with his blood. Nail trimmings, tufts of fur, and whiskers—all hung over his heart to echo with the beating.

Pliers in hand, he started the grisly task of removing the rest of the canines' teeth. More than once, he winced when a tooth cracked free. More than once, he whispered an apology and patted a head gently. Useless gestures that he nonetheless performed.

What he hadn't planned on was a respectful burial. He felt guilty doing nothing, so he piled some sand and rock atop the bodies, a half-assed measure that would do little to protect from desert scavengers and didn't make him feel any better.

He started the truck, which farted out a cloud of black smoke, then twisted the radio dial from one end to the other, getting nothing but static and an occasional Southern-fried brimstone preacher. He sighed, snapped his fingers at the radio, and drove east humming along to "House of the Rising Sun."

Chapter 5
ARRANGEMENT

In southern New Jersey, on a sprawling rural estate, sat a mammoth structure publicly known as Trumbull Manor. Built in 1871, it was a hodgepodge of designs—Queen Anne Revival, American Gothic, and a touch of Italianate Villa—as if created by an indecisive architect with endless funding. The surrounding landscaping, while not gracing the cover of any gardening magazines, was maintained just enough to strengthen the façade of it being the summer home of some reclusive millionaire.

Known privately as the Athenaeum, the interior held one of the largest collections of arcane knowledge in the world. Every once opulent room had been converted into makeshift offices for the army of bustling researchers known as librarians.

The lobby stood bare except for a single pedestal, upon which sat an old-fashioned rotary phone. Ivory in color with ebony numbers, it was simple, elegant, and eerie. All the Athenaeum staff gave it a wide berth, and Isaac did no different. With a shoulder brushing the wall, he made his way past it.

Isaac's assigned librarian, a jolly Norwegian man called Lefse, would have made an impressive Viking on Halloween, albeit one who had done a bit too much feasting and not enough pillaging. With an eager hand, Lefse jotted down every detail, no matter how minute, of Isaac's meeting with Maloc and the Asphalt Devils. Isaac saw that Lefse even wrote down "King Shit."

"So, how many of these vacationing motorcycle enthusiasts did you get killed?"

"What? They were not enthusiasts. They were a hardcore criminal biker gang." Isaac knew his protests were for naught. "Five."

"And the bartender makes six." Lefse scribbled more notes. "Still not as bad as that time at the cultist ranch."

"For the last time, I didn't start that fire."

Isaac was used to these meetings, but initially had detested them. No self-respecting magician would enjoy revealing the nature of their tricks. Doing so was just antithetical to their being. But Lefse's enthusiasm had won him over enough to make it tolerable. Besides, Isaac always left out any personal revelations.

With the tale finished, Lefse closed the folder. The label on it read *Isaac Unknown*. The Norwegian still didn't accept that Isaac truly didn't know his own last name, so he had created the moniker with a good-natured chuckle.

"Now, let's see the goodies." Lefse set an ornate oaken box on the desk—the cloth-lined interior perfectly molded for the Black Tarot card that Isaac placed in it.

Lefse's mouth dropped open. "A real Black Tarot card. The Emperor. I've never seen any in person." He poked it around with his pen as if prodding a dead animal that may spring to life. "He only had the one?"

Isaac kept a plain face. "Just one."

"That's a shame. I sincerely hoped he'd have more."

Isaac shrugged. "One is trouble enough."

"Damn. Oh well, one is better than none, but not better than two, as my grandmother used to say when I stole donuts." He closed the box with a click. "I wish we could have a few days with it. So much to learn."

"What happens to it now?"

Lefse frowned the way he always did when Isaac asked a question he didn't have a long-winded answer for. "It'll go to the basement. All the dangerous stuff goes straight to the basement." Isaac raised his eyebrows in lieu of his obvious follow-up. Lefse's frown deepened. "In the basement is a sign that says, 'no entry' and behind an iron wall that not even the executive staff can get past. What lies beyond..." He let out a snort and tapped his pen a few times before leaning forwards and lowering his voice. "I haven't figured that out yet."

Isaac shouldered his everbag. "When you do, I'd be curious to know."

"I bet. You know it'll be tit for tat, right? You'll have to cough up, oh, I don't know, little details like your real name or who you apprenticed under."

Isaac had no intention of answering, but didn't even have the opportunity to say something pithy before a deafeningly loud phone rang. They both winced. Not just because of the volume. It went deeper than that, piercing the psyche and rattling directly inside one's mind.

"That's for you, my friend," his liaison said, suddenly lugubrious.

"Yeah." The ringing's psychic pokes told him that. Under each spine-vibrating *briiiing,* he could almost hear his name being whispered. As he spent little time at the Athenaeum, the task of answering the calls generally fell to Lefse and his fellow librarians. Isaac decided at that moment that he preferred it that way.

With Lefse on his heels, he headed for the lobby. The uncomfortable effects of each clamorous ring had brought the busy Athenaeum to a halt. People paused their tasks and peeked out of their offices. Isaac imagined this was how it would have been to be a student called to the principal's office, with dozens of apprehensive yet curious faces lining up to witness the gallows walk.

It wasn't that the phone rang rarely. Quite the contrary, it did so rather frequently. It was the ominous power and the haunting otherworldliness it exuded that kept the librarians from acclimating to it. They were charged with cataloging arcane knowledge large and small, yet the greatest source of magic remained completely unknown to them.

No one knew who or what Arrangement was. They didn't know where the calls came from. They didn't know how it knew what it knew or how it created its assignments. Under the stare of dozens of eyes, Isaac answered the phone.

"Hello," he said through gritted teeth, like he was anticipating the tip of an injection.

"Isaac," said the Voice of Arrangement.

An old adage to describe a bad phone connection is that the person sounds like they're talking from the bottom of a well. The voice saying his name was reminiscent of that—a static-laced utterance whispering up through a drainpipe. It struggled to string words together like a winded old man, or maybe it just didn't know how to breathe. He'd long assumed it was something inhuman, attempting to speak like a human, calling from a place where no humans existed.

Isaac listened to its instructions as if tolerating an uncomfortable dental procedure and then quickly hung up. The assembled librarians, disappointed that nothing extraordinary had happened for the umpteenth time, resumed their duties. He rubbed his temples, feeling more of a headache than any of his boozing had ever caused him. The Voice of Arrangement hadn't mentioned the snake-covered card he had left in his everbag, and he deflated like a balloon with profound relief.

"That's why around here we call it the Ivory Migraine," Lefse said. "New assignment?"

"Yeah."

"Any juicy details?"

"Guess I'm going hunting."

Chapter 6
THE HEAD LIBRARIAN

One thing most of the librarians had in common was a disheveled-professor fashion sense. The Athenaeum had no official dress code, and the staff ran the gamut from wrinkled business casual to pajamas. Lefse himself strutted around daily in baggy sweatpants, button-strained cardigans, and sandals.

Fashion sense was only one of many reasons that Lefse disliked the Head Librarian, who called himself Mabahazi. Mid-fifties but aging without grace, as evidenced by his darkly dyed hair, Mabahazi dressed like a stockbroker and acted like a lawyer. Normally he only met with staff members begrudgingly, but today the Head Librarian gregariously ushered Lefse into his office and offered him a seat in an overly expensive leather chair at his overly luxurious mahogany desk. Lefse knew the man's excitement had nothing to do with seeing him.

"Is this the tarot card?" Mabahazi asked excitedly, wringing his hands.

Lefse set the box on the desk. "Yes."

Mabahazi reached for it, hesitated, and drew back. "Can you open it for me?"

Yet another reason Lefse disliked him. If he were an archaeologist, he'd be the kind who sat under an umbrella while hired hands did the digging. At least the man's excitement distracted him from the look of contempt on Lefse's face as he flipped the lid. Mabahazi leaned away skittishly as if he expected a jack-in-the-box to spring out, but when nothing happened, he peered in.

"Amazing," he whispered. "Would you mind flipping the card so I may see the other side?"

This request stunned Lefse and left him half-tempted to throttle the smaller man. "I will not. These cards are as powerful as they are unpredictable. If you want to touch it, then be my guest."

At first, Mabahazi scowled with annoyance, but he quickly relented, either because he was intimidated by Lefse's size or because he realized how dangerously unreasonable the request was. "Yes. Yes. You're right. Just the one card, then?"

"Isaac said it was just the one."

Mabahazi hummed distrustfully but accepted that no contrasting evidence had been presented. "Close the box, please. You may go."

Eager to be away from the man, Lefse did as instructed and headed for the door. He paused to say, "I filed Isaac Unknown's interview."

"Thank you. Did he touch the card?"

"I'm sure he did. Knowing Isaac, he probably shuffled it like he was playing poker." Lefse knew this to be untrue, but had an idea that it would rankle Mabahazi, which it did, as the man's face darkened. He grabbed the doorknob.

"It's a shame, don't you think?"

Lefse looked back. "What?"

"That we have to lock up such wondrous artifacts. Imagine the things we could learn if we had the time to properly study and use them."

While this wasn't unappealing to his own inquisitive nature, Lefse knew his boss used the word *we* loosely. The scenario that popped into Lefse's head consisted of him and his peers delving into dangerous work while Mabahazi watched with binoculars from a bomb shelter. "I guess. Although isn't that why we turn them over to Arrangement? Because this knowledge isn't meant for us mere mortals?"

Mabahazi's earlier enthusiasm vanished, replaced now by his usual generalized disdain. "Yes. Mere..." He waved a hand. "Dismissed."

Grateful, Lefse wandered out, mumbling under his breath, "'Dismissed'? I'll dismiss you with a body slam, you pompous ass."

* * *

Alone in his office, Mabahazi seethed impotently. He cherished his décor too much to willfully smash anything, and his power wasn't such that he could lash out violently. As a manager he knew better than to vent on his subordinates, knowing he'd need their loyalty in the future. So, sulking in his chair was the only method of venting available, and he did that with vigor.

If he could have possessed anything at that moment, it would have been the courage to open the box. Mabahazi was not a brave man. Inquisitive. Intelligent. Rational. But not brave.

It wasn't the tarot card he feared, despite the dangerous legends. After all, if that derelict nomad Isaac had handled it safely, then he should have had no issues. Instead, the act of disobedience terrified him—Isaac stepping out of line when he had no idea where the boundary had been drawn.

But otherworldly secrets were the blood and bane of all magicians, and he, despite his lofty title, was no different. Surely just a peek wouldn't hurt. Mabahazi moved his fingertips to the sides of the box and paused, listening intently for the ivory phone. When nothing happened, he grew bolder and flipped the lid. The silence continued. Giddy with anticipation, he reached for the card.

The lobby phone rang. Despite the distance, the volume was such that it may as well have been sitting on his desk. He nearly fell from his chair and a passing librarian dropped a ream of paper. The phone rang once more before he gathered his wits and snapped the lid on the run box shut. After that, it fell silent.

Already his temples ached. Like everyone on the receiving end, he'd instinctively known the call had been for him.

No. Not a call. A warning.

With a trembling voice, he repeatedly apologized to the air, hoping the Voice of Arrangement heard and forgave. Box in hand, he hurried from his office to the freight elevator that carried him to the basement. It opened to a long concrete hallway that dead-ended into an iron wall. At first glance, it appeared to be a door, but there were no hinges or handles—only a drop slot exactly the size of the box he carried. This was no coincidence. The slot always had the exact dimensions to accommodate a delivered artifact. Be it a jewelry box or a coffin, the hatch preemptively transformed to fit.

He hated it—a complete surrender, akin to handing over a life-changing lottery ticket. He pushed the box a quarter of the way into the slot and a greedy force yanked it from his fingers. It disappeared into the iron wall, and to where and to what purpose he had no idea.

And not knowing was the most infuriating thing.

Chapter 7
SIXTEEN-POINT ELDER TICK

Isaac would have missed the address if not for the giant billboard. Despite the faded and chipped paint, he made out the cartoon rooster wearing an army helmet and firing a shoulder-mounted bazooka. Projecting from the weapon in a cloud of smoke was a large, round breast, hurtling nipple-first at an unknown target.

BOOBzookas!

Isaac parked Maloc's truck under the sign, slung his everbag on, and walked in, glancing over his shoulder several times at the sign to let out puerile chuckles. With a name like that, he may have stopped here anyway, or at least taken a picture of the sign.

The dark interior helped hide the outdated and ill-kept furniture. Three dancers took turns swinging from the pole on the single stage or strolling around looking for tips, exuding all the energy of people bagging groceries. The handful of patrons watched, not with excitement, but resignation, as if they knew this should be arousing but couldn't muster up the spirit for it. They waved dollar bills, tucked them into proffered G-strings, and exchanged smiles with the dancers, but it exuded all the fun of an ATM withdrawal. The music was loud, but not booming. Old speakers hissed and crackled periodically. Not that they could ruin the awful country-rock fusion. Too hard rock to be country but not hard rock enough to be good.

A tall man with a receding hairline accentuated by a tight ponytail picked up his beer and walked over.

"You Isaac? The magician?" he inquired as casually as if asking, *"You the plumber?"* Isaac nodded and shook the man's hand. "I'm Wallace. Follow me."

Isaac tailed the man to a crowded table in the corner farthest from the stage.

When attending a business meeting with clients one has never met, one tends to develop an idea about just how professional these clients will appear. Lawyers would have suits and be sleazy. Artists would be fashionable and pretentious. And so on. These preconceived notions were what led Isaac to believe that this group of professional vampire hunters would be former soldiers or covert operatives or hand-to-hand combat experts or snipers or ninjas. Certainly something different than Wallace's crew.

Who were *hillbillies. Good ole boys. Rednecks.*

They were a collection of men who apparently took the "hunter" part of "vampire hunter" literally. These guys looked like they should be wandering through the woods shooting anything that moved and mounting it on their mantle. Or eating it. Raw.

They were playing poker, smoking cigars, chewing tobacco, and pounding beers. A pretty, dark-haired waitress in mismatched thrift-store lingerie brought them another round. The group did their best to be boorish—drunkenly attempting to grope her—but she deftly maneuvered around their paws, sidestepped failed pinches, and, in one case, just brusquely slapped a hand away. Isaac found her a lot of fun to watch and quickly rooted for her against his new teammates.

"Listen up, assholes!" Wallace called them to order, which struck Isaac as coincidental because that was exactly how he would have referred to this group. "This is Isaac. He's our hired magician."

The crew looked up as one, seemed to do a quick evaluation of Isaac purely on the length of his beard and lack of camouflage accouterments, and returned to their game. Wallace squeezed two more chairs into the table. While he did so, the waitress asked Isaac if he wanted anything.

"Bourbon on the rocks, please." Politeness must have been a rare currency here, as she gave him a genuine smile.

Wallace introduced the men. Slim—a bony man capable of smoking, drinking, and chewing tobacco all at the same time. Drink, spit, inhale, exhale, drink, spit, in rapid succession. Surely impressive even to his brethren. Frank—stocky with a chest-length beard and a Confederate flag ball cap. Lee—almost as stocky as Frank, but with a shorter beard and a camouflage hat, which would surely render the top half of his skull invisible in a jungle setting. Rocky—a mountain of a man, solid and dim-looking. Finally, Cash, who appeared to be the youngest of the crew. He, of all of them, Isaac voted most likely to have been dragged out of a trailer kicking and screaming by police. He had short unkempt hair, bad teeth, and a patchy beard that made his face look unwashed.

"What the hell we need a mo-gician for? We've been on plenty of tick hunts without one." This gem of a statement came from Cash.

Tick. A derogatory term for a vampire. Others included mosquito, tapeworm, flea, and leech. Isaac preferred the term "leech," but had to admit that "tick" snapped off the tongue with fervor. "Mosquito" was too much of a mouthful and tapeworms were just gross. So, tick won the day.

But *mo-gician*?

"Supposedly, this tick is different," Wallace said.

"Bullshit. You kill one tick, you've killed them all," Cash boasted, and he crushed his empty beer can with a ferocity that would surely be intimidating to some kind of being physically incapable of crushing such a can.

"Different? How is it different?" Isaac asked, more concerned with this information than with Cash's amazing strength.

They were interrupted by the return of the waitress, who dispensed cheap beers to greedy hands. She leaned over Isaac, brushing against his shoulder as she set his drink down. She smelled of perfume, sweat, and cigarette smoke—a melded scent that enthralled in strip clubs alone. Again, he thanked her and received another cute smile for it. He would never brag about his social acumen, so if he could get such sweet looks for simply not being a drunken lout, he'd take it as a win. When she moved out of earshot, he repeated his question to Wallace.

"We're hunting an elder tomorrow."

"Excuse me?" If they had been in a sitcom, this would be the part where Isaac spit out his bourbon in a surprised spray.

"The job we have is for an elder vampire," Wallace confirmed.

"Figures to be over two hundred years old." This came from Slim, who said it the same way a fisherman would describe a legendary catfish.

"An elder? An elder vampire?" Isaac repeated, looking from one drunken face to another. He got nothing back but expressions ranging from uncaring to vapid. "Have you guys ever hunted an elder before?"

A couple of shrugs before Lee snapped at him. "What's the big deal? We walk in, find the snoozing sum'bitch, and stake the shit out of him. We've done it before. No big deal. I don't even understand why we need you, 'cause frankly, you don't look like much." This brought some guffaws from the group.

Isaac downed his drink and turned to Wallace. "Why do you need me? 'Cause he's right. I don't look like much, and looks are obviously very important at this table."

"The elder may be protected by traps. Magic traps," Wallace said. The collective table started naysaying and complaining about how such things didn't exist. "So, Arrangement said to have you disarm any traps so we can take out the tick."

"Oh, fucking hell. *Magic*. Next, you'll be telling us that the Tooth Fairy and the Easter Bunny are real," Cash said.

Isaac turned to him. "You hunt vampires for a living. You've seen the immortal, undead, blood-drinking monsters with your own eyes. But you don't believe in magic?"

"They're animals. Just animals. No different than hunting deer or duck or possum or deer..." Cash ran out of animal names.

Isaac sighed. "True. Most wildlife does burst into flames in the sun."

Wallace, enough of a leader to see the conversation boiling into a possible fight, held up a hand. The group respected the man enough to shut the hell up. "Look, I don't like taking on outsiders for our jobs any more than y'all do. But the people paying us say he has to go. So, he goes. He'll do his part. We'll do ours. Get it done and go our separate ways." The table begrudgingly agreed and, happy to be leaving, Isaac stood.

"Hold on there, Merlin," Cash said, impressing Isaac by knowing the famous name. "How do we know you're really a mo-gician? Shouldn't you do some sort of trick? Pull a rabbit out of your man-purse there?" The reference to Isaac's everbag brought more lowbrow laughter.

Normally Isaac would never stoop to tricks for the *oohs* and *ahhs* of rubes, but the purse jab rankled him. Maybe only Indiana Jones could pull off a satchel. He sat back down, took a fifty-dollar bill from his wallet and a pen from the table, wrote something on it, and began folding it.

"You gonna make that appear behind my ear?" Lee snickered.

"No, I like to keep my money clean."

Lee opened his mouth for some kind of retort, but was beaten by Slim, who said, "Don't say nothing. You got the dirtiest ears I've ever seen." This brought several more into the verbal fray exchanging barbs and laughs.

Finally, Isaac held up a money paper airplane. More teasing came when they saw the final product, but the voices stopped when Isaac let the plane go and it just hovered in the air. Then, as he directed it telekinetically with subtle hand movements, it sailed around the table, picked up speed, and performed a couple of loops and spirals. The group watched in quiet surprise. It orbited Wallace's head a few times and then launched off across the bar, sailed over the big hairdo of the dancer onstage, and landed gently on the serving tray of the waitress. She noticed it quickly, unfolded it, read the note, and then looked at their table. She winked.

Satisfied that he had quelled their skepticism without really having to exert himself, Isaac again got up to leave. But no one clings to misguided beliefs quite like morons do, and Cash arrogantly spouted, "A paper airplane? Really? What a crock of shit."

Isaac smiled but had no intention of performing further parlor tricks. "Earlier you mentioned the Tooth Fairy. I've seen a tooth fairy.

Horrible little bastards. Although I think everyone at this table would be safe." He started to walk away, paused when he recognized they didn't get the insult. "Because of the lack of dental hygiene." Still nothing. "Bad teeth." He gave up.

Wallace followed him to the door. "Y'know, the boys have a point. You don't hunt a sixteen-point buck any different than you'd hunt a twelve-pointer."

"I'm sure I'd disagree with you if I had any idea what you were talking about."

"Deer. Those are deer. Points on their antlers." Wallace held his hands to his head and splayed his fingers out as if Isaac didn't know what antlers were.

Isaac sighed, opened his mouth, found no words, sighed again, and said good night.

* * *

What Isaac had written on the money airplane was the name of a nearby all-night truck-stop diner. It had struck him as a good idea at that time and place. But sitting here, sipping coffee, he realized it was dead quiet, which meant if the waitress showed, he'd have to do his part to converse. Simple politeness wouldn't carry the day. So, he opted to chicken out and had just stood up when she walked in.

The waitress had swapped the mismatched lingerie for street clothes, but she had that same sweet grin for him. "I'm Susan. You're leaving? Want to stay for coffee?"

"Isaac. Sure. I'll have some"—and he realized he still stood next to his half-drunk cup—"more of that one right there."

They sat down. Isaac had no head for a give-and-take conversation, especially one with introductory small talk. But he was endlessly curious, so he rattled off questions. Susan proved gregarious, and he listened with rapt attention. She grew up locally with middle-class parents and took the waitress job to save money to split between restoring her mother's Camaro and paying for school. She listed hobbies: watercolors, hiking, and photography. Her answers were enthusiastic, normal, and real, and Isaac loved every minute of it. At no point did her tale include demons or monsters and absolutely nobody died.

Alas, eventually she turned the tide back to him. He couldn't hide in plain sight all night. "So why exactly are you hanging around with Wallace and his crew?"

"I... umm..." How did he not anticipate this question? He had to think of something plausible, and quick. "I'm a professional hunting guide." It was all he could do to not wince at how terrible this lie was. His tongue turned clumsy when talking to regular people.

"Right," she said skeptically. "Those guys have been hunting around here for years. What exactly could you teach them to hunt?"

He only knew how to keep digging. "Deer." He put his hands to his forehead to mime antlers just as Wallace had, and she burst into laughter.

"No way. Look, if you don't want to tell me..."

He racked his brain for a way to sort of tell the truth. That was why he hated these situations. He could never tell the damn truth. It would be so liberating for once. "Part of my job is to work with people who are going to do incredibly stupid things and assist them with not dying."

Susan sensed his sincerity, but couldn't quite acknowledge his explanation as real employment. "So, you're like an all-purpose lifeguard?"

"I guess. Sometimes."

"Well, that's great. You save people. Are you good at it?"

"Not really."

"Oh."

Great, have coffee with a pretty girl and tell her you're bad at your profession. That reset his low bar.

"But it's got to be a really hard job." She was so sweet to attempt this salvaging. "I'm sure you try your best."

Ouch. He contemplated running for the door, but he didn't want to stiff her with the check. "Yeah..."

A realization came to her. "So, does this mean Wallace and Cash and the others might die tomorrow?"

"Yup." Now, *that* he answered with abrupt honesty when he should have lied. He'd never get this right.

Susan leaned forwards. "Is it legal?"

Isaac was thrilled to not technically know and therefore not have to put thought into the answer. "I really have no idea."

"Wow. That's some heavy stuff."

Isaac was socially spent. "Look, I'm sorry. I shouldn't have bothered you. It was just a weird impulse that I should have ignored. As soon as I do this job and save"—he cleared his throat on the last word, so it didn't sound too hopeful—"the hunters, I'm going to move on. My job keeps me from settling down. But it was nice of you to join me." He dished out money for the check.

Susan smiled at him, but he couldn't identify what kind of smile it really was. When it came to expressions, he only excelled at spotting dimwittedness and bloodlust. Was it a sign of attraction or the same look she'd give to a stray puppy? "Thanks for the coffee and the tip and the conversation. It was nice meeting you." She slid to the edge of her seat.

"Hang on."

From his everbag, he retrieved a crudely constructed amulet. Two stones—a carnelian and a citrine—twisted together with wire. A piece of sturdy twine just long enough for a neck finished it off. He handed it to her. "It's good luck."

While it was impossible to gauge the efficacy of such trinkets, he hoped when life got precarious for her, the amulet would give a compensating nudge to her confidence, prosperity, and karma.

"You sure? You don't look like the kind of person that believes in luck."

"That's why I'm giving it away."

She laughed slightly and stood, tucking the bauble into her pocket. "If you're ever back this way, you know where to find me. Maybe we'll see each other again."

Probably best that we don't, he thought, but he only said a simple goodbye.

Back in his hotel, he collapsed on the bed without even removing his shoes. Meeting Susan had gone as well as he could have hoped. An unimpressive date to be sure, but it began and ended in ordinary fashion.

Ordinary was a luxury he could rarely afford.

A small movement caught his gaze from the corner. A web disturbed the shadows as a small spider danced across it. He opened the everbag and retrieved a small glass jar.

Every little thing helped.

Chapter 8
THE GREAT VAMPIRE HUNT

Isaac awoke with the dawn that filtered through the twisted window blinds and beamed directly into his eyes. He sighed, yawned, and, still dressed from the night before, headed out to Maloc's truck with the intention of driving for a quick breakfast. Something had been tucked under the windshield wiper.

A one-dollar bill, folded into a paper airplane. On it was written, "This is a tip for a fun night. Don't die today!" A smiley face dotted the exclamation point.

This may have been the greatest token of affection he'd ever received. The smile didn't fade from his face until the hillbilly hunters pulled up behind him and laid on the horn. At this point, he remembered he was taking a bunch of idiots to fight a vampire and the mood faded. He tucked the dollar bill away for luck, lamented his empty stomach, and joined the surprisingly punctual crew.

In moments he was whisked into the rear seat of a large van, itself part of a small convoy. The riders engaged in no perfunctory chitchat. Everyone kept quiet—not due to any kind of introspective focus but because they were all hung over.

Slim sprawled out on the seat in front of him. Lee drove and Rocky rode shotgun. All three had open beers, opting for hair-of-the-dog cures. Country music twanged its way through the speakers, but thankfully, the headaches kept them from cranking the volume.

As they drove, Isaac grew more concerned. What troubled him most about the job, other than being torn limb from limb, was the implausible setup. Vampires were creatures of wealth and privilege, especially elders. Hiding out in Nowheresville in the lower Midwest typically ranked below their status. For one to reach such a ripe old age meant they were crafty, clandestine, and powerful. Undoubtedly, they had monstrous servants, traps armed with more traps, secret chambers, and multiple safe houses. It was a tall order to even pinpoint one's location. With all that, Arrangement found an elder vampire and then handed the assassination to a bunch of redneck amateurs? Nothing made sense.

"So, an elder," Slim said, obviously toying with some kind of inquiry.

"Yeah?"

"If it's so old, shouldn't it be kind of weak? A withered old man?"

"Vampires grow more powerful as they age. Whatever dark force flows through them is enhanced by time and blood."

Slim let out a low whistle. "So, one that's two or three hundred..."

"Would be a virtually unstoppable killing machine."

He nodded, swigged his beer, and rubbed his chin scruff. "So why you coming along? If you're so sure we're going to die and all?"

The answer that popped into Isaac's head was that he had no idea what the consequences would be for refusing an Arrangement directive. He declined to give Slim such a doom-and-gloom response. "I really doubt there's an elder out here. I expect we'll encounter just a younger one or maybe nothing at all."

The landscape became even more rural, passing only occasional farmsteads or small, dilapidated mobile homes until they pulled into a winding gravel driveway that led to a shuttered-up farmhouse. It showed all the signs of long-term abandonment: boarded windows, overgrown weeds, and peeling paint.

With no regard for subtlety, they parked in full view of the house. Isaac counted himself lucky that they didn't honk the horns to announce themselves. They clambered out and went to work unloading. The first thing opened was a beer cooler, with each proceeding to chug one while they geared up. Isaac watched the preparations, growing more annoyed with each piece of equipment produced.

Things looked up when they pulled out the most efficient vampire-hunting weapons—crossbows with mounted lights. Isaac's spirits lifted momentarily, but then came the rest of the gear. They had nothing else of practical use. Sure, they had pistols, shotguns, and rifles, which might be handy in a pitched fight, able to knock a vampire down and stun it long enough to stake it. But only Wallace had a stake—just one—tucked through his belt next to a hefty mallet.

They had no defensive equipment at all. No chain mail neck guards, no Kevlar vests or padding on knees and elbows. No helmets. Isaac's experience with vampires was limited, actually nonexistent if research were taken out of the equation, but he knew in a fang-fight one was more likely to die from a beating than from a bite. Broken bones, crushed skulls, ripped limbs. Hunting caps and tank tops would do little to prevent such wounds.

They loaded weapons, strapped on knives, swigged beers, and smoked and chewed tobacco. A bunch of good ole boys fixing up for a weekend in the woods.

Slim came and stood next to Isaac. The hunter had a golf-ball-sized lump of chaw in his mouth, making his bottom lip bulge out.

"They talk?"

"Huh?" Isaac replied.

"They talk? Ticks? Can they talk?"

"Yeah. They can talk. They're pretty much the same people they were before becoming ticks. Only fangier."

"Seriously?"

The questions bothered Isaac. "How many have you guys killed?"

"Three."

Hunting vampires was a dangerous profession, so the number satisfied Isaac. "But you never heard one talk?"

"Nah. Wallace staked them all while they were sleeping. Sure enough, they started hissing and flailing about, but they never really talked."

"So, you've never encountered one awake?"

"Nah. I hope we never do. Must be a hell of a thing to hear." Then, as if to purposefully spoil his introspective moment, he spit a giant stream of brown saliva onto the gravel.

Wallace had moved to the front of the convoy and was studying the house intently, one hand on his hip, the other hoisting a crossbow onto his shoulder. He certainly had the look of a battle-hardened veteran. The others waited behind him for the issuance of what Isaac assumed would be a battle plan. After another minute of this posturing, he finally turned and said, "All right, boys, we got a tick to bag," and simply walked up the drive. The others followed, advancing like a Revolutionary War skirmish line. Isaac frowned and followed several feet behind.

They were about a hundred feet from the house when they first felt it. A tingling at the nape. Goosebumps on the arms. One by one they slowed to a stop. Breaths came hard. Hands shook. All macho bravado ceased. Isaac felt it too—a sudden, acute foreboding that intensified the closer he came. His blood quickened, sweat spread under his arms, and butterflies swarmed in his stomach. They were rooted in place, and Frank vomited up his liquid breakfast.

All the symptoms of fear.

It made no sense. They were still outside. These hillbillies were too headstrong, and possibly too drunk, to already be so scared. And Isaac, well, he wasn't one to brag, but he was rarely afraid. The emotion had been harshly trained out of him early in life. If he was fearful when he knew he normally wouldn't be, then the emotion had to be artificial.

A dread spell—fear magic cast on an object, in this case the house, to keep out interlopers. That had to be it. It was a spell that probably generated ninety-nine percent of the haunted house legends in the country. No one with powerful secrets wanted to suffer the indignity of having them discovered by nosey neighbors or petty burglars.

"Stay put," he shouted to the team needlessly, as they kept trembling in place. He advanced on the house, moving normally now that he had ascertained the spell. Still, he marveled at the tangible effects. So strange to feel the physical manifestations minus the emotional ones.

The runes were easy to find. A sequence of symbols had been carved into one of the front porch stairs. No attempt had been made to disguise it. Its designer probably assumed no one would get close enough to the house to see it. The first symbol was a half-circle with a series of lines below. With his pocketknife, he defaced it by completing the circle and adding a smiley face to the middle.

The spell ceased and Isaac felt the fear wash away. The hunters behind him did as well. They straightened up, and looked around at each other, wondering what had scared them so badly, but already pretending it hadn't happened. Fear would never be shared amongst these type.

Beer-fueled courage renewed, they advanced again on the house. Isaac sighed at their brashness. Without scouting the property, they just walked up in a bunch onto the porch. Unable to see inside through the boarded-up windows—to keep out prying eyes and dangerous sunlight—Rocky reached for the knob on the front door.

"Stop," Isaac ordered. "Let me check it." The big man, easily the most affable of the bunch, moved aside. Isaac checked the frame. Next, he moved his hands around the door itself, palms hovering about an inch away from the wood. One of the hunters started to ask something and Isaac silenced him with a hiss. From top to bottom, left to right, he waved his hands.

"Seriously? What the hell you doing?" Cash finally asked, annoyed that he hadn't killed anything yet.

"I'm feeling for spells on the other side of the door. Some magic gives off a wave, a vibration, like holding your finger to someone's wrist to find the pulse. It's faint, but you can feel it if you know what you're doing."

"And?" asked Wallace.

"Nothing here that I can feel."

"Shit, whatever." Cash shouldered past him and reached for the knob.

"That doesn't mean there's no regular trap. A shotgun wired to the knob wouldn't emanate any magical auras." This gave Cash pause. "Go on," Isaac goaded, "break it down." The hunter bristled, clearly struggling with one instinct to kick the door and another to punch Isaac in the face. Instead of either, he stood there like a dipshit doing nothing.

Quickly tiring of the standoff, Isaac moved to the door, standing to the side in case of some kind of projectile trap. He reached for the knob, stopping when he noticed the rest of the team still stupidly lined up in front of it. Resisting the urge to twist the knob and see if a cannon fired and killed them all, he gestured at them like an irritated teacher to unresponsive students, and they finally nudged each other out of the way.

A gentle twist of the knob revealed the door to be locked. He dug into the everbag and produced a key. It was old-fashioned, heavy iron at both ends, but the barrel of it was calcified bone—specifically the index finger of a very talented but long-dead thief. He tapped it on the knob and smiled as it unlocked itself with a satisfying click.

He pushed the door open and peered in but could make out nothing in the gloom. Wallace took point, shining his crossbow light into the house. "Just the first room," Isaac said. "No further." The leader nodded, and one by one they entered. They secured the first room with the most disorganized lack of professionalism Isaac had ever seen. The group just strolled around and shined their lights all over the damn place.

The room was empty. Nothing but run-of-the-mill furniture covered in dust and cobwebs. Three doorways led out. One to a flight of stairs up. One to a kitchen. The last to stairs down into blackness.

"Don't leave the room. Start pulling those boards off the windows. Let that sunlight in."

This order made sense to them, and they got to work at it. Except for Cash, who just leaned against a wall and made childish faces. Isaac ignored him and kept up his inspection. The doorway leading upstairs was clean, the same as the entrance to the kitchen. However, at the top of the basement stairs, he noticed something of interest.

Sunlight pouring in from a newly liberated window highlighted a drop of liquid in the center of the doorway floor. He borrowed a flashlight from Slim and panned the light up one side of the frame and across the top, where he found another. A liquid bubble just hanging there, defying gravity, directly above the spot on the floor.

"What is it?" Slim asked as the curious others gathered around.

Isaac thought for a minute to suggest someone watch the other stairway, in case some kind of monster came down, but figured eh, what was the point? "I think it's a drowning pillar."

"A what?"

Isaac knelt and looked closer for marks he knew had to be there. He found them. Around each drop was a faint circle, a barely visible scratch on the wood. Lines ran from each circle across the floor, up both sides of the frame until they joined with the circle around the drop at the top. "See these? The rest of this place is bone dry. These should have evaporated. But they won't. They're special."

Frank adjusted his Confederate hat. "Like retarded?"

Isaac resisted the urge to furiously rub both temples. "They're magical. To be specific, both drops are probably water taken from a drowning victim. One drop from each lung. The magical lines connect them."

"What's it do?" asked Wallace.

"If someone were to step across the line, a pillar of water would engulf them and drown them on the spot."

"Oh, bullshit!" This, of course, was Cash, continuing to deny the existence of the supernatural.

"For fuck's sake," Isaac said. "Then trip it, Cash. Step right on in. It'll save me the trouble of disarming it. And frankly"—Isaac wrinkled his nose—"you could use a bath."

The hunter took an angry step towards the magician, but Wallace intercepted him. He snatched Cash by the shirt. "Either step in and prove him wrong or keep your mouth shut. I'm getting tired of this crap."

A moment of silence descended as the team waited for Cash to decide. Finally, he said, "Whatever, asshole. Y'all go ahead and do your little magic bullshit. I'll play along."

Isaac sighed. Cash was smart enough to not step into the spell, but too arrogant to admit such intelligence. The trap could have been triggered, he would've been killed, and the world would get just a bit brighter. *Win-win-win.*

Returning to the task at hand, Isaac rubbed his chin. His former master would have advised him to just chuck one of the hunters into it. Not only would that be the simplest way to disarm it, but then he'd have access to two lungs full of water that he could use to make his own dastardly drowning pillars in the future. But Isaac always tried his best to be better than his master. "Anyone got a sponge?"

The group murmured to one another, confused until Rocky raised a hand and said, "I have one in my truck bed."

"What the hell for?" Frank asked as if an instrument of cleaning was acrimonious to the group.

"Washing my truck." The big man shrugged.

Isaac asked him to get it and, when he did, instructed him to cut the sponge in half. He handed one half to Lee and left the other with Rocky.

"Now then, at the same time, I need you both to slap those sponges down over the droplets and press as hard as you can. It may have some pretty serious pressure blowing out, but… *do not let go*."

Now that they were involved, the hunters looked a bit nervous. It was so much easier to not believe in such magical nonsense when they didn't have to lend a hand. The two hunters got into position. Isaac raised three fingers and lowered each in turn. "Go!"

Rocky and Frank pressed their sponges to the spots. A rush of water, like a burst hydrant, sprayed around the edges of their sponges. Water from nowhere gushed like geysers in all directions. The men swore at the sudden velocity and strained their arms against it. The rest of the hunters stumbled back, shocked and splashed.

"Holy shiiiiiit!" Frank yelled.

"Hold it! Not much longer!" Isaac shouted.

A pool of the magical water spread across the floor and flowed down the basement stairs, showing no signs of abating. Isaac cursed, drew his knife, and inserted it between the doorframe and the wall, eyes squinted against the spray. The frame, aged and slightly rotten, gave quickly. He tore a chunk away, breaking the magical lines that ran along it and connected the water spots. Like a shut valve the water stopped.

Both men, soaked to the skin, removed their sponges and wiped their eyes to stare in disbelief at the drenched doorway. Isaac pulled a plastic bag from his everbag to collect the sponges. He wasn't sure if the water had any magical properties at this point, but it couldn't hurt to keep.

"That was the damnedest thing I've ever saw," Slim said, open-mouthed, tobacco juice on his chin.

"Lucky the wood was so old." Isaac tossed the broken piece of frame aside. "Nice work," he said to Frank and Rocky, who both nodded back, still breathing heavily. "Let's check the rest of the house. Then we'll head into the basement. It's the most likely spot."

Wallace had Rocky and Frank guard the basement door as they searched the kitchen and the second floor. They had no problems now letting Isaac lead the way and waited patiently for him to check each doorway. There were three bedrooms and a bath upstairs. All empty. The windows weren't even covered, with sunlight streaming in, illuminating floating dust motes in their beams. This concerned Isaac. He had assumed that any vampire lair would have all sources of sunlight obstructed so that daytime interlopers had no safe haven to flee to.

With the upper floor cleared, the group soon assembled around the dripping basement door. The water trap had rattled them, and no one volunteered to take the lead. They shined their flashlights down the stairs, but barely illuminated more than the steps. No one moved.

"You know what?" Cash said to Isaac. "I was wrong about you. I think it's a great idea that you tagged along so that you could go first and check for traps." He jammed his flashlight harshly into Isaac's ribs. "So, lead on."

A procession of annoyed expressions cycled across Isaac's face. He wasn't sure what was worse—being outwitted by Cash or having to walk point into a basement where possibly lurked an elder vampire.

The Cash part, he decided. That was worse.

He started down the stairs.

Chapter 9
THE BUBBA

Isaac stomped down the steps as if he lived there. Stealth and caution were irrelevant now. Vampires, especially elders, were notoriously deep sleepers. If the volume of the drowning pillar trap hadn't awakened the elder, then his footsteps would matter little. If they were awake, then they were all dead men anyway, so he may as well get it over with. Better to dive into a meat grinder than slowly inch in.

He reached the concrete floor and panned his flashlight around as the hunters followed. Dull cinder block walls with no windows. Dust. Cobwebs. A long-unused oil furnace sat in the center of the room, and the only thing of interest was a weathered tarp hanging from hooks on the eastern wall.

"What the fuck? Where is he?" Cash hissed.

Isaac tapped Wallace on the shoulder and pointed at the tarp. It was large enough that it obscured the wall from floor to ceiling. The leader nodded and moved forwards. The rest followed with weapons aimed.

"Hold up," Isaac whispered. The lights glinted off of a pair of hooks that held the tarp in place. It was probably safer not to get too close. He concentrated, held out a hand, and visualized the tarp lifting. It did as commanded, telekinetically shifting until the right corner fell off its hook and it dropped like a curtain on a magic show finale.

The cinder blocks had been pulled away to form a door-sized hole that led to a roughly hewn tunnel dug into the earth beyond. Each of their lights quickly settled on a giant person standing motionless about five feet inside.

Not just giant, but *gigantic*. Easily one of the largest men he'd ever seen. Dressed in overalls, with one strap buckled and one undone, half of his corpulent torso exposed. The flesh held an unhealthy pale blue. In each hand, he clutched a rusty machete. What worried Isaac more than the dual weapons was the weird mask the man wore—a sack stitched together haphazardly from some kind of leathery material. It had only eyeholes, no slits for mouth or nose, and the bottom had been stitched directly to his neck. None of this seemed to matter, as he didn't appear to be breathing anyway. Dusty spiderwebs stretched from the man to the wooden beams in the ceiling, a testament to time spent immobile.

"Is that an elder vampire?" Lee whispered.

Slim mumbled softly, "I have no idea, but that is definitely the biggest Bubba I've ever seen."

As the group's hired magical consultant, Isaac felt the need to intervene and explain the situation. He should have said something to calm the jittery group, since Wallace seemed as confused as the rest and did little to lead. *This is a trap,* he should have whispered to them, one far more elaborate than the others. This man wasn't a vampire, and if they valued their lives, they should do absolutely nothing to disturb him.

Those were all things he should have said. Instead, in a complete professional lapse, he turned to Slim and asked, "What the hell is a Bubba?"

His answer came with a twang of a crossbow fired by Cash's itchy trigger finger. The bolt whistled by his head and drove deep into the giant's chest with a dull thump.

"Oh boy," Isaac mumbled as the giant stirred and his eyes—milky gray with cataracts—popped open. Cash's shot, idiotic as it was, had flown true and had certainly pierced the heart. The feathered arrow still quivered, but as Isaac had feared, this giant had already kicked the bucket. The sickly-hued skin, the sack stitched directly to him, the fact he was standing in a room unmoving for who knew how long. Oh, and the lack of breathing. *No breathing is always a dead giveaway.* Isaac nearly laughed at the pun.

With cobwebs pulling loose, the masked giant strode forwards. To their credit, Wallace and crew responded quickly, firing off four more crossbow bolts that each found their mark. But the bolts did not even give the Bubba pause and simply became four more quills porcupining from his fleshy torso. He thundered towards them, agilely turning sideways to fit through the doorway, the ends of the arrows snapping off on the bricks.

Isaac, unsure of what they were dealing with, wanted to shout something helpful or reassuring, but could think of nothing that would achieve either. The fearless vampire hunters broke into a panic.

Each man shouted and the small space became a cacophony of ignored orders. The one-shot crossbows were too cumbersome to reload with speed and were dropped for firearms, which had the unintended consequence of the weapon-mounted lights all suddenly shining at foot level. The crossbows were then kicked, turning the room into a disco strobe. Wallace, Rocky, and Slim tried to aim, but were bumped into by the others trying to flee. Isaac stumbled backwards from the cave entrance and dropped to the floor, away from the machetes.

The giant strode with machinelike purpose into the human confusion and chopped with the right machete, then the left. Screams erupted. Gunshots rang, muzzle flashes giving split-second glimpses of violence. Bullets struck the giant, slapping wetly but having no effect. Isaac stuck to the floor, crawling past legs towards the stairwell. Something landed with a splat in front of him and Slim's severed head bounced into one of the fallen beams of light. Dead eyes frozen, a lump of chewing tobacco half out of his mouth.

Damn, he had kind of liked Slim.

He got to the stairs, chanced a view over his shoulder, and saw Rocky valiantly leap at the behemoth. He landed a heavy fist into the sacked face before being hacked down. Frank lay against the furnace, a left arm stump pumping crimson.

Isaac started up the steps. Wallace was hot on the magician's heels until the giant hacked one of his feet out from under him, and Isaac glimpsed the man toppling from the stairs, screaming.

When he burst into the living room, he found Lee had made it out ahead of him. Instead of fleeing further, the hunter just stood there, aiming his rifle back at the basement.

"What are you doing? Keep running!"

Lee pointed at the open window. "Sunlight! It'll burn him up!"

"He's going to curb stomp us, you moron. He's not a vampire..." Isaac trailed off as the Bubba emerged from the stairwell and shrugged off several shots from Lee's rifle, striding through the brilliant sunbeams. Lee couldn't process that his defensive scheme had failed, and he pulled the trigger until a blade caught him in the side of his head.

The Bubba turned to Isaac, dead eyes peering through the holes, machetes dripping. Isaac stood closer to the other stairwell than the front door, and so he went up, taking the steps two at a time. He rushed down the hall, his hands held wide so that his fingertips brushed the walls, casting a telekinetic spell that pulled each bedroom door he passed shut with a bang. He ducked into the last room, slammed the door behind him, and leaned against it panting.

A crack of splintering wood resounded in the hall. The Bubba breaking down the first closed door, he guessed. He was banking on the giant having limited cognitive skills, and he surmised that he would systematically eliminate each hiding spot as he advanced. It bought Isaac some time.

He reached into his everbag and produced the glass jar containing the small brown spider. It sat motionlessly. For a second, he feared it had died. He tapped the glass until it scuttled quickly in circles around the bottom. In the hall, a second door smashed open.

He unscrewed the jar and eyed the spider with disgust, like a child wrinkling his nose at cough syrup. Then, with a down-the-hatch urgency, he tilted the jar up to his open mouth and felt the spider fall in. An intense urge to vomit overcame him as the spindly legs skittered along his tongue and the back of his throat, but he managed to down it with several tough swallows. He was still gagging when he heard the third door go down. Only his door remained.

The spider was small and thus his time was short. He kicked off his shoes and pulled off his socks, all the while repeatedly whispering "Spiders stick and that's the trick"—a silly-sounding verse to be sure, but effective. He backed up against a wall and placed both hands on it. His fingertips stuck as if a layer of double-sided tape lay in between. It certainly didn't feel strong enough to lift him, but that was part of the spell, the nature of the trick. One had to believe in the sacrifice of the spider; otherwise, any clown could choke one down and scurry along.

Hands pressed, he lifted one leg, planted his foot firmly to the wall, and felt it adhere as his hands had. The other leg followed, and he was completely off the floor. As fast as he could, nowhere near spider-fast, he crept along. Moving to the ceiling was the tough part. It required hanging from a horizontal surface while gripping nothing, stuck there only by conviction. But it worked, and when the giant guardian kicked open the door, Isaac hung just above it.

The Bubba stopped beneath him, the sacked head slowly going right to left, scanning the room as best it could with small eyeholes and non-dilating pupils. Isaac knew he had to act quickly. Already, he felt the magical adhesive begin to fade. With a deep breath, he quit the spell.

Isaac landed squarely on the behemoth's back, one hand around the neck as the other clutched a fistful of sack mask. The giant reacted as expected, thrashing and spinning around, swinging both hands up and back, but the angle proved too awkward to bring the sharp edges of the machetes to bear. The flats of the blades swatted him painfully, but bruises were better than cuts.

The magician held on, a cowboy on an enraged bull, and yanked on the mask. He was thankful that at this point the giant didn't know better and dropped his weapons. With a free hand, the giant could have easily reached back and grabbed him, pulled him free, and pretty much choked the life out of him. But he stubbornly, stupidly flailed away with the blades. He floundered around the middle of the room with Isaac on board.

The mask began to tear, dead skin proving a poor fabric for stitches to hold. The seams connecting it to the neck gave first, the skin stretching and then snapping bloodlessly. With one last yank, the sack was pulled loose, and Isaac tore it from the giant's head.

Predictably, the Bubba simply became dead again and dropped with a thunderous boom. Isaac rolled off and lay next to the body, the sack mask in hand. When he'd gathered his breath, he examined the giant. The face, pale and puffy like a corpse, looked otherwise normal. He'd expected a disfigured visage, something terrible to behold, like all the masked slashers in horror movies. In the end, he could only assume that the man was indeed just a large, dead Bubba.

With the adrenaline fading, aches from the blunt machete whacks set in and he imagined that he'd be covered in nasty bruises for several weeks. After stashing the mask in his everbag, he hobbled down the steps and found Wallace on the couch attending to a nasty calf gash.

"Another trap?" Wallace said evenly, asking a question he already knew the answer to.

"Yeah. I took care of it." He looked towards the cellar. "Everyone else?"

Wallace stood, winced at putting weight on his leg. "I can't find Cash. All the others are dead."

There weren't any words for Isaac to use—no consoling, keep-your-chin-up nonsense. They would have been empty platitudes anyway. Wallace needed to handle this alone. They had chosen a dangerous occupation and it had cost them everything. Wallace would either be born again hard, or he'd sink into depression, or he'd get a regular job. *Whatever*. Isaac didn't really give a shit at that point.

Outside they found Cash. He sat in the driver's seat of one of the trucks, staring emptily at the house.

"You fucking ran on us. Left us to die." Wallace dragged him out and slammed him against the cab.

Cash offered up no resistance as he hung in Wallace's grasp like a doll. "Yeah. I did. I would have driven away, but I don't have any of the car keys." He hung his head. "So, I just sat there."

"Gutless fucker." Wallace shoved him towards the van. "Gear up. We're clearing the last tunnel and then burning the place to the ground."

* * *

As they stepped back into the basement, Isaac regretted not offering to do it alone. He doubted that Wallace, being so proud, would have accepted, but now their progress slowed with his and Cash's emotional reactions to seeing, and maneuvering around, their dead comrades. With the amount of blood spilled, it proved impossible to avoid stepping into puddles.

"Should we check for pulses?" Cash whispered.

Isaac scanned the room with his flashlight. Bodies. Severed limbs. He settled the beam on Slim's head. "No. Don't bother. They're dead."

Cash recovered his crossbow and set to reloading it. Isaac watched him wearily before saying, "Listen, do not fire that unless I say so. If you don't hear me say, 'Oh my God, Cash, shoot that horrifyingly dangerous thing and save us all,' and then see me point at the target, do not squeeze that trigger. Got it?"

Isaac expected a dimwitted argument from the man, but post-massacre Cash proved more cooperative. The hunter nodded and fell into third place as they headed into the tunnel.

Wallace led the way, his crossbow light illuminating the passage. It twisted and turned and narrowed at points so that their shoulders brushed the dirt walls. Only a few timbers crisscrossed the ceiling at odd points and Isaac worried about the integrity of the structure.

The tunnel ended.

"What the hell? There's nothing here!" Wallace said vehemently. He panned the light over every inch of the dead end. "Was Arrangement wrong? Did my men die for nothing?"

"Yup," Isaac said too abruptly. When Wallace shot him a stern glare, he amended it to "maybe" with a shrug, but it didn't pacify the hunter in the least.

Wallace slammed a boot into the earthen wall. Clumps of loose dirt cascaded down, and for a moment Isaac feared the roof collapsing. The tunnel stability held, but the shifting soil revealed something. An odd protuberance jutted from the end of the tunnel. At first, Isaac assumed it was a tree root.

"Calm down," he ordered Wallace as he stepped forwards and brushed his flashlight along the bump. More dirt fell away, and he jumped back when an empty eye socket popped into view.

"Holy shit! Is that it?" Cash brought his crossbow to bear but refrained from firing. Isaac felt an odd sense of pride at the man's restraint, and not just because he probably would have intercepted the bolt with his head.

"Hang on." Like an archeologist on a dig, Isaac eased away soil until the top half of a skull was revealed. He hooked a finger through a socket and tugged up gently, wiggling it free from the wall.

"A victim?" Wallace asked.

"Nope." Isaac held up their discovery. From the nasal cavity up, it could not be differentiated from a human. In the lower half, the difference proved obvious. The incisors and canines along the upper jaw extended at least an inch longer and were wickedly sharp. Even buried and unused, Isaac guessed that the fangs could draw blood from a touch. "Definitely vampiric."

"That's it? I expected it to be a lot more *alive*." Cash thought about what he'd said. "I guess that ain't the right word either. You guys know what I mean."

Wallace patted his only remaining teammate on the shoulder. "Go get the gas tanks out of the truck and start soaking down upstairs." After Cash had left, the leader said to Isaac, "All this. All my men. Killed to retrieve a dusty skull."

Isaac felt no need to either defend Arrangement or assuage the man's feelings. "It certainly looks that way." He dropped the skull into his everbag. "I'll turn it in."

Moments later, they stood outside and watched the house burn. They'd followed standard vampire-hunting practice, a scorched-earth policy to kill any hidden ticks they may have missed and to deny them a safe lair in the future.

"One thing I can tell you," Wallace said to Isaac as the billowing smoke thickened. "Next time that damn Voice calls me, I'm not going to answer."

"Let me know how that works out for you." Isaac assumed the answer would be "not well."

Wallace handed him a set of keys. "Leave the van at your hotel. We'll get it later."

Isaac shook hands with the men and drove away, leaving the pair solemnly watching the flames consume the house and their team.

* * *

"All we recovered was a damn skull. How am I supposed to know if it's an elder? I can't carbon-date it," Isaac told Lefse on the phone in his hotel room, examining the Bubba mask he had stretched out on the table.

"This will be my shortest report yet. The vampire you were after was deceased and all your hunters still ended up dead," Lefse replied as if Isaac had somehow failed a test he'd studied weeks for.

"Not *all*. Just most." Isaac argued for a D grade over an F.

"Tell me again about the Bubba."

"Just some kind of undead trap. Big fellow. Machetes. I've already gone over this."

"And the mask?"

"Burned up in the fire. It was too damaged from the fight anyway."

"That's too bad. I've never heard of such a thing."

"Me neither. I'll bring the skull to the Athenaeum tomorrow."

Isaac hung up and returned to his examination. The mask was a grotesque work of art, and he knew without a doubt now that the material was skin. The stitching was a bit rough, and the eyeholes were wonky, but when Isaac flipped it inside out, he found magical runes inked into it. These were intricately flawless and would require much study. Since the Voice hadn't sent him for it, he had felt no need to hand it over. The only reason he even mentioned it was his concern that Cash or Wallace might discuss it if debriefed. For now, he had the perfect place to keep it. He opened his everbag.

Chapter 10
MABAHAZI THE MAGNIFICENT

"This is our elder vampire?" Mabahazi asked disdainfully. He poked the skull with his pen. So perfect was its fit in the rune-marked box that it didn't even shift.

"Apparently," Lefse said. "There's no way to know if it's an elder, but it's definitely a vampire. Everything else lines up to mark the place as a safe house. Magical traps and an undead guardian. No young vampire would be able to acquire those."

Mabahazi flipped through the papers he had already read as if new information would spring forth. Despite his dislike of Lefse, he knew the burly man generated good reports and that the folder before him contained all the possible information on the assignment. The knowledge only made his confusion that much greater. "So, the Voice of Arrangement pairs Isaac up with a team of vampire hunters and then sends them to kill a vampire, except the vampire is already deceased. Have you ever known Arrangement to make that kind of mistake before?"

"No, but I don't believe it did."

"I'm sorry?"

"My gut tells me the Voice knew exactly what transpired there. Its specific instructions, I believe, were to hunt down an elder vampire. It never specified the state it may be in. Think of it as more of a treasure hunt than a killing hunt."

Mabahazi sighed. "I suppose you're right. It's not like we can call out the Voice for word usage. Still, it'd be nice to know the true purpose behind these assignments for once."

"I think we're just not important enough to be in on all of the reasoning."

Statements like that were what kept Lefse on Mabahazi's bad side, and the Head Librarian glowered. "Are you sure you didn't miss anything? Maybe Isaac was less than truthful?"

Now Lefse took his turn to glower at his professionalism being questioned. "Not that I know of."

The Head Librarian huffed. "What the hell is a Bubba anyway?"

Lefse shrugged. "Some kind of undead hillbilly, I guess. I'm unfamiliar with the species."

"Of undead?"

"No. Hillbilly."

Mabahazi snapped and slammed the folder. "Okay, that's enough." He waved Lefse out, not even bothering to say the word "dismissed" this time.

After the librarian had stomped away, Mabahazi leafed through his current stack of reports. The folder below the one marked *Isaac Unknown* had been labeled *Gregory Scott*. Reports for Gregory came in like clockwork, once per quarter, and they did not make for good reads. An avid serial killer, the man preyed on homeless individuals at the behest of the Voice. Mabahazi could not fathom why. The next folder detailed the work of Sophie Eddon, a psychic who most recently helped find a missing child. Then came a magician known as Santeel, who murdered people by means as unexplainable as they were unnatural. Following him was a magician who specialized in the quelling of nightmares and curses. Then came a masked assassin with a deformed face.

So on and so forth. Death and salvation. Horror and hope. Blood and miracles. Every good deed seemingly balanced with something vile. He just didn't see the point.

At least the acquisition of relics remained a part of the job he could understand. Removing these powerful objects from world circulation was no different from taking explosives away from children. This made sense, even if being denied access to these artifacts still rankled him. At least he could briefly see them when delivered and confirm their existence, which satisfied his cravings just a bit.

From childhood, Mabahazi had been obsessed with magic. His mother had been a Vegas showgirl and he spent countless hours at shows on the strip, from headliner acts in casino theaters to sleight-of-hand street corner shysters. His favorite had been a man known by the stage name *The Great Hanzani,* a master of such classics as sawing his assistants in half, levitation, and vanishing, Hanzani's finest moment had been catching a fired bullet with a pair of salad tongs. Mabahazi's wide child's eyes had never grown tired of him, and he later fashioned his own nom de plume in Hanzani's honor.

As much as he loved the spectacle, he was far more interested in, even haunted by, not knowing what occurred behind the stage curtain. Be the tricks real or fake, Mabahazi knew true enlightenment and power resided there. Even as an awestruck youth, he had realized he was just a rube in the crowd, one of the astounded masses who existed with their wool permanently pulled over.

The feelings were no different at Arrangement. Despite his intelligence, his rise in the ranks, and his long list of achievements, he remained on the wrong side of the curtain. Such knowledge, such power, passed through his fingers on a daily basis, yet he remained an impotent spectator. He might as well be tearing tickets for a Vegas show.

It occurred to him that during his reminiscing, he had been glaring with furrowed brow at the office phone on his desk. Mabahazi suddenly feared that projecting his irritation onto an innocent proxy could still be considered a transgression to a power he couldn't comprehend. He coughed into his hand and averted his eyes as if he had misspoken during a meeting with his superior.

Being put in his place by a silent telephone didn't improve his mood. He closed the lid on the vampire skull, and with a dejected sigh, he went back to reading about the adventures of others.

Chapter 11
THE BELIAL FLY

The fly had teeth.

Miniscule, bone-yellow teeth with no proboscis—just a disturbingly humanlike mouth underneath its large multi-lensed eyes. The view through the magnifying glass showed it opening and closing its mouth, almost smacking its lips, sickly green saliva stringing from top to bottom.

Isaac set the magnifier down and leaned back in his chair. He certainly wasn't an entomologist, but he felt confident that no species of fly had choppers. Aside from that and its unusual size—about as big as a bumblebee—it appeared to be a run-of-the-mill housefly. Now it sat in its jar, motionless except for the teeth-gnashing, like a cow chewing cud.

Across the table sat a young man named Randy. No, *Randolph*, as he had snootily informed Isaac. There were three others in the room with them. A bald fellow named Glenn, who carried himself like a tough guy, leaned against the wall by the door of the small apartment. A bookwormy guy named Stu rested his elbows on the kitchen counter. Lastly, a dark-haired girl named Raven sprawled on the couch.

The job he had been assigned appeared simple at first. Pick up a package at this address and deliver it to Arrangement. It sounded like a no-brainer. Even better, the pickup resided in a fairly well-to-do part of town in an upscale apartment. The young occupants were probably living it up on their parents' dime. Isaac got the impression they were persnickety know-it-alls, but not really dangerous.

Easy pickup. Easy delivery. Easy money. No pile of corpses left behind.

However, as he had walked down the hall towards the apartment, his apprehension grew. Claustrophobic spaces didn't usually bother him, but the hallway was small, confining, and dark. Yet there were windows at both ends of the hall, sunlight beaming in, and recessed fluorescents along the ceiling. All the sources of light shone suitably bright when he looked directly at them, but for some reason, nothing penetrated the gloominess. The cramped feeling only intensified the closer he came to Apartment 10D.

Glenn had let him in, staring sourly at him in a bid at intimidation. He certainly had the expression down, but with his thin build, he only seemed as tough as his scowl made him.

Isaac had found the interior of the apartment aped the hallway, and worse. The place was clearly roomy and well-decorated. But again, everything felt cramped, the air thick like a crowded elevator. The windows were open, and a pleasant breeze tussled the drapes. Lights on. Television on. Still, it remained somehow dark. The gloom always framed the edges of his peripheral vision, as if it consciously moved out of his direct sight.

Randolph had introduced himself and his friends with dismissive waves of his hand. Stu grunted. Raven barely acknowledged being spoken to and just kept her eyes vacantly on the TV. The nervous group twitched and jumped at every move, yet gave off an air of being lazy and depressed at the same time. Randolph remained slumped in his chair, but his eyes darted. Raven chewed her nails or pulled at holes in her tights, but otherwise sprawled uncaringly on the couch. Stu paced, albeit slowly, aimlessly around the kitchen, often peering out the window. Glenn looked like he wanted to punch something, but only if it wandered right up and picked a fight so he didn't have to put any effort into it. The whole group behaved like they were afraid of something but too tired to do anything about it.

And now Isaac sat, looking at the jar with the fly. He'd asked for the package and Randolph placed this before him. They even supplied the magnifier as if knowing he'd be curious.

"Where'd it come from?" Isaac asked. He knew he should just grab it and go, but every magician carried the curse of curiosity. It couldn't be helped. He assumed this was what a drug deal felt like: a business transaction where everyone teetered on the edge, each waiting for someone else to do something brash, but also eager for the relief of the merchandise changing hands.

"We found it by accident," Randolph answered.

"That so?"

The man nodded, eyes locked on the jar as if mesmerized.

"My employer will want to know its origins." A lie. No information had been requested, but Randolph here didn't know that.

"Oh, just tell him. Who cares anymore," said Raven, spitting out a hangnail. Isaac glanced at her, but she had spoken without tearing her eyes from the television.

"We were screwing around with spells. Pentagrams. Black magic."

Isaac nodded. "I'm familiar with it."

"We had the dumb, drunken idea of summoning a demon. Asking it questions or for wishes."

Raven snorted derisively. "Like a genie or something."

"Shut up, Raven. This is your fault," Randolph snapped. Or he tried to. His words had no spark to them, just a sense of fatigue. Back to Isaac, he said, "We didn't think it would work. And it didn't really seem to. No monsters. No flames."

"No show," said Raven.

Stu spoke up, his arms crossed as if warding off a chill. "But then we found the fly. Right in the middle of the pentagram. Just sitting there."

Isaac nodded. Things were starting to make sense. The oppressive miasma emanated from the fly, slowly exerting a crushing pressure on the environment. Claustrophobia, shadows, depression, as well as physical effects like the collapsed plastic bottles. He had no idea of the extent of its power. Maybe it had already reached its limit. Maybe it would eventually kill them. "Can I see this pentagram?"

Stu shook his head. "We did the ritual at Raven's place. Erased it right after."

"Where'd you get the diagrams?"

"I found them," Raven said with a sigh. "But I burned the papers. They were complete failures anyway." She still had yet to make eye contact.

"That's a shame. Obviously, they worked."

She finally looked at him. She had pale skin, but everything else about her trended dark: hair, clothing, lipstick, nails, fishnet stockings. If she donned a pointed hat, she'd be wearing a complete sexy-witch costume. Silliness aside, Isaac found her attractive, and he imagined these three clowns had hopped when she said frog. "Really? A fly? Why a fly? What's so demonic about that?" The girl seemed put out, offended that some other-dimensional power had sent her a bug.

"Flies are used pretty extensively in Hell." Isaac thought about how to explain it in mundane terms. "They're infused with information. That way, they can deliver messages."

"It can talk?" Stu asked.

"No. My guess is it has to be eaten. Then the information kind of... leaks... into the swallower." He could think of no more efficient way to explain it.

"Lord of the Flies," Stu whispered reverently, just now making the connection.

"Yeah." Isaac nodded, although what he really wanted to do was line them up and do one consecutive Three Stooges-style slap along all four faces. The link should have been freaking obvious. *Damn weekend demonologists.* Thankfully, his annoyance was temporary and irrelevant, since he intended to take the bug with him. The effects should fade, allowing them to return to whatever god-awful personalities they had previously possessed. It was the kind of good deed he liked, savior as a by-product. One last question, though. "How'd you know someone would come to get it?"

Randolph looked at his cell phone as if it had bitten him. "Someone called me. Said it knew what we had and that someone would come by to collect it." He swallowed hard. "Sounded..."

"Like someone not to fuck with?" Isaac finished for him, and the man nodded. "Yeah, I'm familiar with that too." He picked up the jar.

A knock came at the door.

It echoed through the apartment. Three raps—rhythmically spaced. Isaac imagined each of them would have jumped in fright if not clinically depressed by the evil fly. Instead, they just kind of looked at the door in confusion, except for Raven, still glued to the TV.

"Expecting someone?" he asked.

"Just you," Randolph replied.

Unexpected guests during an evil fly transaction? Probably couldn't be chalked up to coincidence. The ominous knock, like a bell tolling, came again in three more bangs.

"Who is it?" Glenn finally said through the door.

A feminine voice responded with monotone but bold authority. "My name is Ms. Feckle. I have come to collect the property of my lord. Your cooperation would be appreciated. Should you comply, I swear to fatally harm you in the most efficient, and therefore painless, method that I can employ."

A chill itched its way down Isaac's spine. The voice had been almost robotic. No inflections. No emotion. But what really bothered him had been "my lord." *Who says that? People in the service of some kind of Hellspawn. That's who,* he surmised.

The odd language confused Glenn, and he responded to the threat with "huh?" as he leaned forwards to the peephole. Isaac raised a hand to ward against the action, but probably should have yelled dramatically instead.

The ensuing gunshot burst through the peephole and into Glenn's face, popping his head back in a red spray. Glenn fell backwards and landed staring at the ceiling—or would have been staring if his face weren't a craterous ruin. The shot, presumably from a very large gun, left Isaac's ears ringing.

The muted reaction of Glenn's compatriots surprised Isaac. None of them moved, each glaring somberly at the door like they were helpless to resist this violent fate. Isaac leaped to his feet with the jar in hand. "All of you, get into the bedroom!" he hissed, trying to avoid the killer at the door overhearing. But it proved pointless. None of them paid him any heed.

The door was still bolted at the deadlock and locked at the knob. A shape peered through the gunshot-expanded peephole. Again came the level, passionless voice. "In case you question whether I'm a being of my word, your friend has transitioned from this life quickly and without pain. I once more humbly request your cooperation and will happily hold up my end of the bargain."

"Give her the fly. Just get this over with," Raven said. She turned off the TV, annoyed with the interruptions.

Isaac frowned. The weird dark power had depressed them into complete inaction, removing even their survival instincts. He pulled Wilma from his everbag and aimed for the keyhole and the dark, examining eye. He fired but missed the small target, the buckshot splintering the wood but failing to penetrate. The figure at the door ducked away, allowing a shard of light to spill unhindered through the hole.

"I'll take that as a sign that you are disinclined to accept my most generous offer," Ms. Feckle said. A gun blast from the hall blew the deadbolt in. A second, and the doorknob shattered to pieces. No longer secured, the door slowly swung open under its own weight.

Isaac fell back, set the jar on the kitchen counter and aimed Wilma again. Stu still sat on the stool next to him, watching with lazy interest.

"My lord has no interest in your suffering, only that you return his property and then die for this trespass."

"We've already given the fly to someone. He's in the kitchen right now aiming a gun at you," Raven said.

"Seriously?" Isaac glared at her, resisting the temptation to shoot her himself.

"Oh my," Ms. Feckle said. "Another courier? In service of whom, may I ask?"

Isaac thought he caught a hint of enthusiasm in her voice now. He sighed. Oh well, his cover seemed blown anyway. "My client's name is strictly confidential."

"Ah, I assumed as much. It's information I'll have to pull from you, along with flesh and bone." As she finished, she stepped, or rather flashed, across the doorway. A large handgun, silver and gleaming, fired. It caught Randolph in the chest and blasted him from his chair.

Isaac caught a glimpse of a long black coat, some kind of old-fashioned hat, and exceedingly pale skin. "Raven, hide!" Isaac commanded, but the girl ignored him. In the end, she wouldn't have saved herself anyway as another boom from Ms. Feckle's hand cannon sent a shell through the wall next to the door and into her head. Finally moved from her seat, she flew over the arm of the couch, taking down the lamp next to it.

The shot impressed him. Ms. Feckle must have glimpsed Raven's position when she flitted past the doorway and then blindly fired a kill shot through a solid wall. Isaac moved slightly, in case this Feckle character had also gotten a bead on him.

"That's some gun you have there," he shouted to the hallway.

"Thank you. Hell-forged."

"They make guns in Hell?"

"Why wouldn't they?"

This little nugget of knowledge surprised him, even if it made perfect sense. Even Stu said "huh."

Having forgotten about the little fellow, Isaac turned to him. "Hey, Stu, you may want to—"

Ms. Feckle danced across the door again, fired once, and sent Stu violently from the stool and into a row of kitchen cabinets before Isaac could finish his warning. Doors swung open and cookery toppled out with a cacophony of clangs and crashes.

"—duck," Isaac finished. The wound, a fist-sized hole in the man's chest, sizzled and smoked. Hell-forged firearms indeed.

Ms. Feckle certainly seemed to be a foe beyond his skill level, and now he found himself as the only target left.

Chapter 12
THE AUTOMATON

Alone now, Isaac weighed his options. "Well, Ms. F., you've killed off all the amateur demonologists. How about I just roll the jar out to you and call it a day?" He had no intention of giving it up but wanted to keep the killer talking instead of shooting.

"Sorry, my dear boy," Ms. Feckle said, ever so politely. "But the terms were presented at the onset of this encounter. If my lord had wanted to negotiate, he would have sent a diplomat."

"Not an assassin."

"Correct."

Isaac sighed and looked at the fly. It had stopped chewing and now seemed to be smiling. He shook the jar, enough to bounce the smug insect off the sides a few times to teach it a lesson.

Satisfied with the bug punishment, he leaned around the counter and telekinetically pushed the apartment door shut, but without a knob, it only bumped and then slowly started to swing back open. He needed something to secure it.

Glenn's body lay just a few feet away. It would be taxing to move such dead weight, but at least it was dead. All life forces were naturally magic-resistant, which made telekinesis hard to use on living things. With Glenn's soul dearly departed, it became just a matter of heft.

Isaac concentrated and moved a bit at a time. Flopped one arm, then one leg, pushed him like a rolled-up carpet, and jammed him against the door. The *thump* alerted the killer, who immediately shoved it, in vain, as it jammed into now-useful dead Glenn.

A shadow fell across the gunshot hole as Ms. Feckle peered in. "You're only delaying the inevitable."

Isaac dug through the kitchen, snatched out every sharp piece of cutlery he could find, and tossed them onto the counter. The door shuddered as the killer put either a shoulder or boot onto it, nudging Glenn's body across the floor. Isaac adjusted each knife, blade tips aimed. Ms. Feckle was strong, amazingly so, alarmingly so, and she pushed again, moving one-hundred-fifty-plus pounds of dead Glenn aside. The killer stepped into the room.

The only exposed skin on Ms. Feckle was her face. A black overcoat, black boots, and black gloves, topped off with a black pillbox hat, concealed the rest. Unusual attire for sure, and it only made her alabaster skin shine that much brighter. The coloring reminded Isaac of the famous statue of David. Black sunglasses obscured her eyes. The ridiculously oversized handgun she carried shined silver with speckles of fiery red that sparkled like cinders.

"I don't suppose you'll do the polite thing and identify yourself?" Ms. Feckle asked.

Isaac responded by flicking his fingers, like one would do with wet hands and no towel, over the laid-out cutlery. Each knife flew off the counter, rocketing missile-like across the room.

Feckle moved with speed. She sidestepped a couple and swatted another aside with the barrel of her cannon. But she couldn't avoid them all as several tore through her jacket and found skin.

No. Not skin. The knives bounced off her with a metal-on-stone *clank.* All her dodging about did have one aggravating effect, however. Ms. Feckle's pillbox hat fell from her head and ungraciously rolled in several wobbly circles. Her head was as white as her face and completely hairless. Not just lost-her-hair bald, but mannequin-head bald.

Ms. Feckle stared at her hat. Hardly able to read her expressions, Isaac assumed this one hovered between anger and disbelief. "My offer of a relatively painless execution is hereby rescinded," she said.

Maybe she meant the statement to be threatening, to make Isaac panic. Instead, when the killer bent to retrieve her headwear, Isaac telekinetically smacked it and sent it spinning away from her reaching hand.

This seemed to frost Ms. Feckle, and she stood up, ramrod straight, hand cannon ready. But Isaac had already aimed his own. He fired Wilma and scored a hit dead center in her forehead. The strike snapped her head back and sent her stumbling, but more like she'd been punched, not like she'd had her brains blown out. Her sunglasses fell, landed next to the hat, and she raised a gloved hand to the wound.

Her forehead looked like a damaged windshield, with a series of small cracks spreading weblike from the impact point. And now, with her glasses removed, Ms. Feckle glared at him with bloodshot eyes. They moved bizarrely, rotating in their sockets without the muscles of her face chipping in, as if in a mask, constantly irritated because there were no lids to soothe them.

Isaac swore. Ms. Feckle was an automaton—an artificial construct brought to life via nefariously awesome sorcery. He didn't know the specifics of such works. There were lots of different ways to create such beings—crafting a stone body with a smattering of human organs and imprisoning a soul or spirit within it produced this one, he assumed. High-level shit to be sure, and certainly not to be trifled with.

He hopped over the counter and ducked into the bedroom. He slammed the door and crossed to a window that looked out onto a fire escape. Ten floors up. The automaton could move much faster than him, so trying to escape via ten levels of stairs wasn't going to work. Instead, he took the ladder up and swung one leg over the ledge onto the roof just as Ms. Feckle kicked the bedroom door off its hinges.

"Courier? Where are you?" she called out in her annoying, even-steven voice.

Isaac clambered onto the roof, ran left, then straight, then right, then stopped. Nearby roofs were either too far to jump, or wide-open surfaces that would make it easy for Ms. Feckle to pick him off. He had dead-ended himself.

"You should have gone down, courier," the automaton called from the fire escape. "Now you have farther to fall when I throw you."

The black pillbox popped into view, then the pale face, as Ms. Feckle ascended the ladder. One hand came over, then the second. At this range, he'd probably be turned into a red mist by the enchanted hand cannon. No time to do anything but something brash. He had to end this quickly, and nothing seemed faster than falling.

Tucking the fly jar under one arm, he reached into his everbag and produced a plastic baggie of maple tree seeds, the V-shaped whirligigs popular with children. On each seed, very delicately, he'd inked magical symbols so faint one could barely see them.

Ms. Feckle topped the ladder, steadied herself with one hand, and brought the gun to bear with the other. Isaac charged towards her, tearing open the baggie and carefully grabbing each seed, as all were instrumental in the upcoming spell. He leaped, threw his body into the assassin, knocked her loose from the ladder, and sent them both into free fall off the roof. As soon as he cleared the ledge, Isaac chucked the seeds into the air, save one, which he clenched in a fist.

Surrounded by helicoptering seeds, he began a whirling descent, while the alabaster woman dropped like a rock. Isaac had hoped to never use this spell, as it allowed only for complete success or flattening on the pavement. He didn't exactly float like a feather, and he spun faster than he'd anticipated. Fast enough to completely disorient him, sending his world into a dizzying blur until a rough landing in the alley below proved hard enough to stun him.

When he regained his senses, the alabaster woman already stood over him. Ms. Feckle had fared worse. Her precious hat and glasses were gone, and cracks zigzagged across her head. Isaac met the horrible, bloodshot eyes. But Ms. Feckle looked elsewhere, to the magician's left. When he followed the gaze, he saw the shattered jar.

"Nothing for me to return. Flown off or smashed like any insect." Ms. Feckle sounded disappointed. "I suppose both our masters will be angry."

Isaac said nothing, only nodded, lips tight.

"Still not going to introduce yourself?"

Isaac shook his head.

Sirens could be heard now, distant but closing.

Ms. Feckle holstered her weapon. "Lord Belial may have different plans now, maybe involving you. Who knows how these devils scheme and plot, eh?" She spoke like she and Isaac were work chums bitching about their bosses at the water cooler.

Isaac's shoulders slumped at the mention of the powerful being, but he kept his mouth shut.

"Maybe if we meet again, you'll work on your manners and be more polite." The killer turned away, moving slowly down the alley, limping on a twisted leg. A black limousine awaited her on the intersecting street. A man in a dark suit stood by its rear door. Ms. Feckle clambered clumsily into the vehicle, saying something to the man, who ran down the alley towards Isaac. Isaac tensed, ready to defend himself, but the servant instead retrieved the hat and sunglasses.

"Oh, shit," the man said, holding the glasses by an arm to reveal cracked lenses. "Now I'll be shopping forever to find Feckle a new pair. She's so picky. Thanks, asshole," he said to Isaac, and he hurried back to the car.

Isaac stood and waited for the limo to pull away, tapping a foot like a fellow in line to take a desperate piss. When it did, he opened his mouth, reached in with two fingers, and pried the fly off his tongue. He'd scooped it up from the shattered jar, amazed that it wasn't smushed, and hid it in the best and easiest place available. It probably shouldn't have come as a surprise that the evil little thing chomped into his tongue and ground its nubby little teeth back and forth the whole time Ms. Feckle had been talking to him. He had barely kept a straight face. He found a fast-food cup with a lid in a nearby dumpster and dropped the fly in.

* * *

By the time he made it back to the hotel, he burned with fever and doubled over with cramps. The dresser soon filled with empty water bottles from rinsing his aching tongue, and he was dying to collapse into sleep. But he forced himself to stay awake and alert. The moment the fly had bitten him, he knew there would be consequences, and being asleep was not the way to face them.

In the corners of the room, in the open closet, and under the bed, he could now hear the shadows seethe. A disconcerting sound, like a susurrus of eels sliding across each other. The air grew heavy. After several hours he could see their movement in his peripheral vision, undulating masses of tentacles. The fever intensified, and hot and cold flashes tore through him. He couldn't speak, his tongue too swollen to open his mouth. More than once he started to pass out, to fall back into the comforter and succumb to the fatigue of whatever infection coursed through him. But he knew that could be the end of him.

The fly had done more than deliver a message. It had arranged an introduction, but shadows didn't like to be known. He couldn't sleep until he outlasted them.

The hours tick-tocked by as he sat in the middle of the bed, legs crossed. And just before dawn, the shadows—unable to bring Isaac to heel—relented. They silently retreated to their natural spaces in the dark nooks and crannies of the room. Isaac smiled, telekinetically whipped open the blinds, and dropped into sleep bathed in sunlight.

Chapter 13
THE IRON AMBASSADOR

When the phone rang, Isaac kicked off his covers in a momentary panic, thinking it could only be Arrangement calling to bludgeon his already aching head with its psychic hammer. He realized the tone sounded different, and he snatched up his cell phone as it buzzed and vibrated across the nightstand.

Lefse started barking in his ear. "What the hell happened on the fly job?"

Even as Isaac said, "I got the damn fly," he jumped from the bed to make sure the little monstrosity remained imprisoned in its cup.

"You weren't supposed to kill them all!"

"I didn't. An assassin named Ms. Feckle showed up and did that. She was after the fly as well."

Lefse's voice softened. "That's good to hear. I just got off the phone with the Head Librarian. He was pretty worked up, thinking you went on a murder spree. I told him you don't kill people willy-nilly without a good reason. You're just bad luck and lots of people end up getting killed anyway."

Isaac didn't really want to thank the librarian for the backhanded compliment, but at least he'd stuck up for him. "If that's settled, I'm going back to bed."

"No can do. The fly needs to be here ASAP. It's caused a bit of stir."

"Fine, fine. I'm on my way." Isaac sighed and tossed the phone onto the bed.

He turned his attention back to the fly. It didn't seem interested in any escape attempt, or even in buzzing around in its prison. Much like a tiny cow, it just sat there chewing its cud. Isaac had been tossing in bits of whatever foodstuff he could find, and everything—corn chips, lettuce, crackers, and sugar cubes—was readily gobbled up. It became more a game of seeing just how much it would eat rather than an interest in keeping it alive. Still, anxious to be rid of the thing, he hurriedly dressed and headed out the door.

* * *

"That's just hilariously gross," Lefse said as he peered into the jar. "I think it's looking at me." He pressed a finger to the glass and snorted when the fly tried to gnash it. "These things would make great pets."

"So, what happens to it? Arrangement have a bug collection?" Isaac asked. He lazily slumped in his chair. The aftereffects of the fly bite felt much like the day after having a bad flu.

"No. This little fellow doesn't get cataloged. We've made a deal to return it to his rightful owner."

This woke Isaac up a bit. "Belial?"

"Yup. The Iron Ambassador is on the way to pick it up."

Isaac sat up straight. "The Ambassador of the Iron Embassy is on his way here? Wouldn't Ms. Feckle have worked directly for him?"

"Yup," Lefse said as he brushed the end of his beard back and forth on the jar and laughed as the fly moved and attempted to chomp in sync. "The Ambassador sent Ms. Feckle at the behest of Belial." He showed the jar to Isaac as if the magician hadn't seen it. "This thing is actually a lot of fun."

"I'm distressed a bit about the lack of concern you seem to have. Did anyone here think maybe I should run for the hills?"

"Oh, relax. It's all been worked out. The Ambassador chatted with the Head Librarian. Backdoor wheeling and dealing. You know how it is."

"I really don't. But you have the fly, so I'll just scoot on out of here and let you handle the Ambassador."

"Nope. I was told that the Ambassador specifically wants to meet you." Lefse continued making silly faces at the jar like it contained a very small baby.

The idea didn't exactly panic Isaac, but he didn't like such complications. He wanted to finish his assignments, collect his pay, and move along to whatever god-awful mess the next day held. Having a meeting with the mortal voice of Hell held no interest at all for him. "You have any clue why?"

"No idea. Maybe he wants you to pay for the damage to that Feckle character. Like, garnish your wages or something."

Isaac remained annoyed but had to admit he rather enjoyed that last joke, so he chuckled reluctantly before yelling at the man. "Will you stop making googly eyes at that bug for one damn minute?"

With a huff, Lefse set the jar down. "What do you want me to say? When the Ambassador of Hell wants to meet someone, that person gets met. He made the request to the Head Librarian, who, frankly, was probably so thrilled at getting to talk to such a powerful person he agreed without hesitation."

Isaac tapped the phone on the desk. "So, no one asked Arrangement directly?"

"We don't call Arrangement. Arrangement calls us. You know that. And the Voice hasn't called to say anything about you."

Defeated, Isaac slumped in his chair. "You know anything about this guy?"

"The Ambassador? Never met him or even seen him. He has a lofty title, but honestly, I don't even really know what he does. But he is the Hell equivalent of the Pope, so I'd guess he's pretty fearsome. Two or three feet taller than a normal man. Horns. Fangs. Spiky tail. Sadist. Hung like a rhinoceros and probably a rapist." Isaac finally held up his hand for the man to stop. "Aren't you even a little interested in meeting this person?" the librarian asked.

"No. I've found nothing good comes from meeting these types."

Lefse thought about it. "Yeah. You're probably right." He went back to the jar. "I think this thing can learn to mimic people." And he started puckering kisses at it.

* * *

Several hours later, Isaac awoke in Lefse's office with his feet propped on the desk. He'd meant to prepare some kind of defense in case the Ambassador proved hostile, but figured a conflict would be hopeless and took a nap instead. Lefse had gone and dimmed the lights for him when he left.

He had been awoken by some kind of ruckus. The librarians were scurrying like ants whose hill was stepped on. Something was up.

Lefse burst into the office and hissed, "He's here. What's your plan?"

Isaac shook the remaining sleep out of his head. "Huh? There's no plan. You said we didn't need a plan."

"No. I said *we* didn't have a plan. I didn't mean *you* shouldn't have one. You're just going to wing it with Hell's Ambassador?"

Still exhausted, Isaac refused to summon the energy to be upset with Lefse again. "Yes. I'm just going to wing it. I'll sit here until he comes for me."

"In my office? You're going to make Hell's Ambassador come to my office?" Activity stirred in the hallway. Several librarians hurried by, looking back over their shoulders, attempting to satisfy curiosity as well as make sure they were out of the way. "Shit. Too late."

Two men in black suits, indistinguishable from any bodyguard detail for any politician, stepped into the room and looked over every nook and cranny. "All clear," one shouted back into the hall.

"Of course it's clear. Are you kidding me? These people are all bookworms," complained a cranky, high-pitched voice, and in walked what Isaac guessed was the Ambassador of the Iron Embassy. Frankly, Lefse's exaggerated descriptions fell way short.

He was a she and she happened to be a little old lady. Maybe a tad over five feet tall, she walked with a cane and a slight hunch. Her brown pantsuit, while tailored to fit, looked like she could have worn it to celebrate the end of World War II.

"Which one of you kicked the shit out of my Feckle?" she demanded.

Lefse immediately pointed at Isaac, who raised his hand like a child who didn't want to answer a question in class.

"Ah. So, you're Isaac Unknown." The old lady looked him up and down and then cast her crotchety gaze at Lefse. "And who are you?"

"Lefse. I'm Isaac's researcher. This is my office."

"Lefse, huh? Odd name. That your first name?" The librarian nodded. "I figured. Guess what. I already know your last name. It's Out-in-the-Hallway." She rapped her cane once on the floor and her men moved Lefse out of the office. "Now then." The Ambassador maneuvered her way past Isaac's chair. "No, no, son, stay seated. Don't stand up like you're in the presence of one of the most powerful people in the world," she said, despite Isaac making no move whatsoever to leave his chair. She plopped into Lefse's seat, only to discover it was adjusted for the librarian's larger size. From his side of the desk, Isaac could only see her from the nose up. If this scenario had occurred with anyone other than Hell's foremost diplomat, he probably would have laughed out loud. "Okay, this won't do at all," the Ambassador complained, and she looked around the base of the chair. "Is there a lever or something? Or maybe get me a damn booster seat?"

"There's a doohickey on the bottom. Just pull it," Lefse offered up from his banishment in the hallway.

The Ambassador's bodyguards jumped into action with over-the-top enthusiasm and eventually found the right lever. The Ambassador provided so little counterweight that the chair rocketed up, nearly throwing the small woman off. Now she loomed comically high as if sitting on a throne.

"Easy, knuckleheads. Just shoot me into the ceiling, why don't you?" she said. They apologized and set to task trying to adjust her down, but she waved them away. "Out. Out. Out." The guards looked at Isaac. "He's not going to do anything," the Ambassador said. "Besides, even if he wanted to hurt me, how would he reach me all the way up here?" The men did as ordered, nudged Lefse back into the hall, and shut the door to the office behind them.

"Now then," the Ambassador said, "you're the fellow that gave my dear Feckle such a drubbing, eh?"

"Not really. She fell off a building."

The Ambassador chuckled. "That she most certainly did. And she also failed her mission for the first time I can remember."

"Maybe you should bring this up with the Head Librarian. I'm just an errand boy."

"The Head Librarian? Ha! No. I have no interest in talking to him any further. He squirms like a worm if I so much as blink at him."

"Are you going to garnish my wages?" A joke. Sort of.

"You think I want restitution? Hardly. Ms. Feckle is easily repaired. I was just curious to meet you, and it's not often I get the chance to be curious about anything. I'm usually in a position where I know too much about everything. It's taxing."

Isaac could understand. He often wished he knew less. "So, the fly belongs to Belial?"

"Indeed. *Archduke* Belial."

"Wow."

The Ambassador waved a hand. "Oh, don't be too impressed. While it technically belongs to him, it was really just a message carrier from one of his minions to another. Not worth all this fuss. It's more the principle. A devil of his status can't allow such a transgression, even by accident."

"I hope there's no ill will here."

"Not at all. The fly has been returned and it's not like you actually saved any of the amateur demonologists. Feckle will be good as new. Sure, I had to take a long drive, but it was a good excuse to get out of the damn embassy for a change of scenery. This job isn't as exciting as one would imagine."

Isaac initially wanted to point out that his assignment wasn't to save any of the demonologists, but his ego didn't require such massaging. "Sorry to hear. If being Ambassador to Hell is dull, I can't fathom..." Isaac couldn't even imagine enough to finish the sentence.

"Bah. If it was fun, it wouldn't be work." The Ambassador leaned forwards in her chair. "Now then, the Iron Embassy generally keeps a pretty good tab on, well, everything. But our files on you were bare, to say the least. So, tell me—whom did you apprentice under?"

Isaac hesitated at the unexpected and very hated question. "No one special. Different teachers, here and there."

"Now, that I don't believe at all. Maybe you didn't put much work into that lie because you knew I'd see right through it. It's clear you don't like discussing it. But I also think most people wouldn't believe you even if you told the truth anyway. They'd think you were lying or bragging. What to do, then, when your master is a *faceless* myth? 'Keep it quiet,' I suppose, is the best answer." The old woman winked.

"That's what I always go with." He kept his response simple, but her use and emphasis of the word "faceless" made his blood cold.

"Good. Magicians should have their secrets, especially one of that magnitude. Now then, why don't you walk me out? Maybe if I'm talking to you, then all these busybody librarians will leave me alone."

Flanked by her security, Isaac escorted the Ambassador through the lobby to her waiting limousine. While it did nothing to deter the looky-loos, his presence did seem to prevent anyone from attempting to interrupt the Ambassador. More likely none of the librarians would have been brave enough to approach anyway.

Before climbing into the car, the Ambassador turned and extended a hand. "My name is Henrietta. Henrietta Murray."

He shook it. "Isaac. Isaac… Unknown, I guess."

The old woman chuckled. "This Arrangement nonsense can only last for so long. Some of my finest diviners have predicted its collapse, although the specifics of such a calamity have been lacking. When it eventually comes crashing down, all the traditional powers will go back to doing things the old way. The *right* way. When that happens, you come to see me, and we'll find a place for you. It'll be a hoot. Good pay, plus benefits. The HR department can be kind of a bitch, though."

Isaac thanked her for the offer and then asked in a subdued tone, "So what is Arrangement, exactly?"

Ambassador Murray smiled, then held both hands up, palms out, and muttered an incantation. For a moment Isaac felt like someone had pulled a burlap bag over his head, such was the sudden loss of sensory input. In a blink, the sensation vanished as if it had never happened. "Sorry about that. I never discuss such matters without some kind of obfuscation spell. One can never tell when or how Arrangement is listening. But now we can talk. To answer your question, I can't tell you what Arrangement is. I don't know what manner of creature operates those blasted phones or speaks in that ghastly voice. What I can tell you is what Arrangement *does*. It helms the valves of the world and adjusts the pressure as it sees fit. It ratchets the tension up and down, in matters great and small. To what end I cannot say. But that is its purpose."

"So, what did it achieve with the fly? Feckle would have killed the summoners and taken it anyway. What was the point of getting me involved?"

The Ambassador smiled tolerantly as if Isaac were a dense student she couldn't reach. "It had nothing to do with you. It was a message to *us*. A reminder to the Iron Embassy that Arrangement can defeat our servants and successfully interfere in our affairs. Much like your ill-fated vampire hunt made some powerful elders reevaluate their plans simply by desecrating a grave and torching an old safe house. It was a gentle slap to remind us who currently runs the world." The old woman muttered, and the obfuscation dissolved, signaling the end of the spell as well as the conversation. "Be careful, Isaac. You're developing a reputation as quite the albatross. Wherever you show up, everyone dies."

As the limousine drove away, Lefse ran out of the Athenaeum as fast as his bulk would allow. In between panting breaths, he asked, "So how did that go?"

"Complicated. Just like I said it would be."

* * *

In the back seat of the limousine, Ambassador Murray lifted the jar for a closer examination of the fly. It was the silliest-looking little thing, as if whatever Hellspawn had designed it had been a cartoonist in a former life. She unscrewed the lid, reached in, and let the fly bite the end of her index finger. It ground its teeth back and forth until it tore the skin.

The Ambassador studied the small wound and the way the blood ran down her finger. She rubbed the cut with her thumb, sniffed it, and finally touched it to the tip of her tongue. Then she started laughing.

One of her bodyguards turned. "Everything all right, Ambassador?"

"No wonder Arrangement returned it. The fly is empty."

"Pardon?"

"Oh, it's like opening an envelope with no letter in it. The message has been delivered. Or in this case, intercepted."

"Should we turn around?"

"No. Take us home. Curious things are afoot, and I'm going to enjoy being surprised for as long as I can."

Chapter 14
THE NEW VOICE

A dejected Mabahazi sat in his office chair and stared pensively out the window. He normally loved his view of the Athenaeum grounds, peering out across the manicured grass like the lord of the manor, but found the slow acceleration of the Iron Ambassador's limousine aggravating as it followed the twisting driveway to the main road. It wouldn't have surprised him if the old crone herself was driving, just to spoil his view a bit longer. As soon as the vehicle disappeared, he kicked off the wall, spinning his chair back to face his desk.

The Iron Ambassador had spent scarcely three minutes in his office and still succeeded in berating him to the point that he felt as powerful as a summer intern. Her words reverberated in his head, growing more condescending as they replayed.

"Why did the Voice choose to interfere in our affairs?" she had demanded. "Do you know how much it will cost to fix Ms. Feckle and how long she'll be out of commission? Who is this Isaac Unknown person? Do you know his background? Are you able to answer any questions at all? Maybe I should just ask you what time it is? Or maybe some simple arithmetic? Would you have the authority to respond? It's infuriating that I even sit with you when you're obviously middle management at best."

Mabahazi had possessed no answers. He had been a stammering customer service representative unable to placate or reason with the woman. Once again, he felt like a youngster tearing tickets for elitists who could afford to attend the secret show.

Even worse than feeling useless, however, was feeling weak—utterly spineless. In theory, his position at Arrangement should make him one of the most powerful people in the world. He should have an army of magicians, assassins, and monsters at his command and a treasure trove of arcane artifacts and knowledge at his fingertips. Even people like the Iron Ambassador and her ilk should speak to him like royalty, with trembling voices afraid of incurring his wrath. Hell, he'd settle for being spoken to as an equal.

Instead, he continued to be kicked around like the court jester—a punching bag for frustrations that could not be directed at the true power of Arrangement still secreted away behind the damn iron wall. The Ambassador had verbally slapped him around simply because she could. He had a distinct notion that if her anger proved enough to send an assassin to murder him, Arrangement would make no attempt to defend him or even take retaliatory action. He would just be butchered, forgotten, and replaced, probably by that buffoon Lefse.

That he'd watched Isaac and the Ambassador have what appeared to be a cordial chat proved to be salt in his wounded pride. He could barely contain his profanity when the pair shook hands.

With his mind turning to buffoons, his traitorous psyche brought Isaac Unknown to the forefront. The Athenaeum oversaw dozens of field agents, and, with exceedingly rare exceptions, all the assignments ran like clockwork. Even the psychopaths and murderers performed satisfactorily. The only jobs that ever had a hitch involved that milquetoast nomadic magician. Mabahazi had learned that whenever he had a work-related migraine, it was delivered to him by Isaac. Much to his chagrin, like his earlier emasculating verbal undressing by the Iron Ambassador, there was nothing Mabahazi could do about it. He didn't even possess the power to fire a bad employee.

So, he sat there and stewed in his frustration and inadequacy until it boiled over. Not once had he initiated the use of the lobby phone. No one did. If it didn't ring, no one laid a finger on it. But at this moment, rage overtook sense, and the dam finally burst.

He stood from his desk, aggressively straightened his tie, and headed for the door. His newfound anger granted him temporary bravery and he intended to use it by marching to the lobby, snatching the handset from the cradle, and venting his grievances to whatever other-worldly being would listen. Consequences be damned.

Before he could leave the room, his desk phone rang. The ring was ordinary, with none of the brain hammering the Voice normally brought, but the timing shook him to his core. His ire faded. All he could do was hope it was a librarian reporting a clerical issue and not some omnipotent creature calling to punish him for whatever sin he'd just committed. He walked stiffly back to his desk and answered.

"Mabahazi," said a voice through the handset. "Mabahazi, I know you're there. You need to listen to me very closely."

It wasn't the soulless, inhuman Voice. This voice sounded male, and Mabahazi found it somehow soothing. His words flowed together like a crooning melody. It reminded Mabahazi of a sweet taste, like honey, and it coated and dissolved what little remained of his sudden rebelliousness. Even his fear lessened, although it didn't fade completely. He moved his lips to reply, but the words hid in his throat.

"You have to be able to summon the courage to respond. At the very least. For your sake." The new voice somehow threatened and granted confidence, the tones entwined.

"I'm here," the Head Librarian managed to say.

"Patience, Mabahazi. You will be rewarded in due time, but you must stay the course. All will be revealed. Slings and arrows may sting your ego, but they do not cut your skin. At least, not the kind you've faced so far. Losing your self-control and succumbing to pride now will cost you everything. Remember your role and ask nothing of those who sit above you, but shy not from those who lie below you. Fail in this and we'll simply move on to have higher hopes for your replacement. We are nothing if not patient."

He swallowed hard. "I understand."

"Excellent. Now then, let us all get back to work."

Silence followed. No click of disconnection. No dial tone. Just a void of sound, as if he hadn't been talking to anyone at all.

Holding his breath and moving slowly, as if the phone were filled with nitroglycerin, he hung up. Then, like a man reprieved from death row, he let out a whole-body sigh, poured himself a shot of vodka, adjusted his tie, and went back to work.

Chapter 15
THE GLEAMSTRESS AND THE CAT

Her proper name was Britney Whitworth. Everyone called her Brit Knit. Long ago her kind had been called gleamstresses—witches who used their abilities to create clothing with magical properties. Society's elite clamored for these services. What king wouldn't want robes that exuded dread or protected against poisons? What queen wouldn't want a gown that hypnotized and dazzled on the dance floor? The gleamstresses' fees had been exorbitant and their waiting lists long.

But that had been a different era. Noble blood no longer ruled the world. Extravagant costumes were now only for celebration, with very few willing to pay. Gleamstresses still existed, but their numbers had been thinned by the reduction in demand and lack of belief. Much knowledge had been lost. Those outside of the elite circles were called stitch witches and they managed more meager apparel, as well as existences. A scarf became lucky because of blessed yarn. A shawl had an intricate pattern of symbols which warded off bitterness, both of cold wind and cold hearts. The magic became so minor as to not be noticed at all.

Isaac's encounter with the Iron Ambassador had made him long for a simpler outing, and nothing spoke to his baser instincts more than learning some new tricks. Quick research had found the semi-retired gleamstress and, ever the student, Isaac had quickly driven to her small farm. Now that he had met her, Isaac couldn't imagine her dealing in darker magic. She was a small woman, charming but stern, with a motherly aura about her.

* * *

The scarf slithered across the floor, avoiding obstacles like a conscious thing until it reached Isaac's shin and twisted around it, lashing itself with surprising strength to the leg of the chair he sat on. He tugged his foot, and in response, the article of clothing tightened, akin to a python with prey.

"Impressive," he said to Brit Knit.

"I call it the serpent scarf." She retook her seat across from him, having moved previously to give the magic scarf more room for its demonstration. A snap of her finger and the scarf collapsed lifelessly to the floor. Isaac picked it up and examined it end to end. Adhered to it were several reddened scales. Snake scales, with the red being drops of blood.

"Novel idea," he said.

She was too busy sipping noisily from a cup of tea to reply.

"And the scissor spell?" he asked.

She nodded and moved a paper napkin from her tea saucer to the tabletop. With index and middle fingers in a V, she held them above the napkin and closed them scissor-like. The napkin split in two, cut cleanly by nothing.

Isaac nodded again. Simple but effective. He liked things like that. Low effort, handy results. "You teach?"

"It's been a long time since I've tutored anyone. No one appreciates the little tricks anymore."

"I do."

She frowned. "I've been out of the loop for a long time. I cut all ties with the Other World a long time ago."

The Other World. Code lingo for the field of magic. The active community of magicians, witches, monsters, ghosts, blah, blah, blah. Isaac never used the term, as he didn't bother separating the worlds. One world seemed enough of a hassle without acknowledging another.

"I hated the way trouble always found me in it," she continued. "Lots of beings out there take a sick delight in following and leaving a terrible wake. How do I know you haven't brought something awful with you?"

Isaac wasn't sure how to answer, so he lied. "Nothing following me." He supposed it was true enough in a literal sense.

Brit tapped her fingers on the cup handle as she eyed him. Finally, with a dramatic sigh, she made up her mind. "Fine. I'll teach you. It'll take several days, maybe a couple of weeks if you're slow on the uptake. But something tells me that won't be an issue. You can stay in the spare room."

"Thank you. How much do you charge?"

"Oh, no money. You'll pay in other ways," she said as she cleared the table and Isaac's heart momentarily skipped. "Chores," she continued, and he exhaled relief. "Don't flatter yourself. Firewood and raking leaves to start. Finish those and I'll teach you to shear sheep."

Work didn't bother him much. Telekinetic chopping for the wood, wind spells for the leaves, and some kind of balding spell to make the wool fall off. There were ways around toil.

"And don't think about using magic in the yard. I have customers dropping by all the time. I don't need to explain some stranger moving things with his mind."

Damn it.

* * *

Two days into the chore phase of his training, Isaac awoke early to reddish-orange dawn light seeping through the curtains in his room. He dressed with various grunts and groans from chore-induced soreness. His room overlooked Brit's farm, the rustic charm of her small barn and sheep pens. He drank in the view, ignoring the still-too-big pile of uncut firewood. He liked rural. It felt safe. No chaos or big-city confusion to mask oncoming dangers.

He tiptoed downstairs out onto the back porch, intent on watching the sunrise and sipping hot coffee. On the steps sat a large tawny striped cat. It paid no mind to the sound of the screen door shutting or the creak of the rocking chair Isaac planted himself into. It had to be one of the biggest felines he'd seen—brawny, not fat. Its fur, while an attractive color, was damp and matted from woodland roaming.

Isaac liked animals. "Here kitty, here kitty, c'mere girl, here girl," he said, snapping his fingers for the animal to approach and sniff. Instead, the cat turned and hissed, and Isaac withdrew his proffered scratch with a yelp of disgust. The cat had the face of a brawler—several hairless scars, a tattered ear, and one permanently closed eye. The other eye, a shockingly bright and beautiful silver, gave him a once-over, and then the cat hopped off the steps and disappeared into the bushes.

"Don't call him a girl. He hates that," Brit said as she joined him on the porch, a cup of tea steaming.

"He knows the difference?"

Brit guffawed. "Oh, he knows. He's a bright one. Real sharp. Meaner than a shithouse rat, though. I took him to the vet once." She held up a finger. "Once."

"I've never seen a cat with an eye like that." Isaac hesitated, not wanting to pry into a witch's secrets, but curiosity won the day. "Is he your familiar?"

Again, Brit chuckled. "He almost was. He wandered onto the farm one day, bleeding, having lost an eye. Raccoon fight, probably. Even all beat-up, he chased off my ex-husband's hounds. I nursed him back to health. I could tell he was special, that he had some kind of spark most animals don't. A rare feel for things." She leaned over and punched Isaac lightly in the arm to illustrate the cat's pugilistic sense of the world. "So, I started the process of making him a familiar. But it just didn't take. Maybe too willful. Maybe just too mean. But the process imprinted something. Changed him somehow. He's been here ever since, a watchful, belligerent eye."

A guard cat, Isaac mused. *Why not*? He'd seen stranger things. "What's his name?"

"I'll tell you, but don't laugh."

Isaac smirked, thinking the cat was named Cuddles or Mittens, something inappropriately cute. But Brit looked serious. "Okay."

"I mean it." She craned her head, searching the bushes. "If he's listening and hears you laugh..."

Really? Isaac played along and nodded.

"Testiculies."

Isaac didn't laugh. The utterance had been so unexpected that it stunned him. "What?" he asked just to hear it again.

"Testiculies. Like Hercules. Only with more... testicle." Brit sipped her tea quickly to cover her embarrassment.

Isaac couldn't help it. He snickered and Brit swatted him. He held up his hands in mock surrender. "Why the hell did you call him that?" The last word left his mouth with a bit too much intensity.

Brit sighed, and started to explain, but then looked past him at the silver eye peering at them between porch rails, and quickly changed topics. "Want some breakfast?"

"Sounds good, thanks." Isaac waited for her to go inside before he made eye contact with the cat. "Testiculies," he said out loud. "So, do you have big balls? Figuratively? Literally?" Even Isaac himself wasn't sure if he mocked or genuinely asked. Either way, the outcome was a low feline growl, and then the eye disappeared with nary a rustle of bushes.

* * *

It was the wee hours of the following morning when a noise woke Isaac. Enough dawn light bled through the curtains for him to see, with blurry eyes, Testiculies sitting on the nightstand next to his bed. The stand must have wobbled and bumped against the frame when the hefty cat leaped onto it. The single eye glowed, one fang protruding due to an old injury to his muzzle.

He truly was an ugly animal.

Isaac lifted his head. "How'd you get in here?" The door was locked. Windows closed. The feline must have been hiding somewhere when he went into bed. One thing was for certain, he was not comfortable going back to sleep with that cat glaring at him. He threw back the covers and started to sit up, "Okay, I'll let you out."

Testiculies jumped, the nightstand toppling from the springboard force, and landed, with all his brawny weight, on Isaac's crotch. He sat up, only to double over in pain and then flop into a fetal position. The cat scrambled out of the bed, leaving Isaac gasping and attempting not to vomit as pain radiated into his abdomen. Between groans, Isaac managed to say out loud to no one, "Oh... Testiculies. I get it."

Chapter 16
SCISSORS AND SCARVES

"My ex-husband started to sleep with a sports cup on," Brit said the next morning as she set a plate of eggs and bacon in front of Isaac. "That cat used to torture him. Of course, he kind of deserved it for always being mean to the cat. Which probably prompted more of the crotch attacks. In the end, it was just a cycle of genital abuse, so it wasn't shocking who won out. Initially, I came up with the name as a joke, but, well, it's kind of stuck."

Enough time had passed that the pain of the feline assault had faded to a dull ache. "Testiculies somehow got out of the room after his... revenge. I couldn't figure out how."

"Oh, he has his ways. Pretty much goes wherever he wants. Kind of like the cat in *Alice in Wonderland*. Only more of an asshole."

Isaac frowned. "So, do I need to sleep face down from now on?"

Brit chuckled. "I imagine he was paying you back for laughing at his name. Now that he's delivered his message, you two could probably coexist. Just don't poke any more fun at him. That was one of the things my ex couldn't do. Just leave Testiculies be."

Duly noted.

* * *

The next morning Brit informed him the chores were done, and they'd start on his training.

The slithering scarf spell proved relatively easy. A prick of a finger, blood drawn with a quill in a vaguely S-shaped pattern on the anaconda scales, and then affixing the scales to a suitable piece of fabric was all it took. Despite Brit's insistence that he knit his own, Isaac found (when the gleamstress left the room) that the process worked on anything appropriately shaped. He had one of his socks slithering around the room in no time. From there he smuggled a length of rope from Brit's barn and soon had it squirming on command as well.

The scissor spell proved a bit more intensive. Brit ushered him into her knitting room and sat him down at her craft table. She'd stacked several boxes of assorted fabric scraps next to it.

"The first step is to have an appropriate set of scissors." She produced a large pair of antique tailor shears. "The older, the better. Ones well-used. Cut until the metal dulls. Sharpen. Repeat." Brit picked them up, delicately, as if they were made of glass and not steel. She cradled them across her palms, a reverent knight with a holy blade. "All magic seamstresses would have a set. A pair long owned and used only by them. But for you, these will suffice. They have sat unused for a long time and need some love. You will sharpen them and then cut." She nudged one of the boxes next to the table. "Cut, cut, cut. Until they dull again. Then sharpen and cut. Until the pieces get so small they disappear. Use only the hand you intend to cast the spell with. Questions?"

Isaac shook his head. He knew how to listen. He'd been a student most of his life, in much worse circumstances than this. *Much.*

He did as she instructed and sharpened the blades by hand. Then he cut and cut. Linen, cotton, leather, wool, yarn, paper, cardboard, tinfoil, and plastic. Scraps of every material he could think of were in the boxes, and he hacked away at them until his hand ached and fingers blistered. The next day he did more. Brit worked alongside him on her own project—beanies for newborns with stitched symbols to protect against illness.

After hours of cutting, she had Isaac sharpen the scissors one last time until the points were like razors. A self-inflicted laceration followed, to the tips of the index and middle fingers of his right hand, deep enough to bleed heavily but still bandage-treatable. He smeared the blood along the blades and handle, then dropped the shears into a plastic bag.

"Put them somewhere safe, where they won't be found. Mine are buried in the yard. We'll give your fingers a day or so to heal, then see if you can snip."

Isaac nodded and dropped the bagged scissors into his everbag. She looked at him oddly when he did. "Safest place I know of," he said, and he clipped it shut. He smiled.

She didn't.

* * *

The next evening, they dined on meatloaf, mashed potatoes, and green beans. Baked apple pie rested on the kitchen counter. Isaac was getting comfortably used to this country cooking. Across the table, Brit hadn't been her normal, chatty self. She had focused on her meal, barely making eye contact, responding to his attempts at small talk with one-syllable mutterings. He found it odd, but wasn't a gregarious fellow himself under most circumstances, so he certainly didn't begrudge her that.

When the plates were clean, she went into the kitchen and came back, wiping her hands with a dish towel, which she then tossed to him. "Cut it. Let's see if you got it." Her brusqueness startled him, but he complied. He held up the towel with his left, made a V with his right, and snipped the air next to it. The rag fell apart, cut clean.

"Well done. You've picked it up fast. Faster than anyone I ever taught. Faster than me. Faster than the witch who taught me."

She seemed more irritated than impressed, so he made a faux sheepish grin and said, "You're a good teacher, I guess."

"Knock it off." She sat down, eyeballing him sternly. "If we're talking about teachers, name me a few of yours. Who've you studied under?"

Isaac's face darkened as he dropped the act. "It's probably better that I didn't."

"Why am I not surprised? You don't even want to speak a name. That must mean these aren't good people, then. Right?"

"No. Not good... people."

Brit plucked a broom from the corner. "Here, cut this." He hesitated. "Go ahead, just like you did the rag."

Feeling very much like he was being scolded, he did as instructed. He snipped his fingers alongside the broom. It proved more of a strain, but the handle fell in two, as cleanly cut as with a table saw. The harder material did make his fingers ache a bit.

The stitch witch pursed her lips, begrudgingly impressed. "Very nice, Isaac. Only you shouldn't have been able to do that. The spell is confined to the materials you practiced on. All those hours you cut. Those should be the limitations. Those are my limitations. Only now I see we don't share limitations."

"Maybe I'm the chosen one for broom chopping."

Her gaze fell to his satchel, resting against the leg of his chair. "It's funny," she continued, "when you dropped the scissors in, the bag didn't move. It didn't stretch down under the weight. The sides didn't bulge at all. It was like the scissors dropped into nothingness. If I opened it up, I'd find only an empty satchel, wouldn't I? But that's not what you find, is it? When you look in, you see whatever you want. Whatever object you put in there is just there, but only for you?"

Isaac didn't care for the line of questioning, but he stayed in his seat, enduring it out of respect, and hopes they were still going to have dessert. "Right."

"It's a bag of emptiness, then? A bag that can never be filled?"

"I call it my everbag."

"Cute. I've heard of those. Never seen one." She sighed. "It takes a nasty kind of magic to make one, from what I've heard. You have to capture the last dying breath of someone who sold their soul, right?"

He nodded. "It's the ultimate emptiness."

She shook her head. "Foul things. Foul things cast that kind of magic."

He didn't argue. He couldn't.

"We're done here. You've learned what you came to learn. Tomorrow morning, I want you to go." She had a hint of regret in her tone, motherly angst as if throwing one of her children out of the house. "And do me one favor..."

Isaac nodded.

"Forget you were ever here. Forget me completely, and never come back."

Chapter 17
THE WITCH HUNTERS

On a highway about three hundred miles east, a white Cadillac sped along, carrying the Unger brothers to their target.

"A stitch witch? A fucking old lady in a rocking chair making mittens?"

The indignant questions came from the back seat of the Caddy. Fergus Unger adjusted the mirror so he could make annoyed eye contact with Ladd, his younger brother. "A job is a job," he said, with Ladd moving his lips in unison, having heard the line multiple times.

"Yeah, yeah." Ladd sat back with a huff. "These jobs are all just so easy. No excitement. No challenge."

Fergus sighed. His brother, barely mid-twenties, was still a rookie in terms of witch-hunting, and thus still full of untarnished enthusiasm. He wondered if he'd been like that at Ladd's age, but couldn't recall, which bothered him. He was only six years older than Ladd, but the span felt like a lifetime. He sometimes wished he were more like his older brother, Aldo, as emotional as a tree stump.

Aldo sat in the passenger seat. Despite the spaciousness of the Caddy, the lanky man barely fit. At nearly seven feet tall, his knees were drawn up, with his head tilting to the side to not bump the roof. But he never complained. Ever. About anything. While Fergus frequently repeated "a job's a job," Aldo embodied the phrase. The gangly giant didn't care at all about their various employments. He'd sign a contract to weed a garden or fight a demonic horde with the same detached shrug.

They pulled over at a deserted rest stop to stretch their limbs and kill time as they waited for the sun to set. When twilight came, they stripped off their shirts, revealing matching tattoo-covered torsos. To the unknowing eye, they were decorated with generic, pick-'em-off-the-parlor-wall tribal tats. But hidden within the designs, needled with special ink, were magic-resistant symbols. Fergus often wondered how powerful a spell the tattoos could repel. They had yet to fail them, but the brothers had never locked horns with any truly dangerous beings.

"You really think we need the vests?" Ladd whined. "It itches."

"Yes," Fergus replied as he pulled the bulletproof Kevlar from the trunk. "These country witches are more likely to have shotguns than dangerous spells."

Ladd rolled his eyes. "I'm tired of going up against these old, powerless hags."

"Sooner or later, we'll tangle with someone that has real teeth. We'll see if that changes your tune."

"Teeth? Lucky if she has dentures."

Fergus sighed and ran a hand over his bald head. "Balding" may have been a better word. He shaved what little he had left. His one vanity. Aldo was also balding but cared too little to bother with it. Instead, he let his curly hair grow into a clownish, horseshoe-shaped hedge from ear to ear.

"Much further?" Aldo asked. He had a light, airy voice. Not feminine, just soft. A man who didn't care enough about speech to put any effort into it.

"Within the hour," Fergus replied.

"Let's go."

* * *

Isaac lay on the bed in the guest room, arms crossed behind his head, eyes on the ceiling. He'd been lost in thought since his conversation with her.

Never come back.

The words had stung. While he had never had any intention of returning, having it verbalized to him had made an impression. He should have left the moment Brit informed him she had withdrawn herself from the Other World. Like with Susan, he should have been smart enough to not involve her at all. But in the end, learning and moving on had been his modus operandi for years. *Glean what you can and disappear.* Leave the past behind, both literally and figuratively.

But still, one of the few decent people he'd met had rightly pegged him as the kind of person she had changed her life to avoid. Maybe that was what really stung. She was an accurate judge of his character.

The front doorbell rang and interrupted his whiny introspection. He heard Brit going down the creaky stairs, loudly mumbling, "Who's knocking at this hour?"

* * *

The front porch was large enough for all three brothers to line up. They made no attempts to disguise themselves, brazenly carrying weapons, clad in Kevlar. Aldo wielded a two-handed ax, Fergus a shotgun. Ladd carried a 9mm and had used the barrel to ring the bell.

A living room light came on and shone through the picture window. Next came the click of the deadbolt. A short, elderly woman, clad in a robe and clearly annoyed, opened the door. "Who are you and why are you bothering..." Her voice trailed off when she saw the weapons.

"Brit Whitworth?" Fergus asked.

The woman backed up. "This house is protected. Barrier spells on the doors. No one who wishes to do me harm can enter."

"Of course not. Aldo?" Fergus said.

Aldo, ax on his shoulder like a lumberjack, pulled open the screen door and put a foot into the house. He winced, eyes pinched, teeth gritted, at the invisible forces that assailed him. The hunter pushed forward slowly, a mime walking against gale-force winds. The magic-resistant ink in his tattoos flared, glowing, searing, as it fought the protective magic. Brit took a step back, mouth agape. Fergus didn't know how his brother could withstand it. Even with the tattoos, it had to hurt like hell. With a final slow-motion charge, Aldo pushed through and stood before the stitch witch.

"Peasant magic. We're always prepared for peasant magic. No offense," the tall man said, and he brought the ax down.

* * *

Isaac peered through the cracked door just in time to see the weapon fall. Even if he'd been prepared, he wouldn't have been able to intervene. The stairway banister partially blocked his vision and spared him the death blow, but not the sound sickeningly akin to chopping wood. His breath caught, and his heart skipped a beat, but he otherwise physically restrained himself to only a slight flinch. There was no point in further reaction. He could do nothing for Brit and saw little benefit in giving away his position. Instead, he slowly backed up, gathered up his everbag and his shoes, tiptoed into the walk-in closet, and shut the door.

He opened his everbag. Even if he could see, it would be empty until he willed an object out of the everbag's pocket dimension. Just as Brit had said. He pictured a piece of onyx he'd previously placed in it. Black, shiny, smooth. And it appeared, spit back into this dimension by the lining of the bag.

With the stone in his hand, he could cast a spell to camouflage himself in the darkness, the shadows wrapping him like a blanket. He didn't like it. It made for a cold place to hide. But even if the intruders shone flashlights directly on him, they would see nothing but dark, empty space. If the killers indeed hunted for him, they'd have a tough time finding him. If they were only there to kill Brit, then they might never even know he was there at all.

It wasn't fear that bid him do this, just resignation. He'd liked Brit and had no wish to see her die. But she'd been right about the Other World, the one she'd left behind. She'd been right about him. Foul things tended to follow the both of them. Whether the assassins had come for him or her, he didn't know, nor did he care. Brit was dead. It made no sense to engage her killers—no justice to gain and no retribution worth the risk. Other World scales were not built to be balanced.

The house was old, and he could hear them wandering around. They moved freely, unconcerned about wooden floors creaking, uncaring about the noise they made. Their voices carried at normal volume. If they were in pursuit of him, he assumed they'd still be wary of their prey, but they moved casually like the job had been completed with Brit's death.

He heard the guest room door open, and someone rummaged about. Passing feet broke the light bleeding under the closet door.

Then he heard the voice—young, angry, disappointed. It cried, "I knew the old bitch would have no teeth."

The onyx lay in Isaac's hand, cold in his palm. The concealment spell would be quick and easy to cast, but something stopped him.

Teeth. The old bitch had no teeth. It jarred him. Made him think...

* * *

...Isaac had been much younger, maybe a teenager, he couldn't quite remember. He couldn't recall the month or the year. He'd been in a place where time was irrelevant, so there was no need to know. His master stood before him, wreathed in shadow, only a silhouette, an outline of a cloaked human form with a shine in his eyes like jewels. To his right, on a stand made of bones, perched a giant snow-white owl. On the ground before him lay a skull, polished and bright, but inhuman. It had an oblong shape and oversized jaws, with rows of fangs, too many and too large.

"Fangs are impressive." When his master spoke, the voice was flat. Unable to tell if it was a statement or a question, Isaac had remained silent. "They terrify the lesser because they impart a ferocious countenance. One would be a fool to engage such a beast. Yet look where it is. A trophy used as a lesson because it judged me by the size of my teeth. And found it to be a serious misjudgment." Then, finally the question. "Should you fear such fangs?" The skull levitated with the words and rotated in the air.

A butterfly stomach was Isaac's first reaction. Admit fear and be thought a coward. Deny fear and be thought a fool. The master was hard to anticipate. Better to dodge. "It depends on what they're attached to."

Since he could observe no face, only swirling darkness, it proved impossible to tell the reaction. "It's more important for beings such as us to keep our fangs hidden. But those with sharp teeth on display deserve to be met in kind. You must always be ready to bite, and when you do, make sure your teeth meet."

* * *

Isaac didn't cast the spell. He replaced the stone, drew Wilma, and stood in the center of the closet, ringed on three sides by Brit's clothing, her handiwork, her life. Normally he didn't get riled up enough for vengeance, but he supposed this particular situation called for teeth.

Chapter 18
WITH TEETH

The killer in the bedroom opened the closet door. Not expecting to see Isaac, his eyes went wide, and he reached for the gun protruding from his waistband. Isaac fired first, the roar from Wilma proved deafening in the confined space. The buckshot sprayed across the man's chest and hurled him to the floor.

The gunfire echoed through the house. Isaac trained the weapon on the hallway, waiting for the witch hunter's companions to rush into view. And one did. The tall man with the ax stepped from Brit's bedroom. They locked gazes as Isaac aimed. The assassin didn't even attempt to move out of the way—just stood there, seemingly willing to test a shell. Isaac, more than happy to oblige, started to squeeze the trigger.

Before he could fire, the young hunter, not dead, leaped up and tackled him. They fell against a cabinet, then to the floor, grappling as they went. Wilma spun from his grasp.

"Aldo! Aldo! Grab him!"

The tall man, Aldo, strode towards the door at the young man's call. Isaac, from underneath the younger assassin, got one hand loose, waved it with fingers spread, and magically slammed and locked the bedroom door in Aldo's face. He then got the hand to his own face in time to deflect a punch. He countered with a telekinetic lashing, only to be disappointed as it washed around the man ineffectively, like wind around a tree. It must be the same kind of magical resistance that allowed Aldo to force his way through Brit's barrier spell, and he took a punch near the eye for his failure.

The door shuddered from the big man's shoulder but held secure. It wouldn't last long. Isaac twisted his head to slip past another punch from the man on top of him. The assassin was grinning, his eyes alight with an eagerness to hurt.

With a silent command, Isaac brought his new scarf to life. It slithered off the bedpost, flashed through the air like a striking cobra, wrapped around the man's head, and pulled tight. The young assassin fell back, hands snatching at the fabric. A telekinetic pull yanked his pistol to Isaac's hand, and he put a bullet dead center into the scarf. No Kevlar intervened this time. The man stayed on his knees for several seconds, blood staining the scarf around the dark hole, forming a cyclopean red mask, and then he fell, just as the doorframe shattered and the door burst open on twisted hinges.

Aldo entered, long legs making strides that negated his ponderous speed. He pounced on Isaac before he could react, a large hand around the magician's throat, lifting him off the floor and slamming him to the wall. Framed pictures shook and fell from the shock. Aldo snatched Isaac's left hand and squeezed until pain popped the gun from it. He casually glanced at his fallen comrade before moving his gaze to Isaac, studying him like a novelty. Isaac stared back as if he'd just met Bigfoot.

"You killed my brother," Aldo told him in a higher-pitched voice than Isaac expected, a polite, soft tone more suited to a maître d'.

"Yeah," Isaac squeaked out with barely enough air to breathe, much less talk. "Sorry?"

Aldo nodded impassively, maybe not accepting the apology but understanding it. "It's a dangerous business. We all know the risks."

A voice called out from downstairs. "Aldo? Where are you? What the hell's going on?"

"Upstairs, Fergus."

Great, another one. Isaac wheezed his air in and out. Aldo could easily snuff that but didn't. He must have seen the wondering on Isaac's face, because he addressed it with, "Fergus will want to meet you before we slay you."

"Ah," Isaac replied. He heard footsteps downstairs. Mystery Fergus on his way. "He sounds nice. What say I take us all out for beers?"

Aldo shook his head. "We're quite past that now."

Index and middle fingers in a V shape, Isaac snipped them across Aldo's ear. The lobe came off, cut cleanly, with a splash of red. It proved painful enough to make the man flinch and step back, allowing Isaac to twist free. With silent command, Isaac's blood-soaked scarf writhed to life, unknotted from the dead brother's head, and lashed itself around Aldo's legs. While not enough to topple him, it did force him to put a hand on the wall to maintain his balance.

Isaac scooped up Wilma as he ducked out of the room. He turned at the top of the stairs and took aim at Aldo, ready to put him down. Then there was a thunderous bang and the railing post shattered, splinters spraying him. Isaac lost his balance, tumbled backward, caught himself about halfway down the stairs, and saw the man who must be Fergus in the living room aiming a rifle for a second blast. Isaac lashed out with his telekinesis. Surmising that this assassin had the same form of magic resistance his companions did, he aimed at the weapon and not the man. The rifle was pulled from unsuspecting hands and spun across the floor. Isaac brought Wilma to bear, emptying it in the man's direction. He either missed or only managed to test the Kevlar again.

"Who the fuck are you?" Fergus shouted as he retreated to the porch.

Isaac responded by magically slamming the door on him and turning the deadbolt, locking Fergus outside. Clambering to his feet, he hopped down the remaining stairs two at a time. He hoped to retrieve Fergus's weapon, but it had slid completely underneath the couch. He started to kneel for it, until Aldo, freed from the scarf, appeared at the top of the stairs. Outside, Fergus began to kick on the front door.

"You're not walking out of here," Aldo said in that reserved, unexcited voice. It sounded less like a threat, more like a fact, which made it oddly more menacing. He took a step, then another. Slow. Unconcerned.

"Not walking. Running," Isaac said, backing up. His barrage at Fergus had left Wilma dry. With assassins on either side, Isaac realized he'd picked a bad battleground.

Movement on the landing caught Isaac's attention. *Testiculies.* The cat appeared at the top of the stairs, his little head panning back and forth, compensating for having half a view of the world. Then he moved, darting down the stairs and in between Aldo's feet. The giant stumbled and fell.

Isaac didn't wait for him to pick himself up. He took off through the kitchen, burst through the back door, and leaped off the porch. The dark woods beckoned. Testiculies quickly outpaced him and vanished into the shrubbery. He sprinted out of reach of the house lights and concealed himself in the nearby trees. He planned to circle the house and make his way back to his truck—a scheme cut short when Fergus tackled him from behind.

The witch hunter was an established hand-to-hand combatant, as Isaac painfully learned when he took two hard punches to the ribs and then found himself flat on his back after a perfectly executed hip toss. Fergus leaped on him, a forearm across his throat. Isaac went for the scissor snip again, but Fergus slapped away and then pinned his right hand, and the magician would have cursed, if he could breathe, about his dumb ass learning the spell for just one hand.

"Who are you? Whitworth's apprentice?" Fergus demanded.

Isaac shook his head, unable to draw enough air to answer. With his free left hand, he reached... for nothing. Enough trees shielded the moon above them that they wrestled in deep shadows. And that was what Isaac grasped at.

Since the Belial fly had bestowed, or rather, *infected* Isaac with the ability to communicate with shadows, he'd made multiple attempts to wrangle them into greater levels of cooperation, with limited success. They did not respond to any form or verbalization or gesture. He had to *think* at them–a process Isaac disliked as these thoughts were consistently and involuntarily corrupted with his opinion that shadows were stupid and lazy. Despite the truth of it, these impulsive insults did little to inspire collaboration.

Isaac assumed it was the urgency with which he now called to them that spurred them into motion. With sluggish reluctance, the shadows solidified around his outstretched fingers as a gelatinous ooze that flowed around his hand and covered it like a glove. Then it constricted, crushing his flesh. He had to act quickly. As Brit had said before, it was *foul magic*.

With his shadow-wrapped hand, he grabbed Fergus's bare elbow. At first, the assassin just smirked. Isaac, the smaller man with no leverage, was not going to physically overpower him. Then the pressure started with a pincer-like compression on the arm. Fergus pulled away from Isaac's grip, but not from the pain. Isaac grabbed his forearm, then his wrist, each touch leaving behind a black handprint that continued to squeeze with unnatural strength.

Fergus scrambled off, shaking his arm, wiping at his flesh, but the shadow hands clung like stains. The pressure increased, and Fergus howled in pain and stumbled away, heading back towards the house. He only got a few steps away before Isaac heard bones break, and the witch hunter screamed, disappearing into the trees. The magician smiled as he crawled to his feet… and nearly lost his head.

Aldo's ax spun through the air, the blade barely missing his face, but the handle hit his shoulder with enough force to knock him back down. The gangly giant came striding through the trees. Isaac snatched up the ax, scissor-spelled the handle in half, and made quick cuts to one end to craft a rudimentary spear, which he flung at the assassin.

Isaac never considered himself all that athletic, but with a telekinetic boost as guidance, the missile flew true and struck Aldo in the right thigh. It stuck there, maybe not as deeply as Isaac had hoped, but enough to slow the man.

Before he could take advantage of Aldo's exposure, sharp pain constricted his hand. The darkness there tightened, a shrinking glove that curled his fingers to his palm. While its effects were not nearly as dire as they had been for Fergus, Isaac couldn't linger. It was dangerous magic, a kind that would eventually turn on him.

He had to make a break for it, revenge be damned. He'd taken one of them in Brit's name. A life for a life. It would have to suffice.

He picked up Aldo's now much smaller ax, its head still smeared with Brit's blood, and ran. Making it to the front of the house, he found a Cadillac parked there, surmised it belonged to the killers, and promptly flattened a tire with the ax before running to his truck.

The crushing blackness on his left hand grew more intense. He hissed with pain. Flipping on the headlights, he shoved his hand into the beams. Relief came immediately as the shadowy glove melted away, smoky tendrils wafting into nothing. He knew his hand would ache and bruise, but the foul magic had saved his life.

Maloc's pickup was a beat-up wreck, but completely reliable for starting and driving—the only important parts of a vehicle. It cranked to life, farting angry black smoke as Isaac gunned it, spraying gravel as he tore down the driveway. The engine roared, and he didn't hear the gunshots from the house until they banged into the truck with metallic thuds. The truck bulled on and he turned onto the main road, the lights of Brit's farm receding into the night.

*　*　*

On the porch of Brit's house, a seething Fergus lowered his rifle. His fractured forearm had thrown off his aim, and he could only watch as the truck lights faded away. He leaned the rifle against the porch railing, peeled open one side of his Kevlar vest, and tucked his injured arm in the makeshift sling.

The magic-resistant tattoos had failed miserably against the shadowy spell. Maybe they weren't strong enough, or maybe this stranger was too powerful. It wouldn't be settled until he forced a rematch.

He'd solved the crushing shadow hands by sheer chance, stumbling into the house in a blind panic, with the lights then undoing the spell. Damage had been done, but he assumed the spell could have crushed his bones to powder if left unchecked.

Something caught his attention in the trees. A large owl perched silently on a limb, eyeballing him intently. He only noticed it because of its snow-white feathers, which almost glowed in the moonlight. As furious as he was, he almost shot the bird out of spite, but the door opening distracted him.

Aldo came out, carrying lifeless Ladd in his arms, like a new bride across the threshold. Fergus thought he saw some sadness in the tall man's face, wetness around his eyes, maybe a hint of a frown. It was the most emotion he'd ever seen from his brother.

"We should move quickly," Aldo said. "This was a loud encounter. No telling who may have heard."

Fergus nodded. He stared at Ladd's face, focused on the perfect hole in the young man's forehead. It seemed so small, almost a blemish, on his brother's fair skin. But it had been fatal. His brother was over. Fergus had failed him.

"Fergus." Aldo's voice snapped him back. "We need to move. The job is complete. It is not up to us to decide to track and eliminate an unidentified target."

Fergus ignored the last statement and glanced back at the tree. The owl was gone.

* * *

Isaac drove through the night, the direction chosen only by whim and avoidance of big cities. He stopped at dawn, eyes bleary, ready to pass out in a cheap motel. Sitting in the bed of the truck was Testiculies, looking especially surly.

The magician sighed. He didn't want an animal traveling companion, especially one that had tried to neuter him. But he supposed he owed the cat a debt. His owner had been killed, and Isaac had no idea if her death was in any way his fault. Plus, Testiculies had tripped up Aldo, which, even if it didn't help much, had been pretty funny to see.

"Fine," he said to the cat. "You can tag along until we find you a suitable family with bad enough karma to deserve you." Testiculies yawned and licked a paw. Isaac wasn't sure what was more annoying—when the cat acted with almost human intelligence or when he acted like a damn cat. Regardless, he walked into the motel office intending to get two single beds.

Chapter 19
THE SHANTY OF MADNESS

In the weed-laden backyard of a ramshackle house, two ill-tempered dogs snapped and growled at each other. Moments earlier a man had stepped onto the back porch and tossed several chunks of meat to them, which spiked their aggression as they choked down all they could before fighting over the last.

Nestled in a grove of trees on a hill overlooking the hovel sat Isaac. Through an old-fashioned telescoping spyglass, he watched until they had eaten every scrap. Then he scanned the windows. Nothing new to see with the ratty curtains pulled over each. For the umpteenth time, he surveyed the rest of the property: a pair of utility sheds and a backyard littered with junk of all sizes, from abandoned cars to refrigerators.

He set the spyglass aside and went back to his previous project—etching simple fire runes into charcoal briquettes. When he had enough for a small pyramid, he stacked them up, whispered "burn," and waved his hand over them. They glowed, going from red to white-hot in seconds. The campfire burned smokeless, with no heavy plume to give away his position. Minutes later he had hot dogs and marshmallows cooking.

A rustle in the undergrowth paused his chewing, and his hand hovered over Wilma Wagon Fixer. Testiculies emerged from the bushes, sat next to the warmth of the coals, and affixed him with that never-approving eye. Isaac sighed, tore a piece of hot dog, and tossed it to the cat. Testiculies gobbled it up, but never lifted his permanent snarl. He shared his hot dog until the feline had his fill and lay down. Just for laughs, Isaac bounced one more piece of frankfurter off the cat's forehead, which elicited a nasty hiss and probably meant the magician would have to sleep face down for the night.

"So, cat, did you scope out the house for me? Encounter any hostiles and smash their balls?" He picked up the spyglass for a check-in on any activity on the run-down property. Still nothing.

Arrangement had sent him here. Somewhere in the dilapidated homestead below was a magical artifact. The inhuman Voice had described it as a wooden totem carved with crude screaming faces. Isaac hadn't received any information on what it actually did, which he found annoying, but one could never clarify with the Voice. Every word was final. Judging by the state of the house, whatever this totem bestowed, it certainly didn't include good fortune.

Morning turned to noon, but Isaac was patient. Every magician had to be. A few long hours sitting in the bushes were nothing. If anything, he relished the quiet.

Just past noon, something finally happened at the house. The back door banged open and two young, unkempt men strode out. The dogs moved from their path, backs bristling, no love for their masters. The men clambered into an unwashed van and, after several chugging attempts, managed to get it started. A honk of the horn brought out two more people, an older man with an impressive beard and a large woman in a flower-print muumuu. Both walked slowly, due to poor physical condition or age or maybe both. The group clambered into the van and drove away. The dogs paced in agitated circles for several minutes, whining, before they lay down.

Isaac waited long after the van disappeared to make sure that they didn't return right away because someone forgot to put on their fancy muumuu or dressy overalls. Finally, satisfied that they were gone, he moved on the house. An unfinished barbwire fence proved easy to bypass. He jogged from junked car to junked car, pausing behind each for a few seconds to make sure he hadn't been spotted.

The dogs had yet to get wind of him. He had Wilma at the ready, but he really considered the weapon a last resort. He had no stomach for killing animals. People, sure, but not animals. This weakness also left him bereft of any good ideas for how to get by them.

As he brainstormed, Testiculies casually walked by him into the center of the yard, sat down, and licked a paw. Both canines lifted their heads. Testiculies hissed. Isaac thumbed the safety off, certain that he would have to kill the dogs to save the stupid cat. Both dogs were then up and charging, barking furiously. Testiculies took off across the yard, the dogs on his heels.

While the burly cat wasn't particularly fast, he possessed a sixth sense that allowed him to make a sharp turn every time a set of jaws was about to clamp down. Eventually, he made it to the trees and all three animals disappeared, the barking fading into the distance.

Unsure if Testiculies had done this to help him or just out of general feline arrogance, Isaac knew to take quick advantage and moved to the first shed. It held nothing but rusty tools and unused lawnmowers. The contents of the second shed were a bit more disturbing. A variety of nets, ropes, lengths of chains, tarps, rolls of plastic, spools of duct tape, and several sizes of steel animal traps lay strewn about its interior. All the equipment a group of kidnappers would need.

He entered the backyard where the dogs had been lying. Only because he strove to avoid stepping in dog shit did he notice the bones. Large gnawed bones. He'd studied enough necromancy to know human femurs, tibias, and fibulas when he saw them. The meat that had been tossed to the dogs had been human. Apparently, a lot of different humans, he assumed from the state of the yard.

After collecting one intact femur and dropping it into his everbag, he climbed the steps to the back porch. The old wood, rotten in spots, creaked and groaned in protest. Unlocked, the back door swung open easily. No need to bother locking up when you have two big man-eating canines right outside.

The smell of the house immediately wrinkled his nose. Rancid and foul and poorly disguised by a layer of mothballs. It wasn't hard to guess what the source would be.

That was when he heard the whispering—a low, unintelligible slurry of voices that seemed to emanate from the very air. It continued unabated, like a man's dying words made with an unceasing breath. Despite being barely audible, the whispering had a grating effect, like the loud volume on a static screen television. It was both hard to hear and impossible to ignore.

Leading with Wilma's barrel, Isaac passed through the kitchen and its stacks of dirty dishes and then into the living room with its ripped furniture and cracked-screen antique TV. Further searching found three bedrooms, each with only bare mattresses on the floor and piles of unwashed clothing. The house was disgusting, and the inhabitants were obviously slobs, but Isaac had yet to see anything like the artifact he'd been sent for. Then he found the basement door.

The stairs creaked loudly as he descended. The odor of decay grew stronger, as did the ghostly whispering. The combination started to make his head hurt. A light switch turned on several dim-watt bulbs that hung from the ceiling, revealing a hoarding nightmare. Boxes stacked on boxes. Milk crates piled high. Towers were constructed from newspapers and hunting magazines. Mounds of plastic bags with who-knows-what inside.

There were two doors, one on the northern wall and one on the western. He got a lay of the land and then clicked the lights back off before pulling a flashlight from his everbag.

The walkway through the junk twisted almost maze-like. Isaac opened the northern door to a small storage room. Rows of jars lined shelves from the ceiling to the floor. In the glow of his flashlight, he assumed they were fruits, vegetables, and whatnot. But one caught his attention. He pulled the string to the storage room light and let out a disgusted sigh.

Many of the jars were labeled. Strawberry jam. Blackberry jam. Many weren't labeled but were obvious. Pickled eggs and beets. But then there were the rest. Human eyes. Fingers. Toes. Larger containers on the lower shelves contained complete hands and feet. Trophies or ingredients, he couldn't say. He reached to turn out the light.

"Hiding from the cannibals?" a voice suddenly said.

Isaac spun and trained his light on the shelves. Nothing. Just row upon row of ghoulish pantry supplies. "Who said that? Come out."

"I did. You can't see me."

"Invisible?" Isaac's mind raced defensively. Fairy? Ghost? Poltergeist? Shade?

"No, there's a jar of toes in front of me."

Curiously confused, Isaac scanned the shelves until he located a large jar of severed toes. Fearful of a trap, he refrained from touching it. Instead, he concentrated and telekinetically slid it aside, revealing a small demonic face directly behind it. Startled, he took a step away and bumped the shelves behind him, setting the jars to rattling.

"Boo," the voice said. "How are you doing?"

Isaac leaned forwards and studied the demon. It had clearly just talked to him, but nothing on the face had moved.

"Yeah, I'm a possessed jug. What of it?"

Intrigued more than wary, Isaac moved several more jars aside to get a better view. It was indeed a jug—sculpted and fired clay, painted garish orange and green. The side facing him had a carved face—devilish, two small horns on the forehead, tongue sticking out childishly between two fangs, one eye small and beady, the other popped in permanent surprise. A cork stopper adorned its head like a top hat.

"Seriously?"

"Yes. Seriously. My spirit has been bound to this vessel, shit, longer than I can remember." The voice emanated sans movement of the face.

"If I pull the cork, you'll be released?" That certainly seemed too simple, but Isaac felt the urge to inquire.

"Hell no. I'd have been free long ago if that were the case."

"So, what's inside you?"

"My owner's choice of unlimited libations. Wine, whiskey, mead. Whatever they fancy. Just pour something in and I become like a bottomless well."

A grin broke across Isaac's face. "An ever-full flagon," he said. This was a find to be stoked about. Even if he didn't find the totem, it made this venture into the cannibal basement completely worthwhile.

"Yes, I'm an ever-full flagon. It's my lot in life." It paused. Isaac assumed it was thinking. "The smile on your face says you're a drinking man. Take me out of this stinking cellar and I'm all yours. Deal?"

Despite the elation from finding a never-ending source of free scotch or bourbon or whiskey, or some taste-test-worthy combination of the three, he knew better than to blindly trust a random spirit. Someone had probably bound it to the vessel as punishment. He'd have to be cautious.

"I'm not committing to any deal, but I'll take you out of here. We can discuss long-term partnerships later."

Isaac thought he heard it sigh, but as it had no shoulders to slump, he couldn't really tell. "Fine," it agreed. "What are you doing here anyway?"

"I'm looking for an artifact. Some kind of totem."

"I figured. It drove the people who live here batshit crazy. Also, the reason I'm locked in here."

"The totem caused this?" He tapped a finger against the pickled toes.

"Yup. Don't get me wrong, this family didn't need much help to go full-on psycho, but that stupid totem pushed them right over the edge. Don't you hear it?"

The whispering static. *Of course.* It made sense now. His ability to use magic provided a measure of resistance to it. He also wore several protective amulets around his neck. Without them, he bet that instead of having a headache, he'd be brainwashed into murderously poor dietary choices. "So, tell me from the beginning what's going down here. Quick version."

"To sum it up, the patriarch of this family found me at the scene of a highway traffic accident and brought me home. I explained how I work. He used me to make domestic beer, so I knew he was stupid right off the bat. Things were going as well as I could hope. I don't aim high because I'm a jug. Then one day, one of his sons comes home with this wooden statue. Not sure how he came to possess it, but I knew right away it was bad news. It spoke to them, but not out loud, with impeccable clarity and astute advice like I do. It whispered. They really couldn't even hear it on a conscious level. But it mumbled constantly, droning on and on, like a goddamn moron, telling them to do the most deplorable things that didn't even involve copious amounts of liquor. I kept telling it to shut the fuck up, but I don't think it understood because it's a stupid cursed wooden totem and not a fully functioning flagon like me.

"Before too long, the whole family started to change. More prone to non-alcohol-related anger, violence, and depression. And less likely to drink, which irritated me to no end. As its influence on them grew, mine waned. I tried warning them that this thing was leading them down a far darker path than me, and one that was a lot less fun. But they didn't listen. After a while, they didn't even hear me. They'd just go out and hunt down people and then eat them while staring vacantly at their broken television, with blood all over themselves, and I'd say, 'Hey, wash that person you just ate down with a few beers,' but they couldn't care less about me. Eventually, they stuck me in here behind the jar o' toes. So disrespectful. Now they're ravenous, but for human flesh and not the cheap beer they put in me."

Isaac held up a hand. That was enough. "Where is it?"

"It's in the next room. That's why you're here?"

"Yeah. I've been sent to collect it."

"Well, I hope wherever it ends up, it's worse than being behind a toe jar. What are you waiting for? Scoop me up and let's go kick its ass."

Isaac hooked a finger through the jug's handle. "So, what should I call you?"

"I have many names. When I roamed the Syrian steppes, I was known as Hundrid the Undying. In Europe during the plague, I went by Crastor of the Black Cloth. But you may call me..." A dramatic pause. "Jughead."

Isaac stifled a laugh. "Really?"

"Yeah, I don't give a shit anymore. Being a jug is humbling. Now, let's go. We got some sissy totem butt to kick."

Chapter 20
THE DIPSHIT IN THE PIT

Guided by flashlight beam, Isaac crossed back through the trash-filled maze and stopped in front of the next door. The stench of death and the insane whispering both strengthened.

"Any idea what's in there? Victims? Traps?"

"Maybe the *remains* of victims, but these people couldn't even spell the word 'trap.' Before we go in there, you sure you don't want a drink? Settle the old nerves? I only have domestic beer churning around my insides, but beggars can't be choosers in cannibal cellars."

Compared to "domestic beer," Isaac wasn't sure if "churning around my insides" was more, less, or equally unappetizing. But oddly, he did feel a pang for a drink—a sudden thirst—like he hadn't had one in a long time. He shook his head, in part to decline the offer and in part to dispel the weird craving.

The door was locked, but a tap of the skeleton key clicked it open, and a nudge pushed it wide. Some kind of low flame flickered the shadows within. Wary of sticking his head in, Isaac lifted Jughead around the doorframe and asked him what he saw.

"The coast is clear, you coward."

"Sorry."

"Eh, no big deal. I'm indestructible."

"Really?"

"Yeah. My jug is unbreakable. Can't even be chipped. No point in being locked in a prison that can be cracked on the floor. Funny story, I once took a tumble off a Grand Canyon ledge. I was with a bunch of hikers and..."

"Hush. Let's get this done." Isaac stepped into the room and panned the light around; "wow" was all he could say.

"Yeah. Not a pretty sight. Although to be fair to that moronic totem, these people were already pigs before it made them into psychotic cannibals. This mess isn't totally its fault."

The family had dug out the basement floor to create a large pit. In the center, a stack of wooden pallets and boxes had been built into a crude pyramid. Lit candles of various melted sizes littered it, and atop the peak sat the totem. Surrounding this makeshift altar lay the remains of many a human being. Isaac couldn't identify a single intact corpse. Just bits and pieces of hacked limbs, bones, flesh, and organs, strewn around the earthen pit—presented as sacrifices or just dropped from greasy cannibal fingers.

The whispering grew strongest here. Isaac couldn't understand it at all. His innate magical ability combined with his amulets destroyed the message, not the voice. Even still, it made him wince.

Jughead let out a vehement hiss. "There it is. Look at this dipshit, perched on his throne like he's lord of the flesh pit. Yeah! I hear you, you son of a bitch!" it shouted. "Isaac, lift me up so I can see him better." The magician complied and held the jug up. "There you are. Now, shut the hell up! Damn, I wish I had arms for punching."

Isaac set Jughead down on the edge of the pit, carefully positioning the flagon so it could see the altar and continue to rain a surprising storm of profanity down on the totem. He approached the altar, carefully stepping around the worst of the offal but still getting gore on his boots. The totem continued its buzzing whispers—in fear or anger, or maybe stupidity as Jughead suggested. He circled the altar, looking for DIY-engineered traps, but found nothing.

"Seeing such horror probably makes you want to have a drink, right? Alcohol is the best cure for fear. It's a soothing balm for the mind," Jughead called to him.

Isaac started to say something to the effect of "that's a terrible idea," but the words caught in his throat because, for some reason, it suddenly didn't seem like such a terrible idea. A part of his brain agreed with the jug and a sudden craving took him, just as it had earlier. The magician suppressed it with a shake of his head, but the fact that he felt the notion at all troubled him. He shushed the jug and focused back on his work.

He found no evidence to make him think that there was anything more to this altar than cannibals stacking garbage and lighting candles. So, like the quick rip of a bandage, he snatched the totem off the altar.

Nothing happened. No activation of a trap. No release of magical energy. No corpses springing back to life. Isaac couldn't help being vaguely disappointed. The totem continued its subconscious chatter, but it remained unaltered, not reacting at all to Isaac's taking hold of it. He realized it had all the intelligence of a television infomercial, mindlessly spouting its message, whether anyone listened or not. About the size of a beer bottle, it had a variety of screaming or laughing faces meticulously carved up and down its sides. He opened the everbag.

A noise came from above—the bang of a door, followed by footsteps.

"The cannibals are home," Jughead whispered.

"Shit. I counted four earlier. Is that all?"

"Yeah. There's Roy Senior, Roy Junior, Billy-boy, and *Momma*." Jughead said the last with reverence, as if it were written in some mystical text that her name not be spoken aloud.

"Why'd you say her name like that?"

"Because if I were an edible human being, I'd be more scared of her than any of them. But I'm an indestructible jug, so I'm good. In fact, one time I got a bunch of gangsters drunk and they pulled their pistols, and I took a bullet right in..." Isaac shushed him again and Jughead begrudgingly finished his story under his breath.

Heavy steps moved back and forth on the floor above them. Loud, deep voices carried. They sounded angry, very angry. And dull, very dull. The house was small, which meant a lack of hiding spots and four sets of angry, dull eyes to avoid.

"Going to be hard to sneak out of here," Isaac said.

"Sneak? Why should you sneak? You should most definitely murder your way out of here. These people certainly deserve it. Cheapass beer drinkers, oh, and they also eat people. I mean, really, could humans actually taste that good? I can't imagine they're worth the trouble when these yokels could just drive to the grocery store for steaks or burgers. Stupid totem..." Jughead paused as the wood above them creaked with cannibals walking. "Whatever you're going to do, you better do it fast. They'll be prepping for dinner soon, if you know what I mean."

Isaac took the jug's words under advisement. A minor telekinetic wave snuffed the altar candles. No sense in the family noticing right away that the totem was gone. With Jughead under his arm, he hurried into the trash room, making sure to shut the sacrificial chamber door behind him. As he crossed the room, he unscrewed both of its light bulbs just enough to ensure they wouldn't turn on. Isaac froze then as footsteps clomped heavily past the basement door. There was no way he wanted to risk climbing the stairs to disable that last bulb. He retreated to the storage room and crouched behind a stack of boxes. He set Jughead down and then opened his everbag to drop the totem in.

Bad idea, he realized. The totem flooded the house with a constant drone. He had sensed it the moment he entered the house. It stood to reason then that the killers above could hear it even now, even if they didn't register it as an actual voice. The everbag interior contained a gate to a miniature dimension of its very own. He couldn't take the chance that the totem's call would be silenced if he dropped it in. That would most certainly alert the family. Instead, he set the totem down next to Jughead.

"Seriously? Get that turd away from me!" the jug hissed.

"Better you sit next to it for a few minutes than spend the next few years back with the toe jar."

"Fine. Fine. Fine."

"You're sure the totem can't tell them I'm down here?"

"I'm sure. Remember it can't speak directly; it just radiates its make-everyone-an-asshole power. Its effects are all psychological. Because it's a morrrooooon and can't talk," Jughead taunted. "That's right, I'm talking to you, bitch."

"Me?" Isaac said.

"No, not you. The totem."

"Ah. Just confusing because you're looking right at me."

"Yeah, that's because I can't turn my head or move my eyes. You're going to have to get used to this. Remember I'm a jug." It paused. "You ready to get drunk yet? It'll make you a better fighter for when the family comes downstairs. Plus, you'll be more pain-resistant if Momma bites you."

As before, Isaac felt an odd nudge towards saying yes, despite Jughead still only having domestic beer and the obvious bad advice of getting drunk for battle with cannibals. "No. Thanks. I don't drink on the job."

Jughead started to protest, just as the basement door opened. Isaac slapped his hand over its mouth and hunkered back into the shadows.

"Just for future reference, that doesn't work," the jug said around Isaac's hand. "I don't really talk through my mouth. I've got the whole disembodied voice thing going on."

"Fine. Whatever. Just quiet down."

Jughead finally acquiesced just as someone started down the steps.

Chapter 21
AT HOME WITH THE CANNIBAL CLAN

The light at the bottom of the basement stairs clicked on, and someone took several steps down but halted when a gravelly female voice called out. "Billy-boy, grab our big Crock-Pot while you're down there. Thinking I'll do some slow cooking with this new meat for tomorrow."

"Right, Ma," Billy-boy yelled back, and he came down the basement stairs. He let out a litany of southern-fried curse words when he flipped light switches to no avail.

The bulb at the base of the stairs created a perfect oasis of light that deepened the darkness in the rest of the trash room. Isaac put his hand into the shadow of the boxes and pulled the darkness to him. It constricted around his fingers, eellike and cold, and encased his entire hand like a living glove.

The cannibal moved slowly into the room, then stopped and snapped his fingers energetically, as if he'd just had an *eureka* moment. He yelled back up the stairs, "Ma! The lights are out. Toss down my night-vision goggles!"

"Seriously?" Isaac whispered to himself. The family didn't own a working washer and dryer, but Billy-boy the cannibal had night-vision goggles. Footsteps came to the top of the stairs. Billy-boy said "thanks" to someone, and then the only working light in the basement clicked off, plunging everything into total darkness. Isaac assumed that the man had his night vision equipped.

Through recent practice and study, Isaac had found that the shadow magic was particularly dependent on environmental conditions. Too much light washed the spells out, weakened them, or dissolved them outright. Too little light and the spells couldn't conjure at all. Pulling shadows from total darkness was like trying to take water from a lake with a fist. The level of illumination had to be perfect.

And now it was too damn dark. He had to be able to see to wield it. The skin of shadow on his hand tightened. He'd grown more resistant to it over the weeks and could tolerate its presence longer before it started to hurt, but he couldn't withstand it indefinitely.

Somewhere in the dark room, Billy-boy said, "Sooo green," and started giggling. Jostling noises came as Billy-boy rummaged through all the rubbish. Following this were footsteps going back towards the stairs, then his voice calling, "Hey, Ma! Where's the Crock-Pot?"

Momma called back, "Check in the storage room."

Jughead whispered to Isaac, "Oh, shit. She's right. It is in there. I used to flirt with it. It's got curves."

Although he couldn't see it, Isaac knew the storage room door was to his left, with nothing to block the line of sight to his current hiding spot. He was going to feel awfully stupid when Billy-boy plainly saw him crouched there in that green night-vision light. He had no seconds to waste as he heard Billy-boy's footsteps coming his way.

From the everbag he produced a clear glass marble and proceeded to rub it vigorously between the thumb and forefinger of his non-shadowed hand. Then he whispered, "Lite and fly." The marble began to glow and flew away, its path carrying it to the storage door, where it floated in place. The luminescence wasn't enough to brighten the whole basement or even overload the sensitive green field of night vision. It hung there like a single Christmas light in the dark.

"What the hell?" Billy-boy said aloud.

Next from his bag of tricks, Isaac pulled a length of rope fashioned with a noose on the end. His own variation on Brit Knit's slithering scarf spell, this nasty creation was indeed foul magic. It needed no spoken instructions, only Isaac concentrating to set it to task. It levitated up, like an angry cobra, and slid sidewinder-style across the ceiling.

Billy-boy passed the last row of boxes, and the marble cast just enough glow for Isaac to make out his silhouette. If Billy had turned to the left, he'd have seen Isaac crouched there plain as day. Instead, he stared in open-mouthed wonderment at the marble. He pulled off the goggles to see it in real sight. "That is one big lightning bug," he said.

Isaac sent the rope in. It dropped down, slipped around Billy-boy's neck, and hauled him up. The loop tightened as it suspended him in midair as efficiently as dangling from the gallows. While it clearly worked as intended, Isaac frowned. The spell didn't have that quick-strike neck-break capability that dropping through a hatch would have. Instead, Billy-boy just swung around, slowly being strangled to death, legs dancing in the air. It was a fairly ugly way to go, and Isaac would have almost felt guilty if the man weren't a murderous cannibal. Billy-boy couldn't scream out, but his kicking legs knocked over a stack of boxes that toppled with a loud thump.

"Billy?" the gravelly voice of Momma called down the steps. "What was that noise? Did you get the Crock-Pot? While you're down there, get a hock from the pit. This new meat won't be ready for a while." Then silence. Billy-boy's kicks started to slow, and his hands fell away from the noose. "Billy? Whatcha doing? You down there? Damn it, boy, you better not be naked in the pit again!"

"I just threw up in my mouth and I don't even have an esophagus," Jughead lamented. Isaac agreed and suddenly felt very okay with murdering the now motionless man hanging in the air.

"Fine. I'm coming down there and I'm gonna tan your hide. I gotta do everything myself around here." The stairwell light clicked back on, and Isaac sighed with relief that he had his shadows again.

The hanging man's movements ceased except for the occasional death twitch. Isaac moved past him, snatched the marble out of the air, headed into the storage room, grabbed the Crock-Pot, and carried it to the center of the room. He found the tallest stack of junk and set it on top before hurrying back to his hiding spot.

At the top of the stairs, two large, dirty slippers stepped into view. Going up from the footwear were two cankles, ascending to beefier legs. The hem of the flower-print muumuu fluttered into view. She took one step, then another. Either unable or not caring enough to hurry, she thumped down the steps one at a time, wood creaking beneath her.

Isaac's first impression of Momma pegged her as old and out of shape. He couldn't fathom why Jughead held her in such dangerous regard. Still, better to play it safe and take her out of the equation quickly. As she took her next step, Isaac telekinetically snagged her heel and pulled it forwards. She missed the next step, did as much of a leg split as someone of her size could, and toppled down the stairs, bellowing like a bull the whole way.

"Ooh, what was that?" Jughead asked, and Isaac picked him up and held him to see Momma lying on the floor. "You knocked her down the stairs? Really? Oh, that's not going to cut it."

Before Isaac could argue his apparent success, the woman moved. She groaned, got to her hands and knees, and then used the banister to haul herself back to standing. With an adjustment of her glasses, she peered into the darkened rear of the basement. "And now I fell down the damn stairs," she growled. "Billy-boy, wherever you're hiding, I'm gonna find you. You're gonna have to carry that Crock-Pot up the stairs with two broken hands."

A threat of such violence against her own kin made Isaac wonder what she'd do to an actual interloper. Next to him, Jughead whispered, "Oh, shit, we're screwed. I mean, you're screwed. I don't have a body for them to eat."

The stairwell light cast enough of a glow into the room that Momma's eyes adjusted quickly. She saw the Crock-Pot teetering on the junk tower. As she reached for it, Isaac telekinetically lifted the appliance and hurled it as hard as he could into her face. The distance and the size of the pot made it a headache-inducing strain, but the irony of blasting a cannibal with her own cookware proved irresistible. The blow dropped her like a rock, and she hit the floor hard, one slipper flying off. He had assumed, with her obesity and advanced age, that the blow would have rendered her incapacitated or even dead.

Instead, Momma immediately sat up, unfazed, blood streaming from her nose. She narrowed her eyes into the darkness. "So, someone down here thinks it's fun to throw Crock-Pots at people, eh?" She clambered to her feet, kicking off the other slipper as if it would vastly improve her dexterity.

The magician debated just aiming Wilma and blasting this woman to death. However, the noise would certainly draw the rest of her kin, and he'd prefer to get out of the basement and catch them unawares if he had to take them on.

"You may as well come on out, whoever you are," Momma said to the shadows. She picked up a slipper and slapped it threateningly into her palm. Isaac stifled a laugh. At least he thought he did. Momma might have heard him, or maybe she realized her slipper threat wasn't the least bit intimidating. She dropped it, rummaged through a box under the stairs, and then turned back to face the dark room with an old clothes iron in her fist. "Don't say I didn't warn you," she said. She looped the electrical cord around her forearm and then made a few surprisingly impressive practice punches in the air.

Isaac started to understand why Jughead had whispered her name with such fear. Momma advanced again on the storage room. He concentrated and lifted the Crock-Pot once more, intent on dropping it on the woman's head. Momma simply knocked her traitorous cookware out of the air with an iron-fisted haymaker. The magician was wearily impressed with her ferocity and disturbed that she hadn't seemed at all startled by her Crock-Pot floating. She may as well have been swatting a large bug. The totem had twisted her tether to reality.

Momma moved slowly through the basement debris, the iron held out as both sword and shield. Eventually, she found Billy's body. "Billy-boy? There you are. Just hanging around like the lazy ass you are." Her magically swinging dead son didn't shake her in the least. "Not only did you not get my pot, you somehow got killed while trying. Jesus Herbert Christ. That's fine. I always told you that if you ever got yourself killed that I was gonna do a barbeque with you. Ribs with spicy sauce. Maybe I never told you that out loud, but I know I wrote it down somewhere."

Isaac released the rope spell and Billy-boy's body collapsed onto Momma, who ended up on the floor under the corpse. With Jughead in one hand, Wilma in the other, and the totem barely fitting in his pocket, Isaac sprinted by her, dodging through the hoarded junk to the stairs. "Roy! Roy Junior! Get down to the basement! We got a trespasser!" Momma screamed.

He made it to the top step when the man who must be Roy Junior appeared in the doorway. Following a brief moment of mutual surprise, Isaac attempted to bring Wilma to bear one-handed. The cannibal enacted a faster and simpler plan by pushing him backwards. The shotgun discharged into the ceiling as he toppled, the boom reverberating. Heels over head, he tumbled until he landed roughly on the basement floor. Jughead unleashed a string of profanities as it flew from his grasp.

"Pa! Pa!" Junior shouted as he came down the stairs. From his belt, he pulled a hand ax still wet from some violent usage.

With all limbs aching but none broken, Isaac dragged himself to his feet, fumbling along the floor for his weapon. His groping hand found Jughead first and, more by instinct than design, Isaac brought it up to deflect Junior's first swing of the ax. The jug hadn't been exaggerating when it claimed to be indestructible, because it survived with nary a scratch, but it started swearing as if fatally insulted.

Junior came with rage and Isaac could only retreat, blocking several more hatchet swings with Jughead. The savage attack drove the magician back across the basement through the hoarded junk. Finally, a jug counterattack managed to catch Junior's fingers and jar the hatchet from his hand.

Isaac had little time to take advantage as the man grappled him, threw several painful punches into his torso, and knocked Jughead out of his grasp. A diet consisting of humans must do a body good, because Junior was as strong as an ox, despite his wiry frame. Isaac quickly deemed it a losing strategy to trade punches with him. Instead, with his shadow-wrapped hand, he went for the throat. But a last-second twist from Junior resulted in Isaac missing and grabbing the man by the lower face instead. Junior slipped free of his grip, but not before the shadow magic left a painted-on replica of Isaac's hand across his chin and cheeks.

Junior immediately felt the wrongness of it. He pushed Isaac into a stack of boxes, sending the magician tumbling to the floor. The cannibal put both hands to his face, wiping at the damp, icy sensation stuck to his skin, but he may as well have been rubbing dried paint.

Then the shadow hand started to squeeze. Junior began clawing at his jaw, swatting with desperation at the unseen force. He fell to his knees, screaming in pain. His howls were muffled down into a sick gurgling noise as his jaw compressed. His jawbone broke with a deafening crack, and several shattered molars shot from his mouth. Junior somehow stayed conscious, weakly pawing at his face as the shadow hand continued, its merciless viselike crushing, grinding his mandible into pieces. Blood speckled with bits of teeth leaked from his lips. Finally, he collapsed, whimpering in the incapacitating pain.

"Wow," Isaac muttered. "I only meant to strangle you to death. That looked a lot more painful than I intended."

With Momma still ungracefully pulling herself free from Billy's dead weight, Isaac scooped up Jughead and tried again to run for it. This time he found his path hindered by the cannibal patriarch, who stomped down the basement stairs, shotgun in hand. With only one route left, Isaac ran back to the altar room and slammed the door behind him. An instant later Roy Senior put two shells into it, leaving fist-sized holes in the cheap wood and spraying Isaac with painful wooden shards.

"So, let me sum up our first adventure together," Jughead whispered. "I've been hit in the face with an ax about fifteen times and now we're trapped in the flesh pit."

"At least you're off the toe shelf."

An eerie silence, minus the constant buzz of the totem in his jacket pocket, filled the basement. Isaac chanced a look through the damaged door. Momma and Roy Senior were moving calmly through the mess, seemingly in no great hurry to chase him. They knew there was no other way out of the basement.

Isaac had cornered himself.

Chapter 22
MOMMA UNLEASHED

"**W**hat the hell's going on?" Roy Senior asked his wife.

"Burglary," Momma hissed as if the crime carried less respect than murder and cannibalism. "That fella is trying to steal our divine wooden prophet."

Jughead started sputtering despite Isaac's attempt to shush him. "Divine? Prophet? Oh, for fuck's sake. He's a babbling imbecile. They think he's a god? I've suffered some grave indignities in my life, becoming a jug being near the top, but this is just ridiculous." Isaac ignored him and continued watching the couple through the shotgunned holes in the door. They stood over Junior, who was still semiconscious and moaning.

"What's his problem?" Roy asked.

"Crushed face. He had some kind of black hand of death on his jaw, and it disappeared when the light shined on it. Of course, he was just carrying on and on about it like a giant goddamn baby. At least your other son had the decency to go quietly."

"Huh?"

"Oh yeah. Billy is lying over there all choked to death. Hung himself, I guess."

"No kidding." Roy didn't even bother to look.

Momma bent to her son, roughly shoved his hands away, and surveyed the damage. "Well, damn it. You better just go ahead and die because if you think I'm gonna be making meat milkshakes for you from now on, you got another thing coming. We don't even own a blender."

Roy stood next to her. "One rule around here—we all gotta pull our own weight. There ain't nothing wrong with having fewer mouths to feed. It'll make things easier on the rest of us."

"Yes, you're certainly right about that, Roy."

Isaac couldn't make her expression out in the bad light, but he could tell by the tone of her voice that she'd just had a murderous epiphany. The clothes iron swung, connected tip-first with Roy's temple, and dropped him inert with a single blow. Like any good cannibal, she continued to wail on her victim, either to ensure death or to tenderize for a future recipe. In either case, Isaac could still hear the crushing blows when he turned away from the door.

"What just happened?" Jughead asked.

"Momma got a Kentucky divorce."

A snap of his fingers brought one of the altar candles back to flickering life. The flame then arced to an adjacent candle, and then the next, hopping from wick to wick like a flaming sprite, until the altar was completely aglow. The combined glows proved enough to dissipate his shadow hand when held close, and he sighed with relief as the pressure subsided.

He surveyed the room—nothing but bodies and stench. As if reading his mind, Jughead said, "So what's the plan for when she busts in here and beats the shit out of you?" On cue, Momma began hammering on the door.

"Here you go, here's your chance to be a deity for a minute." Isaac set Jughead on the altar spot previously occupied by its nemesis.

"Behold! Your fearsome god! Kneel before me and become acquainted with alcoholic despair!" Jughead proclaimed in a surprisingly booming voice. While the jug playfully lorded over the pit, Isaac pulled a small knife from his everbag and, with gritted teeth, cut into the back of his left hand just enough to get a free flow of blood. "Suicide, eh?" Jughead said. "A bold, if counterproductive, plan."

Isaac let it run to his fingers and drip from the tips before he started flicking his hand, sending droplets into the pit. Satisfied with the spread, he then drew a bloody pattern on the back of his right hand. Concentric circles, with the last layer growing arrow-like tentacles that traveled up each digit. A long slow breath on it, as if he were drying freshly painted nails, came next. Finally, he held the marked hand out over the carnage, closed his eyes, and focused his will. The foul magic immediately made his stomach retch with nausea.

It started with a twitch. The larger, more complete pieces exhibited it first. A leg, severed at the knee, moved its toes. An upper arm, chopped at the shoulder, started bending at the elbow. The smaller bits, hunks of meat, skin, and scattered internal organs moved like slugs, undulating across the floor and leaving trails of decayed ooze. All the human remains crawled in whatever way they could towards the center of the pit.

The door shuddered under repeated blows from Momma. Isaac felt sure it'd burst open any moment, but either the wood was sturdier than he gave it credit for or Momma had burned her cardio limit pulverizing her husband.

The offal pulled itself into a pile, flesh adhering to flesh, splintered bones knotting together with tendons and skin. By the time Momma pounded through the door, the remains of her victims had assembled into a thing resembling a skinned pig with no head. It dragged its bulbous body to the edge of the pit with makeshift limbs. Momma stomped into the room, bloody iron in hand, and stood before it as it reared up.

A carrion abomination.

He'd learned the spell years ago but had never had the cause nor the means to cast it. Ending up in a room with a large pile of human offal tended to be a singular experience. It had been too good to pass up. But while the putrescent creation impressed Isaac, it wasn't having the desired effect on his opponent. The abomination existed solely to horrify its victims beyond the limits of a normal human psyche, to snap their hold on reality. It was a nightmare made into a semisolid-gelatinous undead monstrosity.

This may have been a miscalculation, as Momma couldn't seem to care less. She sized the abomination up as if selecting cuts at the butcher. It was disgusting and scary, but beyond that, it really didn't have much going for it. It moved slowly. It couldn't see, as it had no eyes. It had no mouths to bite or fully functioning hands to grab and claw with. So, for the next minute and a half, Isaac watched with a stunned fascination as Momma beat the unliving shit out of his creation.

The bloody clothes iron crashed down repeatedly. She kicked and punched and stomped. The abomination didn't even have a skull, but Momma managed to find a way to utilize a headlock. At one point she even bit the thing and chewed down a mouthful. In short order, she reduced the magical monster to quivering, flattened pieces strewn about the room. Momma stood victorious in puddles of gore, her iron raised like Thor's hammer.

"Holy shit," Isaac said.

"Yeah," Jughead said. "Looks like I may have hitched my horse to the wrong chariot in this battle."

In between labored huffing and puffing, Momma said, "You think you can beat me with my leftovers? I don't think so. Now, put... it... back."

It took a moment for him to realize she spoke of the totem. In the heat of battle, he'd forgotten it. With his attention drawn returned to it, the whispering static flooded back into his ears. It really was annoying. No wonder it drove these people mad. Well, even if he got ironed to death, at least he could spare the poor woman a future of the maddening noise. With that, he dropped it into his everbag.

The whispering ceased, which made perfect sense. The everbag was a pocket between worlds. For all intents and purposes, he just dropped the damnable artifact off the edge of the Earth.

Momma stopped dead in her tracks. She cocked her head to and fro, like an animal disturbed by sound, or in this case, the lack thereof. She searched every corner of the room, and the air itself, as if she had previously been able to see the totem's mad ramblings floating about. When she finally accepted that the whispering had faded, her gaze drifted to the carnage, the pieces in the pit, and then to the doorway, where beyond lay the bodies of her kin. Confusion crossed her face. She panted and swallowed hard several times.

Jughead said aloud exactly what Isaac had been thinking. "Really? That's all it took? Dropping that stupid thing into your bag was enough to knock her back to her normal life? Wow. Of course, it's going to be a solitary life, since all of her family have been savagely killed. Oh, and she's definitely going to jail for the rest of her days. But hey, she's not crazy anymore. Think she wants a drink?"

A pang of guilt shot through Isaac as he imagined this wretched woman coming to her senses and realizing what she'd done, whom she'd killed, and what she'd eaten. Then, amidst her total psychological breakdown, she'd collapse (or slowly sink down, depending on what her knees could handle) amid the human remains and, with her head in her hands, weep for her unforgivable sins. How horrible would that be and how could she live with it? He realized he'd have been better off leaving the totem exposed and letting her stay crazy.

And so he breathed a sigh of relief when Momma's eyes lit back up with rage and she regained her insanity, pushed too far by the totem to need its urging anymore. She let out a battle cry that would have curdled the blood of a Viking and pointed her iron at him.

A shuffling sound distracted them. Junior staggered into the room. The lower half of his face hung slack, like a blood-soaked towel. In his hands was Wilma. His attempts at speaking came out like B-movie zombie moans.

"Junior, shoot this trespassing thief," Momma ordered.

For a moment Junior hesitated. The shotgun came up but aimed at the empty space between Isaac and Momma. The barrel waved back and forth with undecided hands. Isaac hoped that Junior might opt for matricide due to that meat-milkshake crack earlier. Jughead echoed this thought by whispering, "Ooooh, the kid is going to shoot that bitch." But familial ties won over and Junior finally swiveled the shotgun at Isaac, to which Jughead said, "Well, damn."

"Shoot him in the head, Junior. I hate pulling all the pellets out of the chest meat," Momma ordered.

Junior clearly remained in a state of reduced consciousness from his injury. His eyes were unfocused, and the shotgun dangled so loosely in his grip that he couldn't raise it to his shoulder. However, strategically this brought no advantage to Isaac. Buckshot at this range made aim almost irrelevant.

With much effort, Junior finally got the shotgun pointed at him, but just before he pulled the trigger, Isaac used his telekinesis to nudge the weapon to the left. The barrel discharged into Momma's back, blasting her off her feet and into the carnal pit.

"Ha! Take that, you bitch!" yelled Jughead.

A slow moan escaped Junior's disfigured mouth. The shotgun fell from his hands, and he sank to his knees. He swayed back and forth, tilting his head this way and that, searching for something Isaac couldn't see. Hallucinations, maybe? Ghosts? Or maybe Junior just now realized he couldn't hear the totem calling to him. The whispering madness had fallen silent. He reached for the knife on his belt but missed it with fumbling fingers several times before snatching it up.

"Look at that. He wants to have a knife fight. Isaac, you should have a few drinks from me before you accept this honorable challenge. The liquid in your belly will keep your innards moist in case of substantial blood loss via stabbings," Jughead suggested.

"Huh?" Isaac said. He most certainly had no intention of dueling Junior in any way, but once again he felt the sudden urge to accept Jughead's offer. Just a few gulps to take the edge off, his mind told him. Isaac liked his booze to be sure, but here, amidst the carnage with a knife-wielding cannibal still alive? Under no circumstances would he even consider it.

Junior tried to talk. A curse, a challenge, a dying declaration? Isaac had no idea and didn't really care. In the end, the point proved moot, as the man had nothing left. His eyes drifted shut and he slumped face down on the floor. A pool of crimson spread quickly around his head. Isaac wasn't sure if he had died, and didn't bother checking. Death or being a cannibal with no jaw—both seemed fitting punishments.

"That was anticlimactic. A good old-fashioned pigsticking match would have been better. But *c'est la vie,* at least it's over. A drink to celebrate?" Jughead asked happily.

Chapter 23
THE JUG PLAN

The air outside the cannibal shanty chilled him refreshingly after all the time spent with rotting corpses in a stuffy basement. The sunlight made Isaac blink as he opened the rear doors of the cannibal family van. He'd heard Momma say something about "the new meat" and here it lay—a body under a tarp. He pushed back the plastic just enough to find a wrist with no pulse.

"That's a shame," said Jughead from under his arm. "Poor thing probably died completely sober. What a tragedy. You should have a drink in his or her honor. Maybe even a few, considering he or she or they, or whatever, was so, so innocent."

Isaac had known it was coming. Not just the verbal encouragement to drink, but the weird, mental shove he suddenly felt to comply. "So that's your game," he said to the jug.

"Hmm? What's that? Did you say you wanted a shot?"

"You create and feed addiction and then make life-threatening suggestions. That's the only reason you were so pissed at the totem. It overrode your scheme to make the family into self-destructive alcoholics. It had a stronger ability to dominate minds. So, you ended up getting pushed aside." For the first time since they met, Jughead didn't respond. When it fell silent, it became easy to forget the flagon was cognizant and not just pottery. "You may as well fess up, because this subtle psychic power you wield isn't going to work on me."

"Fine. Fine. Yes. That's my game. Don't pat yourself on the back too much for figuring it out. It's not like I'm quiet about it. Yes, I take people of low will and dull demeanor and make them dependent on my fine libations. Then eventually, through no real fault of my own, they overdo it and die from various drunken tomfoolery. For example, one time I convinced a bunch of drunken skateboarders to try surfing. In Lake Erie. In December. In the nude. But I was starting to catch on to the fact that you may be resistant to my tricks. You like to drink, but I can't seem to magnify your desire for it."

"No, you can't. It took me a little while to figure out your angle, but that's only because the cannibals distracted me."

"I assumed as much. Well, sadly it appears that our relationship really can't progress past this point. Your being immune to my domination power kind of negates the very point of my existence. You get what you want, which is free liquor. I don't get what I want, which is to see you go rocketing through a windshield at high speed after convincing you that seatbelts are a violation of your constitutional rights. This partnership really isn't equitable. Sooooo, this is kind of like an awkward breakup, I know, but you can just leave me here. Eventually some new suckers, I mean companions, will come along and find me. Maybe the police. They're usually big drinkers."

"And then you'll eventually kill them."

"I don't kill anyone. I'm a bodiless head. I can't even blink. But yes, they usually end up dead. Or maimed. Or in jail. But they'll be happy drunken clams until then."

Isaac shook his head. "No, leaving you here would be as wasteful as it would be irresponsible. I think you need to go with me."

"What? Why? If I can't influence you to skip, cartwheel, or moonwalk down the alcoholic road to ruin, then what's the point?" Jughead asked. Then Isaac's plan pierced the jug's narcissism. "Wait a minute. Oh, I get it. You're going to abuse your immunity to my power and just use me for free booze. That kind of arrangement could go on indefinitely. No, no, no. You dirty son of a bitch. You leave me here. It's not fair. I may not be able to make you dead, but I can make you miserable. I can be an around-the-clock asshole. I don't even sleep. I'll talk shit twenty-four-seven. I'll ruin every sip you ever take with my horrible personality."

"I've drunk with worse company. Besides, I'm just going to put you in my everbag. I won't hear you say a thing. You can scream your jug out in there. I'll pull you out every so often, fill up my flask or a few glasses, and then drop you back in until I need you again."

"You... how... is there no bottom to the diabolical depths you'd sink to? You'll just leave me floating in some etheric pocket with the rest of your junk? That's just a terrible thing to do to someone. In fact, it may be the worst punishment I've ever been threatened with, aside from having my soul put in a jug. I mean, hard to compete with that one. But this easily makes you at least the second-biggest asshole I've ever met." The disembodied voice lowered to almost a growl. "And I specialize in hanging out with assholes."

Disregarding the odd insult, Isaac picked him up, pulled the cork with a pop, and proceeded to pour in the last bit of bourbon from his flask. It wasn't the highest-end stuff, but he could rectify that later. For now, he just wanted to get rid of the domestic beer.

"Ooooh, much better," Jughead cooed, in a disturbingly sexual tone. "That's like a colonic cleansing."

Ignoring that, Isaac swished the jug around and then refilled his flask. Bourbon poured out, and it flowed until his flask was overfilled. Jughead was truly bottomless. He screwed the cap on and put the flask away. He certainly wasn't drinking any until he could verify its safety.

"Look, Jug, you're going in the bag, but I'm willing to work with you on positive reinforcement. If you behave, I'll let you out more often and for longer periods. You act up, I'll leave you in there."

Silence for a minute as it considered the offer, then, "Fuck you! You think you can break me? Bring it on. I just spent six months in a Kentucky cannibal cellar, staring at a pile of pickled toes, and getting the cold shoulder from a goddamn Crock-Pot. I've been trapped in this jug for centuries for crimes that I probably committed. I can float around in your purse for decades, no problem. We'll see who wins this battle of wills." Isaac opened the bag. "Wait, isn't the totem in there? I'll be in there with that turd? Does the bag have little subdivisions? Will I have my own pocket? Or am I going to be roommates with a madness-causing totem? Wait. Let's talk. We can come to some kind of…" Isaac stuffed Jughead in and watched it magically seep into the lining of the satchel. Then the bag was empty again. And even better, it was quiet.

Isaac sat on the bumper of the van. The sun shone in the blue sky. Birds chirped in the trees. Conversely, the house before him held a basement of horrors. The van he sat on contained a dead person. An artifact that would drive people to madness floated in his bag.

Moments like these rankled him—the incongruousness of the foul existing within the serene. The world just ticked on, beautifully uncaring, shining its warmth on all the miscreants like him as well as the innocents.

He tucked the victim's hand back under the tarp and shut the van doors to keep the wildlife out. He debated doing a sweep of the property and collecting more odds and ends that might prove valuable as spell components, but ultimately chose to skip it. The meager value of anything he could hope to find wasn't worth subjecting himself to that shithole again.

He headed towards his makeshift campsite and trudged halfway across the yard before he saw the dogs. The pair appeared at the tree line, made their way through a gap in the barbwire, and plodded languidly towards him. First instinct had him open his satchel, ready to pull Wilma to defend himself. But as the dogs drew nearer, he noted a lack of enthusiasm from them, considering they were violent man-eaters, and he stood in the open like free lunch. No growling. No snarling. They never even acknowledged his presence. As they passed him, with lolled, panting tongues, he saw multiple, deep scratches on their muzzles and ears. Whatever trouble Testiculies had led them into, they had clearly had enough of it.

The cat lay next to the fading heat of Isaac's briquette fire when he got back. Looking none the worse for wear, he regarded Isaac with his one silver eye and standard annoyance. Isaac felt a measure of gratitude and reached to scratch Testiculies between the ears. The cat responded just as he should have expected—an energetic hiss and a swift paw to his outstretched hand. He sighed with disappointment before realizing no blood flowed from any of his fingers. "You hit me with retracted claws. That's a start. We'll be best buddies any day now. I'm making great, new friends all the time now, it seems."

He had parked Maloc's truck several miles away on a backcountry road. "You coming?" he asked the cat, who replied with another low hiss.

He shrugged and started walking.
The cat would catch up. He always did.

Chapter 24
THE SLOW AND THE CURIOUS

"So, it drove the whole family crazy?" Lefse asked as he furiously scribbled down details. Taking notes remained the only thing Isaac knew the man could do with speed.

"That it did."

"And made them into violent cannibals?"

"Yes."

"Did they mention if we taste like chicken?"

Isaac chuckled. "I think the matriarch had a recipe book, but I didn't have a chance to grab it."

"Shame. I'd have loved to read that. I bet that we taste more like pork, although I base that on absolutely no research at all. I'd imagine we'd need a lot of seasoning too. Possibly a marinade as well, for simmering. Their using a Crock-Pot was probably a good choice. Taste-wise, I mean." Lefse set another ornate wooden box on his desk. Much like the one used previously for the Black Tarot card, it had been perfectly molded for the totem that Isaac pulled from his everbag. Lefse made a face like he'd been poked with a needle when the static-fueled whispering reached his ears. "Damn. I can see how this could drive you mad if you were dumb enough to hang around with it. Put it away."

After laying it inside like it was a body in a tiny coffin, Isaac sealed it in the box and the whispering vanished, blocked by the runes etched in the wood. "Just go ahead and wire my pay to the usual accounts." Thinking they were finished, he started to stand but paused when Lefse pushed the box to him. "Huh?"

"You can deliver this one yourself."

"To the basement?" Isaac's curiosity bristled.

"No. Upstairs. To the Head Librarian. His name is Mabahazi."

"Maba-what?"

"Mabahazi. It's obviously not his real name. You magicians and your silly fake names." Lefse made an unimpressed *pfffft* sound.

Isaac faked offense. "You're the one who gave me the last name Unknown."

"Yeah, well, it certainly has a better ring than Isaac Smith," Lefse conceded.

"Maba-Fake-Name a magician, then?"

"He is, although I've never actually seen him do any hocus-pocus. His ability to pick out fancy suits is strong, and his condescension talent is off the charts, but other than that, I have no idea what he's capable of. So, I couldn't tell you if he had the power to wipe out a house full of crazy cannibals." He scooted his chair back. "I'll walk you up."

"Before that, I wondered if I could ask a favor of you?"

Lefse paused mid-rise and then flopped enthusiastically back into his chair, eyes wide with delight. "What's that you said? Pray tell, is the independent and mysterious nomadic magician with no last name asking for help from one of the few people who get paid to help him?" He leaned across the desk to facilitate his secretive whisper. "Is it dangerous?"

"Seriously? Dangerous? I don't recall you being Captain Bravery when the Iron Ambassador came looking for me."

Lefse sat back with a huff. "That's too damn dangerous."

"That's what I thought. All I need you to do is make a call and check on someone."

"Is it a dangerous phone call?" he asked with a snicker.

Isaac resisted the urge to telekinetically swipe things from the desk. "Just grab a pen and write this down. Her name is Susan..."

"Last name?" Lefse cut him off.

"Unknown."

"You got hitched?"

Isaac should have seen that quip coming. "Ha. No. I don't know her last name."

"Good. Now you know my torment. What's her number?"

"I don't have it."

Lefse chewed his pen cap. "I'm a good researcher, but Susan is a common name in almost every state in the Union. You know where she works?"

"I do." Isaac paused there, not wanting to say the infantile business aloud to the man, but not having any choice. With a sigh, he said, "Boobzookas."

Lefse cocked his head as if having trouble hearing. "What's that?"

"Boobzookas. It's a strip club in that town where I was sent to hunt the vampire elder."

"Right. One more time. It sounded like you said..."

Isaac sighed. "Boobzookas." He glanced at the clock on the wall and began to count ticks of the second hand. Lefse laughed for thirty-seven seconds straight—longer than Isaac anticipated.

When he finished and caught his breath, Lefse said, "Okay. I'll call Boobzookas and ask to speak to a stripper named Susan."

"Not a stripper. Waitress."

"Right. *Excusez-moi,*" he replied with a snort. "What do you want me to talk to your fair maiden about?"

"Nothing. You could hang up after she says hello."

"Well, that'd be impolite."

Isaac rubbed his temples. "I didn't think you'd make me work this hard for a favor."

"You thought wrong. What if I can't get ahold of her? Can I talk to someone else there? Honestly, I'd be interested in talking to just about anyone who answers the phone at a place called Boobzookas."

"I bet you would. You can start an entire file on the place if you want." Isaac stood up and tucked the artifact case under his arm. "Will you do it?"

"Sure." Lefse's face softened in a rare departure from his usual mirth. "Mind if I ask why you just don't make this call yourself?"

Isaac paused in the doorway. "It's no secret that I've been a bringer of bad luck to a lot of people lately. I'm hoping I spared her that fate, but reaching out to her directly may just bring her back into my karmic orbit."

"Your checking on her safety may be what makes her unsafe," Lefse simplified. "I get it. I'll be subtle."

Isaac doubted the giant man understood fully how to be subtle but could only leave that to chance.

* * *

Within seconds of meeting him, Isaac knew he wasn't going to mesh well with the Head Librarian. Mabahazi had the smarm of a car salesman who had faked a magician's resume. The suit he wore was just stylish enough to show that he didn't get his hands dirty. Magicians shouldn't have the time or ego for such indulgences.

"Isaac Unknown," the man said. His voice dripped with syrupiness as if they were longtime friends. "It is a pleasure to finally meet you. Your reports from Lefse are always must-reads."

"He takes good notes."

"That he does. He's one of our best researchers. And you have been one of our busiest field agents."

Isaac mumbled a half-hearted thank-you as he digested the title of "field agent" and found that he didn't like the taste. It made him sound like a real employee, whereas he considered himself more of a freewheeling contractor. He set the totem box on Mabahazi's desk.

"Ah, the latest relic. Is it true that it drove the whole family mad?"

Isaac found this question disappointingly redundant, but he played along to satisfy the man's morbid curiosity. "Prolonged exposure to it seems to cause violent madness. I don't know if it unlocks subconscious evil desires or totally creates them. From what I gathered, this family wasn't a bunch of winners before they somehow ended up with the totem, but they weren't eating people either."

"How did it do it?"

"It speaks, sort of, with a nonstop, migraine-inducing whispering."

Mabahazi's eyes lit up. "That's fascinating. Did you hear it?"

"I did, but it was just garbled nonsense to me. I got the notion that it's more effective on the weak-minded, and even more over a prolonged period."

"How would such a powerful artifact end up with such an insignificant group of people?" Mabahazi's voice mixed equal parts condescension and jealousy.

Isaac had no answer for this. He resisted the temptation to needle the man further by informing him that the cannibals had not one, but *two* relics in their possession. No one appeared to know about Jughead, and the magician preferred keeping it that way. Once he ascertained that the liquid that poured from the possessed jug was untainted, he had no desire to part with the little bastard.

"It's a shame that all the cannibals were killed. It would have been of great interest to speak to one—to hear firsthand about what madness they were experiencing. But then, you do have an uncanny knack for leaving nothing behind but corpses."

Isaac's eyes narrowed just a hair. "Well, it's not like I can carry them with me. They don't fit in my bag."

"How glib," Mabahazi replied. "Seeing as how the Voice has been choosing you for so many heavyweight assignments, I decided to get better acquainted with you."

"Oh, good." Isaac tried not to lace the words with irritation and wasn't sure if he had succeeded. It didn't matter, as Mabahazi paid little attention.

"A few months ago, you completed an assignment that brought us a Black Tarot card. That's easily one of the most powerful artifacts I've seen during my tenure. That encounter with the demon..." He started snapping his fingers to jog his memory.

"Maloc."

"Yes. Maloc. That must have been horrifying. The way he slaughtered all the patrons of that bar without you being able to save a single one must have been difficult to deal with."

Isaac didn't appreciate the way the man framed the statement with failure, but the accuracy proved enough to deter a retort. "I coped."

"Following the tarot card, you've collected the skull of an elder vampire, a messenger fly sought after by Hell itself, and a madness-inducing totem. No agent in history has had such a run. Never has the Voice depended so much on an individual."

Isaac sensed this was no compliment. He waited for the other shoe to drop.

"Why you?" Mabahazi asked. "I have over a dozen agents, each better-suited to every single one of these assignments. If the choice had been mine, you would have been the last resort for each. Here. This guy"—he picked up a file from his desk, waved it around, and slapped it back down—"is a shape-shifting savage. A bloodthirsty animal. He'd have torn through a bunch of cannibals in seconds. Why take a greater risk of failure by sending you?"

Isaac reached over and tapped the file. "Maybe he's an asshole."

"That's beside the point. I've been here long enough to study how Arrangement operates. Clearly, the Voice seems to prefer you." He cleared his throat. "That bodes badly for you."

"I figured as much."

Mabahazi rested his elbows on the chair's arms and tented his fingers. "If all that isn't enough to scare you, the Iron Ambassador herself seems to have taken an interest in you. After you threw her favorite servant off a roof, she requested a meeting with you. As a professional courtesy, I allowed this."

Isaac didn't think that the scenario he referenced happened like that at all. What was it the Ambassador had called him? A worm? Something along those lines. "She was a lot nicer than I anticipated."

This compliment didn't sit well with Mabahazi, and he failed to hide his scowl. "That woman is as powerful as she is dark-hearted. I can guarantee she doesn't have anything but ill intentions for you."

Isaac drummed his fingers impatiently on his leg. "This is a terrible employee pep talk."

"I didn't ask you here to boost your morale. I invited you here to offer my help."

Isaac impressed himself by not snorting. "How so?" he asked, curious about how ridiculous the answer would be.

"My most useful skill is the ability to see through people. I sized you up immediately. Your lack of power is matched by your lack of motivation. You're expendable because that's your true value. But one thing I underestimated about you is your level of craftiness. Behind that clownish personality, there's a wisdom that allows you to somehow navigate these assignments that should be the death of you."

"Powerless. Unmotivated. Expendable. Clown. Your idea of offering help is kind of insulting."

Mabahazi ignored his statement. "I know you're hiding something. You have an excellent poker face, but I've been peering through curtains my whole life. I know you're withholding things from Lefse's reports. All I ask is that you come and tell me. If I don't know all the facts, I can't help. It's literally you against the world out there."

Isaac froze his expression into place. "Lefse knows everything."

Mabahazi slumped back into his chair with a sigh. "Then there is nothing I can do for you. Continue your work for us, Isaac Unknown. Keep pulling off miracle wins until the day you don't."

Interpreting that as a long-winded dismissal, Isaac got up and headed for the door.

"Remember, Isaac," Mabahazi called after him. "The time is coming when you'll need allies more than secrets. When that day arrives, you'll know where to find me."

Chapter 25
FIRE AND ICE

Isaac drove west until sundown and pulled off the highway at a motel near the Ohio-Pennsylvania border. It wasn't the fanciest of places, but had amenities that Isaac preferred—all first-floor rooms with exterior entrances and a willingness to accept cash without identification.

He parked directly in front of his room. As he unlocked the door, he shouted over his shoulder to Testiculies, whom he'd last seen asleep in the bed of the truck. No response came, and with a shrug, Isaac entered the room. If the cat wanted to sleep outside, and maybe even wander off forever, that was fine by him.

Testiculies sat in the middle of the bed. Isaac looked back at the truck, then to the cat, and repeated this several times in disbelief. "Someday I'm going to figure out how you do that," Isaac said. The feline responded with a short hiss as if to challenge the statement before kneading his claws into the comforter and curling into a comfy ball. Isaac tossed his everbag onto the table, used the restroom, and then sat down to think.

The conversation with Mabahazi unnerved him. It reinforced the notion that Isaac had been wondering about himself—that the Arrangement assignments were connected somehow. He more and more believed that the point of each was not the artifacts he'd turned in, but the ones he hadn't.

He removed the unidentified Black Tarot card from his everbag. It remained wrapped in the same cloth from when he acquired it. He had no idea what the card did, so mishandling such power could be catastrophic. Hence, he'd left it alone, secure in the bag.

With the tips of his index finger and thumb, as if changing a dirty diaper, he flipped back an edge of the cloth, just enough to see the upper half. In the center of the card, the ball of snakes he'd glimpsed outside the Devil's Hole continued to writhe in spasmodic twitches. When nothing cataclysmic occurred, he peered closer. The only new detail he noted was that he saw no tails while the heads were all visible, as if the ends of each were lashed together and hidden under the mass. The reptiles continued their silent undulating, eyes shining red and tongues flickering. Loath to touch the artifact, he lifted it up with a pen.

The opposite side of the card was identical.

This reveal made Isaac sit back and rub his chin. As far as he knew—albeit with limited firsthand experience—Black Tarot cards should have divergent faces. The card Maloc had attempted to barter with, the Emperor, was designed as such, with a king in glory and a flipside in ruin.

He wrapped the card and placed it back in his bag. Next, he brought forth the Bubba mask and turned it inside out. This artifact he'd studied a bit previously. While he recognized many necromantic symbols amid the etched runes, there were others he was unfamiliar with. The mask consisted of four pieces, with the runes in the middles to avoid the stitchwork. From a "raise an undead hillbilly" perspective, it was beyond reproach. That didn't tell Isaac why it had fallen into his hands.

Annoyed with the lack of progress, he absentmindedly tugged at a loose thread. It pulled free, creating a gap. Inside this gap, he saw writing. Fingers held in a V, he scissor-spelled along the threads, taking his time to preserve the cloth. When finished, he stretched out the four pieces and examined the writing that stretched along these newly revealed edges.

The words were not English, nor in any language Isaac was familiar with. They were heavy with a's and e's, which, if pronounced out loud, would have given them a rhyming cadence. He felt certain he'd found a ritualistic chant, one probably meant to invoke a spirit or curse, or even summon something otherworldly. However, without any other clues, they were just useless gibberish.

Nothing aggravated a magician more than unraveling a mystery only to uncover another. With only one more artifact left to fail at studying, Isaac pulled out Jughead and set him on the table.

"All right, I'm going to be bluntly honest, I really hate floating around in your magical bag. I thought that damn cellar was bad, but this... holy shit."

"Good. Cooperate and you'll get more free time."

Jughead let out a deep growl that seemed to vibrate the table. "Fine. Fine."

"What's your story?"

"Once upon a time, on a dark and stormy night, I was a magician that became a jug. Thus ends my riveting biography."

Isaac sighed. "That's not what I call cooperating."

"I really don't like discussing it. Honestly, it was all so long ago that I barely remember all the juicy key details you may gather pertinent information from. I don't... hey, what are these?"

Isaac had placed the vessel so that the pieces of the Bubba mask fell into its peripheral vision. "Just another artifact I've been trying to decipher."

"Any luck?"

Isaac detected a lift in the jug's voice—not quite happiness, but at least a momentary lapse in surliness. "Not really."

"Why am I not surprised? Of course you haven't figured it out. I'm just going to assume that you've been at this for hours, wallowing in stupidity like a pig in the mud. A pig that's considerably dumber than all the other pigs. And now I'm going to be offended by this preconceived notion I just made up. Tell me what you know, and then hold the pieces up so I can see them."

Too worn out to be careful and desperate to put at least one secret to bed, Isaac filled the jug in on how he came to possess the Bubba mask. The only details he omitted were Arrangement and the vampire hunters he failed to save. He maneuvered the jug and the mask pieces around so it could get a good look.

"Okay. Stop groping me." After Isaac complied and set the jug down, it said, "What we have here are all the ingredients to summon a creature from another dimension. Specifically, the Pandemonium dimension."

Isaac stood over the table to get a bird's-eye view of the pieces. "Where are you getting all that? I figured the writing could be a summoning chant. But where are the symbols for the magical circle?"

"They've been deconstructed and hidden, quite masterfully, within the working runes that granted unlife to that… what did you call it?"

"The Bubba."

"Yes. The Bubba. Sounds fearsome." Despite the lack of lungs, Jughead fake-coughed to better display his derision. "Many of these symbols are irrelevant to the Bubba spell. But if one were to take these extra symbols and assemble them in the correct order inside of a magical circle, they would create a functioning gate."

"How do you know it's Pandemonium specifically?"

"See that one?"

"This one? Or this one? Or this one?" Isaac traced his finger around several symbols.

"I can't fucking point at it, can I?" Jughead snapped. "The one that looks like an eye with multiple pupils." After Isaac located it, Jughead continued, "That's a symbol representative of the dimension."

"Are you sure?"

"Quite. As I said, I was once a magician, and a much finer specimen than you, I should add. Alchemy was my specialty, but I dabbled in many fields of sorcery. Summoning was a lucrative side endeavor and Pandemonium a popular target."

"Why's that?" Isaac asked. The magical discussion had lifted Jughead's personality. Isaac might yet wring some secrets from it.

"As the name implies, Pandemonium is a realm of complete chaos. Every being that dwells within it is a feral animal, usually psychotic. While still physically dangerous, their low intelligence and lack of social hierarchy make them safer quarry."

"If they're unintelligent, what good would they be?"

"Spell crafting materials, of course. The flesh and blood of other-dimensional beings are especially useful in alchemy. Admittedly, some powerful people just wanted them as trophies. I held a deep disrespect for those ones, but they paid well."

Isaac sat down with a huff. Burgeoning excitement at solving the secret of the mask had been dulled by its apparent purpose. "I don't want to summon up a crazy monster, even a stupid one. My luck is bad enough as it is." He shuffled the mask flaps into a stack. "What the hell do I do with it?"

Jughead let out a long "hmmmmm." "Considering my extensive knowledge on the matter, may I suggest reassembling the mask as it was, soaking it in gasoline, putting it on your head, and setting it on fire."

Isaac sighed. "That's too much work."

"Fine. Just sell the damn thing. It's probably worth something. Someone went through a lot of work to disguise it. Nobody hides worthless secrets. Let someone else make their mistake with it. If I could go back in time, I'd take that advice myself. In fact, I think you should sell all your artifacts. Hint, hint."

"Funny that you mention that. Do you have any experience with the Black Tarot?"

"Absolutely not," Jughead said with a vehement snarl that may have sprayed spittle if it possessed a tongue. "Those are too powerful and leave too much to random chance. Why? You don't have one of those, do you?" Before Isaac could answer, Testiculies hissed loudly, prompting Jughead to ask, "What the hell was that?"

Isaac ignored the jug and looked at the cat. "Damn it. You got the middle of the bed in front of the television, what else do you want?" The answer was another, more truculent hiss, punctuated by several deep-throated growls. Isaac nearly threw his pen. The cat stood up with his back arched and fur on end. "You don't bring a whole lot of positives to this partnership, so shut the..." He trailed off when he realized the cat wasn't looking at him. Instead, he followed his angry gaze across the hotel room to the closed bathroom door.

He didn't remember closing it, and, while Testiculies spent a good portion of each damn day hissing at things for no reason, this time it sent a chill up his spine. Looping the everbag over his shoulder, he slid from his chair and tiptoed towards the door. After three steps, he froze in place at the sound of water running. Casting aside the idea that someone or something could have snuck past him, Jughead, and Testiculies with the purpose of taking a shower, he opted to not care about this new enigmatic event.

At all.

If some mysterious power wanted his cheap hotel bathroom, it could have it. He had enough problems.

Having chosen discretion as the better part of valor, he snatched up Jughead, tucked it under his arm, yelled for the cat, and headed for the door. When he twisted the knob, he let out a hiss of pain, snapped his hand away, and waved it furiously in the air.

The knob was searingly hot, and as he watched, the heat intensified until the metal glowed red and warped into an unusable lump. He moved to the window, intent on shattering his way to the parking lot. When he threw back the curtain, he found that path obstructed as well. A layer of ice, dense enough that he could not see beyond it, coated the glass.

"You mind taking my face out of your armpit?" Jughead asked.

"I thought your nose didn't work," Isaac replied as he replaced the jug on the table.

"It doesn't, but it's still disrespectful. Mind telling me what's going on?"

"We have a visitor. Keep quiet until I get it sorted out or you might end up someplace worse than my bag. Much worse." Isaac's tone proved dire enough that the jug heeded the warning and fell silent.

Fire at the door. Ice at the window. The symbolism confirmed his suspicion and sent the butterflies in his stomach into a flutter. He turned to face the bathroom and, possibly, the music.

Chapter 26
REFLECTIVE REUNION

The bathroom door swung open of its own accord—an invitation—and he was met by a billow of steam and a rush of hot, humid air. Peering through the sauna-like haze, he saw that both the sink faucet and the shower were on full-blast, the unfettered hot water clouding the small space.

He stepped into the sauna. As if in greeting, the shower and sink faucets squeaked shut and the steam parted before him, swirling into a slow tornado with him at the calm, clear eye. He nudged aside the shower curtain, expecting a nude, eldritch horror to be standing there, dripping. But the tub stood empty. Unless someone was hiding in the toilet tank, there was nowhere else to search.

The mirror had fogged over completely with the humidity. He had the momentary notion to wipe it clear, as reflections often revealed the presence of unseen spirits. Maybe he'd get lucky, and all this was just the work of some restless ghost of a traveling salesman who died in the room. He reached across the sink.

A hand wiped the mirror, clearing a swath of steam.

Not from his side of the room.

His reflection greeted him, but the image washed out and became translucent. Ghostly. More window now than a mirror, the glass let

Isaac see not only through himself but beyond. A figure stood in this new depth. Shadows in a shroud, two pinholes of light, ruby red and sapphire blue, burned in place of eyes. Behind this shrouded figure, red sands swirled as if it stood in a shaken, crimson-colored snow globe. Isaac's image overlapped with this being, morphing into a combination of the two that made his skin crawl to see.

The instinct to flee gripped him, but he suppressed it and stood his ground. Just as he knew the identity of this being, he knew running would not only be unsuccessful, but painfully consequential.

"Mast..." Isaac's voice broke. As far as he was concerned, the title no longer defined their relationship. The being in the mirror might view that differently, so with trepidation, Isaac used the only other name he knew the Faceless Magician by. "Bizot."

No response came. The glowing eyes lined up perfectly with his own in their mingled images, and his own facial features translucently filled in the shadows below them. The swirling reds and blues made him slightly dizzy.

"Why are you here?"

The apparition did not respond, which came as no surprise. Direct questions often proved pointless. Isaac could recall many conversations in which his former master never uttered a word, leaving the apprentice to stammer his way around anticipating the demands of a chaotic mind.

Hands, molded from the red sand, stretched inhumanly from the swirling storm and slapped the glass in unison. Isaac flinched but held his ground. The hands wiped at the steam until the glass was crystal clear and Isaac stared through a window into another world.

The Red Wastes. Isaac had been there and had no desire to ever return.

"What do you want?" Isaac asked.

A red arm extended around the apparition, twisting snakelike via multiple elbows, then put a hand to the glass and traced letters. In a reversal of someone writing on a fogged mirror, the finger made letters of steam that dissipated as Isaac read them.

Repay your debt.

The words irritated Isaac, but he knew to keep his response measured. "I don't need a reminder. Your appearance here is a waste of time and energy."

New words were etched with fog. This time they came with a fingernail-on-chalkboard scraping that made Isaac wince.

Is it?

He couldn't tell if the response was sarcastic or indifferent, but wouldn't have been pleased with either. "I've upheld my end of the bargain so far. I've stuck to the plan, which is pretty impressive, I think, considering I have no damn idea what the plan is."

More fingertip scraping produced a longer response.

Ignorance is the point.

"You should have sent Ludworth, then." Isaac almost smiled at the crack, but knew better than to think his sardonic quips would improve the situation.

A figure drifted into hazy view next to Bizot as if on cue. Bare-chested, the man bore more scars than a patched quilt, the result of the magical stitchwork used each time Bizot put his favorite undead servant back together. He smiled wickedly at Isaac and then drew a finger along his throat, tracing the ragged scars there.

Ludworth. The Patchwork Man. Bizot's right hand. Assassin. Bodyguard. Errand boy. Garbage man. Spiteful prick.

"Considering how many times you've been decapitated, I wouldn't use that gesture so casually," Isaac said, proud that he got through the sentence without his voice cracking. He turned back to the Faceless Magician. "I don't understand how this repays my debt. All I'm doing is running dangerous errands for a power that appears to be beyond either of us." Isaac winced as soon as the last word left his mouth.

Us.

He should have known better than to insinuate any equality between them.

The punishment came quickly. The red sand hands writhed in a frenzy, growing and shrinking, fingers elongating, falling away in a dusty shower, then regrowing. The mist on Isaac's side of the mirror billowed and swirled before a crowd of hands emerged and snatched at him. In the narrow space, he could not avoid them, and defensive swings of his arms simply passed through them immaterially. Where the hands grabbed him, however, they proved quite solid. Misty fingers squeezed him painfully and lifted him from the floor, pulling his limbs at awkward angles, barely holding back from breaking bones.

"Give me a direct order," Isaac hissed through agony. "Let me in on this stupid game. I'm getting tired of it."

One new word steamed into view.

Albatross

"Such a shitty nickname, but I can't really argue its validity, can I?"

A word appeared before the moniker.

My Albatross

Isaac gritted his teeth. "Not for much longer."

Ludworth laughed silently, the sound not carrying from beyond the glass. It must have annoyed Bizot, as a red hand cut it off with a smack that left sand bits across his face. Ludworth glowered, eyes full of hate, and Isaac knew from experience that he'd blame the act of discipline on him.

"Tell me what you want," Isaac repeated. "Or else put me down and give me back my fucking bathroom."

One word was erased and two replaced it.

Fly on, Albatross.

The many hands of the mist hurled him from the room. He sailed through the open doorway and slammed into the adjacent wall. The impact knocked the breath from him and left him gasping and rolling on the floor in pain. When he could finally breathe, he sat up just as the bathroom door slammed shut with a bang that shook the cheap framed art on the hotel walls.

Isaac had left Jughead on the table with a perfect view of his aggressive dismissal, and the vessel laughed heartily. "I'm not sure what just happened, but it was one of the greatest things I've seen. Clap, clap, clap, clap, clap."

Isaac gingerly got to his feet. "What are you saying?"

"I don't have hands, so I can't applaud. Clap, clap, clap."

"Knock it off." Isaac limped across the room and plucked the jug up. "We're leaving."

"What's the rush? I'm sure it's not the first time you've been violently thrown out of a steamy bathroom encounter."

Before the jug could insult further, Isaac crammed it into the everbag and turned his attention to the door. The heated knob had reached the point of liquefaction and melted to the floor, leaving scorched wood in its path. Isaac undid the chain bolt, and the door swung open. Outside, only a large puddle remained of the block of ice that barred the window.

Sitting on the hood of the truck was Testiculies. Not even the magical barriers stopped the cat's disappearing trick. It was just further disrespect that the cat waited for Isaac to open the truck door to climb in.

Isaac peeled out of the lot. He checked the rearview mirror several times, expecting some kind of monstrous power to be on their heels. But nothing came. There were no flashes or flames to denote the pursuit of a powerful being, and the motel was soon swallowed up in the distant night.

Chapter 27
THE HALL OF CHAINS

The long and lonely walk.

That was how Mabahazi always thought of the hallway leading to Arrangement's iron wall.

The chat with the strange new voice had boosted Mabahazi's confidence and eased his mind, but his thirst for knowledge remained unsatiated. The recent conversation with Isaac hadn't helped. In the past he hurried, often sprinted, along the needlessly lengthy hall, ever fearful that he might be devoured by some otherworldly fiend or that the elevator might simply vanish behind him, leaving him stranded. Now, secure in knowing that Arrangement possessed at least a mild interest in his continued service, he strolled more casually down the hallway, the box containing the cannibalistic totem held across both palms.

The slower pace allowed him to make several odd observations that had previously avoided him. As he oversaw the Athenaeum's janitorial services, he knew no one ever came down here to clean. Despite this, the hall was spotless. No dust. No cobwebs. The floor shined as if freshly waxed. Above him, halogen lights hummed, spaced evenly so that he never had to pass through shadow. In the years of his supervision, not a single bulb had been changed. Yet none had burned out or even flickered or weakened. Maybe he should buy stock in the manu-facturer, he thought with a suppressed laugh.

Nothing in the hall ever changed. It was like walking through a three-dimensional photo.

Until today.

When he arrived at the iron wall, he found that it had altered itself, but not in the way he had anticipated. Instead of a specialized drop slot for the totem case, there was a full door within the wall. It was tall enough for a human, with an old-fashioned knocker but no knob. He froze, open-mouthed, and if he'd been carrying something more mundane than a magical relic, he may have fumbled it from trembling fingers.

Mabahazi prided himself on his intellect. He knew what this meant. It was a backstage pass—a parting of the curtains. Finally, an invitation to the inner sanctum. Knowing this gave him the courage to bang the knocker. But only once.

It sounded with the deep resonance of a cathedral bell, and the entire iron wall vibrated before the door swung open, with a haunted-house groan of unused metal hinges.

Stepping through was like passing through an immaterial veil. One instant he was in the Athenaeum basement, the next he was someplace completely different. The door did not close behind him. It simply reabsorbed itself, and when he turned, it was just the same solid metal wall he'd grown accustomed to, only now he viewed it from the opposite side for the first time.

Where he was, he had no idea. The metal wall gave off a faint luminescence, but that provided only enough to see where he had come from. Darkness blanketed everything else. In a near panic, he tucked the case under an arm, fumbled for his phone, used the screen for light, and jumped with a scream at the corpse that stood next to him.

No. Not quite a corpse, as it stood on two legs. But if this thing was alive, then Mabahazi couldn't imagine a more torturous existence.

The eyes were milky white with cataracts, and the skin was dark and wrinkled like dried fruit. The body had no muscle tone or fat as if a powerful vacuum had sucked everything from it, leaving only the desiccated flesh over a frame of bones. It was sexless, although impossible to tell if the genitals had been removed or if the wretch had never possessed them. Both arms were extended, palms up as if they had been indefinitely waiting for a gift. A single length of thin, dull gray chain dangled from its back and trailed off into the shadows.

Mabahazi tried to say something, a greeting, an exclamation of fear, but his mouth froze in place. It was apparent what the wasted thing waited for, and so, half expecting the withered arms to snap off, he gently handed over the case. The thing proved stronger than it looked and took the weight with no issue. Once Mabahazi had fully relinquished it, it snapped to life, turning on its heels with the robotic precision of a parade soldier. Now he could see that the chain was not manacled or tied. It protruded from under the skin as if it were a fused extension of the spine. It began to walk away.

"Hey, wait," he called after it. His phone light proved feeble in this space, and the thing would quickly be out of sight. As horrid as it was, the prospect of being alone seemed somehow worse. He moved after it, keeping it just in his range of light.

The hall they traversed was dull concrete, not unlike the basement halls of the Athenaeum, but he instinctively knew they were now far from there. As he followed the thing, he noted that the chain never slacked. It remained taut as if being winched up at its unseen source as the wasted thing walked. On they went until the hall turned a corner and opened into a massive chamber.

Without taking his eyes from the new sight, Mabahazi slipped the phone into his pocket. It was unneeded now, as this great hall was dimly illuminated by high rows of sterile halogen lights. What he saw inspired complete awe and horror at once.

Rows upon rows of desks stretched across the hall, and at each sat a being identical to the wasted walker that had greeted him. Motionless, their cloudy eyes stared straight ahead, transfixed on nothing. From the back of each ran a similar chain, although there were variations in color. Some were golden, others gray like the totem carrier's. Many were black, so dark they almost appeared to be shadows. All of them ran along the floor in the same direction, opposite the way Mabahazi entered from, into another doorway at the far side.

He had stopped, and now the totem carrier had gotten away from him. Halfway across the hall now, it headed down an aisle between rows, following the chains. Mabahazi was reluctant to hurry after it, afraid that any sudden movements would bring attention from the others, but also knew he had nowhere else to go.

Like a man entering a minefield, he proceeded, each step a test— slow, heel to toe, followed by a sigh of relief. Each test was passed, as the gaunt beings never acknowledged him. Eventually, he reached the point of no return, deep enough into the hall that if they suddenly took notice of him, he was too far from the doorway to run back. Knowing this, he picked up the pace and soon passed the rows of workers to the other end of the room. Here the chains converged and lashed into thick bundles that disappeared down the opposite doorway. It was the same direction the totem carrier had gone.

Faced with a new unknown, Mabahazi's confidence waned. The confines of the chain-lined hallway were another test of his newfound courage, and for the moment he faltered, not enough to flee. Unable to advance, he stood trembling with indecision.

"Mabahazi! Welcome!" someone called out loudly, nearly making the Head Librarian wet himself. "I see the totem has made its way here. An excellent addition. I doubt it will ever come in handy, madness rarely does, but it's safer with us in the long run. It's always been amusing to me that most magical artifacts in this world cause insanity in mortals. As if humankind needed much of a push."

The most handsome man Mabahazi had ever seen strode, seemingly from nowhere, across the hall towards him. With his golden hair, sparkling teeth, and bright eyes, the man was almost radiant. He wore an immaculate suit, and his dress shoes were loud on the concrete floor.

I'm so glad you took me up on my offer." He was still at such a distance that he needed to raise his voice, and Mabahazi flinched at the thought that his volume would rouse these ghouls. Seeing his concern, the man said, "Oh, don't worry about these fellows. They attend to their task with single-minded devotion." He demonstrated by tapping one on the shoulder and getting no reaction. "See. Drones. Worker bees. Ironic, really. They monitor the world but are dead to their surroundings. Not much for conversation, but they don't need coffee breaks either."

The man laughed, and the sound rang pleasantly in Mabahazi's ears, like the twinkling of bells. He extended a hand, which Mabahazi slowly grasped. It shocked him how strong the man was, as he was not much bigger than himself. "My name is Dansil."

The Librarian had so many questions they bottled up in his mouth. Finally, with Dansil's parent-like encouragement, he croaked out, "Are you the Voice? Are you Arrangement?"

"Me? Dear lord, no. I am..." He paused. "I don't really have an official title. So, think of me as the general manager of this facility."

"It was you I talked to on the phone. You're the one who told me to be patient."

"Indeed. I was worried that your growing frustration could lead you to some rash decisions. We go through so many promising staff members because of that. And now is not the time to start grooming another."

Mabahazi nodded, as that had been exactly the case. "What is this place?"

"This is the nexus of Arrangement, and these"—he waved a hand at the seated zombies—"are its eyes and ears. Hundreds of ever-vigilant sentinels, collecting and processing the world's thoughts, feelings, and heartbeats and passing them on." Dansil pointed along the chains that snaked out of the room.

Curiosity buoying him just above his fear, Mabahazi leaned closer to one of the workers. "Who are they?"

"*Who?* Dansil repeated with a smirk. "They are no longer anyone. But in anticipation of your next question, once upon a time, they were exceptional beings. Each was a psychic in the service of Arrangement. The problem with employing psychics is that eventually they all learn things you don't want them to. Sadly, our secrets are not meant to be their secrets. It invariably led to rash decisions on their parts. However, they were also too valuable for us to release, so we developed a method of ensuring their continued service."

"What was done to them?"

"Becoming an extension of the Voice has its price," Dansil said nonchalantly, as if their condition resulted from something as mundane as agreeing to work overtime. "Think of it as a physical and spiritual lobotomy. We left just enough of their minds to control their psychic abilities. Every other part of them was severed from existence."

"So, they watch the world here and pass the information to..." Mabahazi motioned down the dark hallway. "What's down there? It's the Voice, isn't it?"

"It is. The Voice absorbs their observations and decides how best to manage the world. No issues are too large or too small to possibly be addressed."

Mabahazi turned in a full circle, getting another panoramic view of the room. "I have so many questions. I don't know where to even begin."

"There will be plenty of time for questions and answers in the future." Dansil looked along the hall where the chains led. "For now, we must be delicate."

"But why was I finally allowed to see this?"

Dansil smiled that radiant, magnetic smile. "As a reward, of course. If we're going to expand your role here, then it's time to start being more transparent. You've done excellent work as our Head Librarian and have, as of late, exhibited a trait that I find most valuable." This was the greatest news Mabahazi had ever received. He straightened his spine, then his coat, then his cufflinks, giddy for this incoming praise. Until Dansil continued with, "You are not a brave man, Mabahazi. But you're not a full-blown coward either."

This brought the librarian's preening to a screeching halt. He said nothing, as he had no idea how to respond to this backhanded compliment, but his face betrayed his unhappiness.

"Oh, apologies, Mabahazi," Dansil said, and he made a slight bow. "I meant no disrespect. An abundance of courage would not serve you well in this endeavor. Fear is an integral part of the human psyche. It's there to keep you alive. If you were a bolder, confident man, you may have allowed your frustration and curiosity to get the better of you." The beautiful man placed a hand on his shoulder and Mabahazi felt tender warmth spread through his body. His indignation melted away. "There is a lot to fear here, and we need a smart man to respect that. The fearless ones are less controllable, so we let them bleed for us on the front lines."

And Mabahazi continued to smile dumbly as Dansil put his arm around his shoulder and walked him back to the iron wall.

Chapter 25
THE RELIQUARY

The woman seated near the entrance had no eyes. This is not to say she was blind or had suffered some form of terrible injury. The blank skin of her forehead extended around her nose on both sides, seamlessly and naturally. Her eyes had never been meant to be.

Bookending her were two men. To her left sat a squat fireplug of a man with a face molded by a lifetime of street fights. To her right stood a thin, well-dressed person whose gender was either secret or nonexistent. Angus and Berry respectively—bouncers and bodyguards for the gatekeeper named Omary.

"Hand," she commanded, and Isaac put it palm-up on the table before her. No form of identification existed that would permit entry here. Only Omary's judgment would suffice. After tracing the lines of his palm, she said, "Isaac. Welcome. You're always a little different with each visit. This time, you have a new layer of shadow in there." She slapped his hand lightly and pushed it off her table. "You may enter." A grunt of approval came from Angus, and Berry nodded curtly as he passed.

While Isaac respected anyone skilled at their craft, he had never been a fan of psychics. Soothsayers. Fortune-tellers. Palm readers. The

218

only thing worse than a charlatan was the genuine article. Mind reading—just a method of stealing secrets rather than earning them, as far as Isaac was concerned. At least Omary maintained enough professionalism to keep all the juicy bits to herself.

The hall ended at an elevator with no buttons. The doors slid shut, and it moved with a mind of its own, ascending to a level of its own choosing: the main hall. The doors slid open to the cacophony of a party that would make Dionysus smile.

The Reliquary—a supernatural mash-up of burlesque and Mardi Gras, illusions, striptease, circus feats, and artistic spellcraft. A place where fantasy fused with reality into a magic-laced New Year's Eve party performed nightly.

It was an eclectic crowd—from formal wear to casual, to leather and lace, to costumes fit for a rave or Halloween party. It had a dress code limited only by one's imagination. But the diversity went far beyond clothing. People from all walks of life and every rung on the social ladder were in attendance. Isaac couldn't say with any certainty what the criteria were for admittance, aside from the judgment of Omary.

The only thing more varied than the clientele was the staff. Most of the entertainers were somehow connected to the Other World. Many had made a home here, whether wielders or victims of magic or the supernatural.

There were few instances when Isaac could tolerate, let alone enjoy, being in a crowd. In fact, when he paused to consider it, the Reliquary was the only crowded place he'd voluntarily attend. The location provided a rare sense of security. With the nightly spectacles and otherworldly attendees, he didn't stand out. Even to those here who knew him, he was nothing special. If he weren't a former associate of the owner, they wouldn't know him at all.

On the main stage performed a woman named Nekane who may have become the mortal stereotype for a sultry female devil. She was red-skinned, with pointed horns, cloven hooves, and a prehensile tail. Her act consisted of fire-breathing, sans combustible fuel. Each deep breath expelled a gout of flame that she then molded to her will. Fiery belly dancers swayed through the air, followed by a dragon that looped and turned, making the crowd duck away. She would then drink the flames back down and repeat.

Isaac made his way to the bar and ordered a scotch. Just as it arrived, so did a short, stocky woman with shockingly pink hair and horn-rimmed glasses.

"Isaac!" she said, and she hugged him. Her name was Lucille, and they exchanged greetings and how-are-you-doings. Pleasantries concluded, she said, "Did Hellebore know you were coming?"

"No. I haven't spoken to her in a while. She still miffed at me?"

"Hard to tell with her."

"Yeah. She here?"

"In the building somewhere. On business. But she left me in charge of the hall, so I'm not expecting her back anytime soon. Maybe it's best you continue to avoid her anyway. We haven't heard from you in months." She leaned in to whisper the next sentence as if anyone could overhear in the din. "There are rumors you signed on with Arrangement. Tell me that's not true."

In a flat and unconvincing tone, he said, "That's not true."

She punched him in the shoulder. "Oh, you damn liar. How'd you last so long in this business being so bad at telling untruths? Are you insane? Everyone knows Arrangement agents are expendable. Any group with an unknown overseer isn't going to care about your life. If you were so desperate to keep up this kind of work, why didn't you come to us? We could have found you plenty of opportunities, with highly vetted contracts and safer employers. Relatively speaking, of course."

Isaac had no immediate response. The truth could not be shared, and further lying, even done with conviction, seemed pointless. "I got sucked in by their healthcare package. Good dental as well."

Lucille crossed her arms with a sigh. "Fine. If you want to keep your secrets, then you do that. Something tells me I'd be safer not knowing anyway."

The bartender handed Isaac his glass just in time for him to toast Lucille's statement. "How's business here?" Isaac asked, willfully ignoring the size of the crowd.

"Booming," she said curtly. Despite his attempt at changing the subject, she wasn't ready to end the interrogation. "What are you doing here?"

"Just needed a night in a safe harbor. Good food. Comfortable bed with silk sheets. Some entertainment. And this." He held up his glass. "Lots and lots of this."

Lucille's eyes trailed from his face to the scotch and back again. "You know that people like us can't drown our sorrows."

"I'm not trying to drown them. I just want to stir them around for a night."

She smiled sadly at this. "That's it? Just a one-night vacation away from it all?"

"Yup." He downed his glass and ordered another.

"Then I'll leave you to it. I'll probably be busy the rest of the night with Hellebore being occupied. So, I'll say goodbye now. It was nice seeing you, Isaac." Lucille turned to leave.

"Wait. Hang on. Okay. There's one other thing I came here for."

She whirled with surprising speed and pointed a finger. "I knew it! There's always an ulterior motive with you. It's the reason Hellebore is so mad at you."

"That's not the only reason." He meant it as a joke, but it came out of his mouth like a correction. "I need access to Hellebore's personal library."

Lucille's eyes went wide. "You're kidding, right? That would be a tall request for someone she currently liked, much less you in your particular situation. This isn't an Arrangement assignment, is it? If Hellebore were to find out that you were snooping around here on behalf of those puppet masters, I'm sure... well, we can both imagine how she'd react to that level of betrayal."

He held up his hand. "No. This is a personal matter for me. Just some research."

"Why not research it at the Athenaeum, then? I've heard they have one of the largest collections in the world."

"They do. It's also one of the last places you'd want to try and keep your research a secret." It occurred to him that with the Voice's ability to be supernaturally aware of the world, if not wholly omniscient, Hellebore's sanctum might not be any more secure. An adage popped into his mind—the only way to hide from a god was to hope the god was too busy to look. It didn't fill him with confidence. With a dearth of options, it was still his best chance at achieving any secrecy.

"Is your life in danger?"

"Eh, probably," he said with a shrug. He accepted his new glass of scotch from the bartender.

She shook her head at him. "I'll get a message to her. I'll even hint that it's a matter of life or death, without actually saying it that way. But her answer, whatever it may be, is final. And I'll enforce it as such. Just so we understand each other on this."

He felt the threat hidden within her words. He knew Lucille genuinely liked him, but her loyalty to Hellebore remained unquestionable. Given the command, she'd stab him to death with her horn-rimmed glasses, before arranging an elaborate funeral and crying over his coffin. "I understand. Thanks, Lucille."

She gave him a half smile and walked away. No sooner had he said goodbye than a pair of boney hands wrapped around his head and covered his eyes in a guess-who. In this case, "boney" didn't mean thin. "Boney" meant bones. Fleshless, skeletal hands. In any place on Earth other than the Reliquary, Isaac would've lashed out in self-defense. But here one had to expect such things. Besides, he knew whom the hands belonged to, and not just because he could see through them.

"Hello, Husk," he said, and he turned, the hands over his eyes transitioning into a friendly hug.

"Isaac." She stepped back and looked him up and down. Not in an admiring way, Isaac knew. She just disapproved of his casual dress. Isaac did the same, but his once-over was purely gratuitous. With the looks of a starlet, catwalk grace, and flawless porcelain skin, Husk was simply beautiful. The whole world would probably know her name (or whatever her real name happened to be) if not for her shortage of flesh.

Fleshless from the shoulders down, her arms were nothing but bone. No skin or muscle or veins. Simply bone, aged to a yellowish-brown color, like a dug-up fossil. Where her skin ended, it flapped in bloodless tatters, like a T-shirt with frayed sleeves. Her legs were the same from the knees down, skeletal feet daintily pushed into high heels. It had to be some form of powerful curse, although she'd never discussed it with him. He thought it could very well be a punishment for past vanity, although she certainly hadn't learned her lesson.

"How are you?" he asked.

"Similar to you, except more fabulous, much happier, much sexier. The list goes on."

The dig was her way of being friendly, and Isaac couldn't argue it anyway. As he had in the past, he offered to buy her a drink from the bottom shelf liquors, knowing she would scoff snootily at him. Husk had a taste for only the finer things, and it was an ongoing joke between them that Isaac in no way made the cut.

He didn't know her well, but she'd always been friendly with him, albeit in the manner of a condescending older sister. Rumors abounded that prior to her Reliquary employment, she'd been a serial murderer who preyed on the wealthy, particularly old money elitists. He had no idea if this was true and had no intention of finding out. That remained the beauty of their conversations. They were short and pointless. Husk didn't ask anything meaningful because she didn't care. He didn't ask because he feared she'd actually tell him.

"Mind your manners tonight," Husk told him. Before she left him, she playfully pinched his cheek and he winced at how much it hurt with fleshless fingertips.

On the stage were a magician in a top hat and her two lovely assistants. They performed a slapstick skit, with each failed magic trick resulting in the exaggerated loss of clothing. No real magic, just good sleight of hand and tear-away clasps. Always a sucker for such shenanigans, Isaac found an empty table with a better view. Flagging a server, he ordered another drink and a burger.

By the time he finished his meal, the next act began. A blonde-haired woman named Lavaliere performed with multiple lengths of thin silver chains. Like living snakes, they followed her unspoken commands, swinging and spinning her around the stage, several times letting go to the crowd's gasps, only to snatch her up moments before a crushing landing. Isaac found himself impressed with what he assumed were more complex versions of his slithering scarves.

The warmth of the scotch spread from his belly to his limbs and then to his head. His vision swam and the room began to sway. The stage shows continued, and he clapped for performances he knew he wouldn't remember.

In between sips, faces emerged in his memory. They didn't come unbidden, forcing their way through his alcohol-weakened defenses. On the contrary, Isaac pushed each into the forefront, one after another. Asshole bikers. Amateur vampire hunters. Weekend demonologists. Brit Knit. Each of them roamed around his blurry thoughts.

Lucille had been right about one thing. He had no intention of drowning his sorrows. He didn't drink to numb the pain but to find it. The voices of the dead didn't need to be silenced when they couldn't be heard. They should be shouting. Deafening around the clock. They should be screaming blame into every fiber of his being. Instead, they were only nagging whispers that he heard in his most intoxicated state. Their passive faces just looked at him as if he shared no blame for their fates. As if he actually were an albatross that soared overhead, blissfully unaware of the doom it left behind. The faces reminded him of the tremendous guilt he should feel.

Brit Knit. Her death had stung more than the others. But not enough. Not nearly enough.

He drained his last glass and got up. Nearby, the sultry devil Nekane had summoned a rotating halo of flame that customers were using to light cigars for some celebration. He tried to watch the display while simultaneously walking in the opposite direction, and tripped over a chair. He stumbled into someone who hissed animalistically at him, caught his balance, took two steps, and then crashed into a couple wearing matching robes and porcelain masks. Drinks spilled with the sound of shattering glass. Someone swore at him, and he responded with an unintelligible babbling that he would later recall as witty.

"I think you've had enough for the night," Husk said as she appeared next to him and locked a skeletal hand around his wrist. He attempted to pull away but found he may as well have been manacled to her. With no flesh or muscle, her strength remained amazing. He didn't understand the physics of it.

"I agree."

Husk tugged his arm and led him towards the elevator. "When I saw you order your sixth drink, I put a room on your card."

"Good call. Does it have silk sheets?"

"It does."

Isaac mumbled his thanks. By the time they reached the elevator, he'd passed out completely.

Chapter 29
THE FINE ART OF SKINNING

Something rare happened that night—Isaac dreamt.

Most magicians were trained early on to repress such unintentional sensory experiences. A cautionary tale told to many was that of a young pyromancer who dreamt of fire and woke up in flames. The subconscious could be a powerful thing, the emotions it provoked even more so.

Upon waking, he remembered little more than bits and pieces that leaked into his consciousness, like quicksilver through grasping fingers. It struck him as unfair that nightmares were the only dreams strong enough to punch through the repression training. A dream about being old and retired in Scotland near a distillery? That one never made the cut.

Just as they had invaded his bathroom, the Faceless Magician and the Patchwork Man intruded on his slumber. Their appearance had undoubtedly stirred up unwanted memories, and the alcohol binge probably didn't help his moment of subconscious weakness. While Bizot loomed like a shadow, an unseen oppressive weight, it was Ludworth that plagued his night.

Frankenstein was a myth, a story meant to frighten and entertain, but the necromancy it had been loosely based on worked well in pow-

erful enough hands. In the modern world, such beings were colloqui-
ally known as stitches. Isaac considered it a vulgar term and had used
it as such when dealing with Ludworth, but he couldn't think of a
better descriptor for an undead being constructed from spare human
parts.

His nightmare had flashed pieces, emotionally jarring snippets
from years ago. A full-day hunt. A game of cat and mouse. Isaac had
been amongst a group of fellow apprentices tasked with surviving
twenty-four hours with murderous Ludworth on their heels and that
damn white owl floating above outing their every hiding spot. There'd
been eight of them to start the game. Only Isaac survived.

It had been the first time, but not the last, that Isaac "killed" Ludworth. He'd never been prideful, but made a mistake that night
destined to haunt him. Influenced by youthful inexperience and post-
bloodshed anger, he'd returned to his master carrying Ludworth's
head, his index finger and thumb buried in sockets of eyes he gouged
out. Like a bowling bowl, he'd tossed the head and smirked as it rolled
to Bizot's feet.

The shrouded being, skin fluctuating between darkness and reflection as if coated in a liquid mirror, contemplated this act for an
agonizing length. The desired effect had not been achieved. The Faceless Magician remained unimpressed.

The punishment, novel in its departure from the usual physical
trauma, came swiftly. In an adjacent chamber, Bizot had constructed a
makeshift morgue. Seven tables held seven bodies. The corpses were
fresh, with bloody wounds still wet and skin not yet cold. The best
condition for replacement parts for Ludworth.

Isaac received a crash course in necromantic surgery, although he
was so exhausted that he retained almost none of the teachings. Bizot

had stood over his shoulder, hands folded behind his back—directing but never helping as Isaac sawed apart the seven bodies of his fellow apprentices killed that very night.

As further punishment for Isaac's disrespect, Bizot forced him to start by removing the eyes.

Now Isaac sighed and pushed the memories out of his mind. He rubbed his temples which had begun to ache. He doubted he'd be able to get back to sleep but reached to pull the blankets up anyway. His hand patted around but found none. Maybe he'd kicked them off the bed during his nightmare.

Nope. He wasn't even in bed. He lay on the floor, still dressed in the same clothes, with his everbag firmly strapped on. Figures that he paid extra for silk sheets and then fell out of bed. He got up, his head alternating between aching and spinning as it tried to decide if it remained drunk or had advanced to the hangover.

Wrong again. The bed was neatly made. He'd never even managed to get that far. The last thing he remembered was waiting for the elevator with Husk. It would have been nice of her to at least throw him onto the bed or even the couch, but he supposed expecting a vain undead maybe-serial-killer to lovingly tuck in a drunk was a bit optimistic.

Awake now, he made his way to the bathroom to take a suddenly urgent piss. One of his footsteps landed not on thick carpet but on something cold that crinkled underfoot. A blanket-sized piece of plastic had been spread out on the floor. He patted it with the sole of his foot curiously. Maybe it had been placed there by staff in case he vomited. Although not placing him on top of it seemed counterintuitive.

After flushing the toilet, he walked into the TV area, intent on catching some news while lying on the couch. On the coffee table lay an unfurled leather knife roll which contained a wide array of shiny and very sharp instruments. His eyes roamed over the assorted filet knives and scalpels, leading him to check himself in fear that something had been sliced off during the night. He counted all the appendages that normally numbered ten, two, and one.

A knock came at the door. He spied through the peephole and then let Husk in. She had swapped her evening wear for a tracksuit, exposing only her skeletal hands and feet. She carried a tray with a cup of coffee and a covered plate.

"Morning, sunshine," Husk said as she set the tray on the coffee table, nonchalantly ignoring the plethora of cutting tools, and then took a seat. "I figured you might be struggling this morning, so I brought you up some breakfast."

After a sideways glance at the knife roll, he sat down across from her and lifted the metal cap off the plate. The aroma of bacon wafted up, making his mouth water despite both his hangover and apprehension. A croissant and bowl of fruit completed the dish.

"How are you feeling?"

He shrugged. "Not the worst I've been. It would have been nice to sleep in those damn silk sheets."

Husk dismissed that with a boney wave. "I carried you from the elevator, down the hall, and into the room. I wasn't tucking you in like I was your mother."

"Fair enough." He dragged out the stirring of his coffee, not wanting to test the food with Husk and a bunch of sharp tools in the room. "What's this early morning visit all about? I know you didn't care enough to bring me breakfast in bed. Or on the floor."

"I have good news, and I have…" She tapped her chin in thought. "I guess I only have good news. From your perspective, anyway."

"That's a rarity. Lay it on me."

"Hellebore has granted you permission to use her library." Husk folded up the knife roll. "Turns out I won't be needing these after all. I really misread the situation."

His elation at the first sentence fizzled with the second. "What exactly was your plan?"

"Don't be dense. I assumed that if Hellebore didn't acquiesce to your request, she'd order me to kill you. I prepped ahead of time."

"I'd like to think there'd be some options in between those two extremes. Like a simple 'no,' for instance. Even an 'Oh, hell no.'"

Husk giggled, a sound perfectly balanced between cute and maniacal. "You should know better than that. We know you're working for Arrangement. She had to decide if she still trusted you or not. If she no longer trusted you, then there's really no benefit to her letting you walk out of here, is there?" She secured the binding on the knife roll with a perfect bow.

"I guess." He couldn't escape his morbid curiosity. "You were going to cut an artery? Bleed me out?" In his head, it seemed reasonably painless, at least. Dying in one's sleep while drunk sounded like a decent enough way to go out. Preferable, actually.

"That's not what I do."

"Ah. Okay." Once again, his momentary relief turned dark. "You were going to skin me, weren't you?"

"Yes. That's what I excel at."

"While I was sleeping?" His indignation rose at her casualness.

Husk put a skeletal hand to her chest. "Of course not. Death is a sacred thing. The vast majority of people only get to experience it once. I remember mine quite vividly. Painful but memorable. It was a defining moment in my existence. I would not have denied you that."

"You were going to wake me up from a peaceful, alcohol-fueled slumber so that I could experience being skinned alive." Isaac took a bite of the croissant and chewed nervously. He had no need to worry about poison. If the Reliquary wanted him dead, he would be so. "I suppose it's just business, right? Nothing personal?"

"Well, business would be the reason, but the act would have been incredibly personal. I would have worked on you for hours. Friends deserve our best, especially when it comes to fine art. When I have my tools in hand, it's much like sex. It would have gone on for hours and been very, very, messy. And I would have kept choice cuts as mementos." She looked him over. "Maybe just one or two. You don't take very good care of yourself. I debated presenting your face to Hellebore, but I don't think she would have appreciated it. She's still a little soft for you. Which is why your request was granted, and I must continue being bored."

He crammed the rest of the baked good into his mouth and said between chews, "You know what? I'm going to look at the bright side of this situation. I got permission to use the library, you didn't skin me..."

"Yet," she interrupted.

"Hellebore still trusts me..."

"For now," she interrupted again.

"And that was a great croissant."

Husk smiled. "You're welcome." She clapped her hands, which without flesh made a sound more akin to whacking wooden sticks together. She stood to leave. "I forgot my sheet of plastic. Be a lamb and roll it up and leave it for housekeeping, won't you? Oh, and next time, remember the Reliquary Hotel has a no-pet policy unless cleared in advance."

Isaac immediately turned to see Testiculies sound asleep on his expensive unslept-in bed. He'd last seen the animal curled up in the bed of the truck. Somehow, he had navigated his way out of the parking garage, through countless locked and guarded doors, and into the room. Out of sheer respect, he let the cat snooze on.

Unnerved by the interaction with Husk, Isaac ambled around aimlessly for a moment, pausing eventually at the window to take in the New York City skyline. The suite was luxurious and would no doubt put a dent in his Reliquary account. Historically, before his falling-out with the Reliquary owner, he'd unwind for at least a couple of days before the wanderlust got back into his blood. Knowing he came close to being a bloody mess on a sheet of plastic marred the experience and now the opulence seemed cold and sinister.

With Isaac still dressed from the night before, getting ready consisted of finishing his coffee and tightening the strap on his everbag. Before he left for the library, he took a petty delight in hacking Husk's plastic drop cloth into the tiniest possible pieces with his scissor spell.

Chapter 30
THE JOURNAL OF UBLESH

As Isaac stepped off the elevator, his phone dinged with a series of texts from Lefse. The first was a picture of a pair of pencil-sketched breasts, cartoonish in dimensions and probably drawn by Lefse himself with his non-dominant hand. A photo of a soldier aiming a shoulder-mounted rocket came next. Finally, Lefse wrapped the thread up with a simple thumbs-up emoji.

Isaac felt spoiled with all the good news as of late. He didn't get skinned alive overnight. He received permission to use Hellebore's library, and now he knew that, thus far, Susan had dodged his karmic chemtrail. Still, he knew better than to get too optimistic. Little bits of glad tidings were usually just precursors to a tsunami of bad ones.

Down the hall, Lucille, still clad in an early-morning bathrobe, stood outside of a large steel door. She made a dramatic show of yawning to get Isaac moving faster.

"I haven't gotten up this early in months," she complained while punching a series of numbers into a keypad on the wall. The door unlocked with a click, leading them into a small, bare alcove. Yet another door barred their path, this one made of stout oak and wrapped in iron banding. A large, old-fashioned padlock secured the handle. Lucille removed a key reminiscent of one carried by a medieval jailor and handed it to him.

Isaac nodded his thanks and inserted the key. It twisted hard and the metallic sound of tumblers shifting filled the alcove. He needed both hands to pull open the heavy oak. The comforting musky-vanilla smell of old paper wafted out, and he took a few deep inhalations. "How long do I have?"

"Hellebore didn't say. I'd make efficient use of your time if I were you, though. She's been mercurial as of late, especially where you're concerned. She may give you all day, or maybe she sends Angus and Berry to haul you out in an hour."

"Will do. I certainly don't want to be Angused or Berried." He took a step, but Lucille held a hand in his path.

"Sorry, but you can't take your bag of many mysteries, or whatever you call it, with you."

Isaac reflexively clutched the strap of his everbag. "What? Why?"

She put her hands on her hips. "Because you could fit every single book she owns into it and walk away whistling."

"I'm a thief now?" He thought about what he just said. "Okay, I have a history of thievery. I wouldn't steal from her, though. She trusts me to go into the library but not to steal from it?"

Lucille poked him in the chest. "Hellebore trusts you to not try and run off with a priceless book tucked under your shirt. She wouldn't trust anyone with a bottomless magical bag around her collection." She crossed her arms. "And neither would I."

He knew further resistance was futile. If he didn't want to follow the rules, he'd just be thrown out of the Reliquary, probably from the top floor. With a sigh, he handed the everbag over. "Just promise me you'll keep it with you. Don't hand it off to anyone else. Just you."

"You have my word," Lucille said. "You don't need to tell me any specifics, but if you can give me a general idea of what you're looking for, I can at least point you to a decent starting place."

"Artifacts. Unique ones with unpredictable powers."

"Oh. That sounds ominous. Start on the furthest right shelf. Best I can offer."

Isaac entered the study. Lucille pushed the oaken door shut behind him, sealing him in with an ominous thump. The space had been expanded since his last visit, and he took a moment to orient himself. Shelves lined the walls and ran in aisles across the room in a crisscross pattern. At the center of them sat a simple wooden desk and leather chair.

While the collection was easily worth millions, it contained no actual magical tomes. Hellebore was not a spellcaster. Her abilities lay elsewhere, chief amongst them being information gathering, and the books here reflected that. Isaac perused each aisle, taking mental notes on new herbology, poisons, and art sections. He loved books and could have lost himself for days poring through each volume, but he knew he had neither the time nor the freedom.

The books also brought unbidden memories. In Isaac's past apprenticeship, the Faceless Magician would often present him with boxes upon boxes of encyclopedias, textbooks, novels, biographies, romances, and just about every conceivable collection of pages between two covers. He'd search and search for any worthwhile piece. There were other complications, of course. Painful punishments if the time elapsed. Booby-trapped books. Cursed pages. He'd once seen a peer lose both hands to a well-concealed acid trap in a cookbook. It had rarely been pleasant.

He scanned through the shelves, tapping his finger on each leather-bound spine. One by one he flipped through those that looked encouraging. Some had full titles and authors. *A Guide to Relics* by Norman Bahn. *Fragments of Heaven* by Alexander Montgomery. *The Infernal Encyclopedia* by Memphis O'Dell. *The Pyrrhic Devices of Cecil Wells* by Samantha Wells. Some were faded to illegibility. Others were not labeled at all. Most of them he dismissed right off the bat. Those that held promise he set on the desk, assembled into orderly towers so he knew which to delve into first.

Stacks constructed, he sat to read. He flipped through pages as expediently as possible, reminding himself not to get lost in curiosity at the sheer volume of information. The early hours proved fruitless, and before he knew it, half of his book towers were exhausted. To add to his frustration, over and over he had to remind himself to soldier on when he encountered a truly interesting but unrelated entry that would have only distracted him.

His first success came in the form of an encyclopedia titled *The Alchemist's Field Guide*. There was one entry describing ever-full flagons, barely a paragraph in length. An unknown writer described such artifacts as prized possessions of both alchemists and assassins, as potions and poisons requiring rare ingredients could be produced in endless supply. That usage certainly made more sense than a bunch of yokels filling it with moonshine and sort of jibed with Jughead's description of his past. Isaac had hoped to find something to shed some light on how or why a soul could be placed in such a vessel, and given at least minor psychic abilities to boot, but no luck.

The next three books failed him, and if he weren't a guest in a dangerous house, he'd have thrown them across the room. He snatched the next from the stack. Very thick, with cracked leather binding, it was an oddly assembled work—put together with more of a scrapbook aesthetic than a true encyclopedia. Unalphabetized and written by a variety of hands, it must have been a collaborative effort, although none of the writers were identified. Some entries possessed illustrations that ranged from exquisite artistry to childlike doodles that were hard to identify. His interest piqued by its unusual format, he began flipping through it. About midway through, his fortune changed.

Black Tarot Excerpts from the Journal of Ublesh crossed the top of the page. Below it was a pencil rendering of a tarot card that Isaac had never seen before. It depicted a line of shambling figures, humanoid and skeletal, trudging from an unknown location to an unseen destination. While done by an expert hand, the illustration remained a crude copy of a true card. The magical vibrancy proved impossible to capture in a quick sketch and he could glean little meaning from it. He read the description next to it.

The March of the Damned

The restless dead.
What do they crave?
A vengeful return,
Or the peace of the grave?

That was it. At the very least, it identified the poor bastards on parade. The last two lines of the limerick made him think the card could cause or quell some kind of undead outbreak. He supposed either of those outcomes could prove handy, depending on one's situation or emotional state. But it wasn't the card he was interested in, so he moved on to the next page.

Most of the following entries proved incomplete. Pages were labeled with tarot names, but no other information had been recorded. Spaces were left for illustrations that had never been drawn. *The Echoing Void. The Iron Gate. The Chained One. The Starlight Ladder.* Tantalizing titles with no satisfaction.

The next entry complete with an illustration was identified as The Scarlet Deep. The drawing proved hard to interpret. Just a series of dark ink swirls and slashing lines. A whirlpool? A hurricane with driving rain? A black hole? An abused toilet? There was no way to tell. He read the poetic annotation.

The Scarlet Deep

There is coming a day
When the sky will rain blood.
The world that you know
Will be consumed by the flood.
Will you learn how to swim?
Or sink with your sins?
There's no way to know
If you'll be gifted with fins.

That card sounded miserable to Isaac. A blood-soaked apocalypse that also required introspective decision-making and self-reflection? He'd just as well not survive such a calamity from the onset. He flipped the page with vigor to display his disgust with the entry.

He hit pay dirt.

The still-life drawing of the entwined snakes lacked the drama of the hyperrealism he'd glimpsed on the card. However, this second-hand depiction had added something, a piece of artistry to provide context. The image was not just a ball of reptiles floating in space. Underneath their mass extended a human neck, thin and apparently feminine, sloping into a pair of bare shoulders. Anyone with even the most basic grasp of mythology would recognize the back of that head.

The Gorgon

Look to our dearest Medusa.
She'll point out the path.
Frozen in time
By her unbridled wrath.
An irresistible weapon.
Her eyes always ablaze.
The question will be
Which way will she gaze?

Isaac sat back in his chair and let out a long breath. He had wondered if he was being overly cautious with his approach to the card, but now that prudence paid off. If he interpreted the limerick correctly, the Gorgon card currently residing in his everbag could be the single most dangerous artifact he'd ever heard of, let alone possessed. Just as the severed head of Medusa vanquished the legendary Kraken, this card was a weapon that could potentially defeat anything, so long as the wielder gambled on Medusa's whims. Now the design of the card made sense. Snakes on both sides until she decided which way to face.

The relief that came with discerning the card's true nature eroded with the realization that he had no idea what to do with it. He certainly had enemies out there he wouldn't mind using it on, but had no desire to engage in a battle that had the same odds as a coin flip. Maybe he'd take Jughead's advice and sell the damnable thing. The price it would fetch would be beyond imagination.

There was one additional Black Tarot entry, and curiosity led him to flip the page. Its illustration depicted a jester, easily identifiable by the three-pointed hat and curly-toed shoes, skipping merrily down a cobblestone street. In a cruel juxtaposition, the avenue was lined with prone bodies he assumed to be peasants, dead or dying. A wagon could be seen in the background, stacked high with corpses loaded by three men in black robes. Isaac looked back to the jester, specifically the wide smile he wore. Was this a man reveling in death, or one who remained true to his jovial nature despite it? Isaac didn't like any of these cards and hoped to never encounter more, but this was the first to make him shiver.

The Festering Jester

Alas, dear reader,
I found this one vague.
Simply a man who finds laughter
As he is consumed by the plague.
My interest is piqued.
This one I shall test.
And if it costs me my life
I'll depart with a jest.

It struck Isaac that this was the only limerick written in the first person. He shuffled back through the pages to reread the name of the original author of the journal these entries had been transcribed from.

Ublesh.

It didn't ring any bells. Probably not the name on an official birth certificate or driver's license, Isaac mused. Lefse's sarcastic joke about magicians having silly, fake names popped into his head. While he still agreed with the premise, something about this moniker kept him from laughing. The name felt wrong somehow. It was foul on the tongue. That the only limerick to be in first person was also the last entry struck him as no coincidence. He wondered at the fate of this Ublesh but had no intention of researching the person further. "Don't go looking for the dead, lest you disturb them" would be one of Isaac's mottos if he ever remembered to write any of them down.

Having found the information he sought, the angsty energy that drove his research evaporated. His brain decided that this was also the best time to remind him that it nursed a significant hangover. He replaced the books and exited the study, locking the doors behind him.

Back in his room, he found Lucille sitting in the kitchenette scrolling through information on a tablet. Spreadsheets covered the counter before her. The business of running the Reliquary never slowed.

"Did you find what you were looking for?"

He shrugged. "You know how it is. One can never find out enough."

Lucille waved a hand at him. "Oh, please. Just say you don't want to tell me. You magicians and your secrets," she chided, as if she didn't belong to the club. She gathered her belongings, removing a folded piece of paper and leaving it on the counter. "Note for you."

"Thanks."

"No problem. You checking out today?"

"Yeah.

"It was nice seeing you. Be careful, Isaac." She pointed out the window. "That's where the animals roam."

He absorbed the dual warning-insult with a half-smile. Only after he heard the door click shut behind her did he unfold the note.

Isaac,

I was planning on meeting with you this morning, but business comes first, and frankly, you annoy me. Working for Arrangement? Every time I think you're not a halfwit you prove me wrong.

That scumbag movie producer in California called here looking for you. I'm sure he'll be willing to overpay you to do something stupid since that's what you enjoy.

See you down the road. If you live that long.

—Hellebore

Isaac folded up the note and tapped it repeatedly against the counter as he dwelled on the message. Even in their best of times, his relationship with the Reliquary owner had waxed and waned like the moon—warm and friendly one day and awkwardly contentious the next. Despite her declining to see him, he took some solace in knowing she had softened a bit in her stance. He'd used her study and not been skinned alive by her handmaiden. That qualified as true friendship compared to his past acquaintances.

Speaking of acquaintances, he switched his train of thought to the movie producer. While Isaac begrudgingly got along with the man, he certainly wouldn't defend him against the "scumbag" title. Still, as the note insinuated, doing something stupid of his own volition sounded like a nice change of pace.

Chapter 31
B-Movie Mania

The killer had a giant onion for a head. Maybe not quite giant, but it was still the size of a normal human head, making it one big onion. He wore denim overalls, carried a scythe, and stood superimposed over a field of corn. Above the onion head, the word "Vidalia" was written, and below his feet, in dripping red letters, "He'll do more than make you cry."

Hands clutched behind his back, Isaac studied the framed poster as if it were fine art in a museum. Such posters lined the hall, a veritable gallery of terrible B-movie perfection. A two-foot puppet swathed in bandages titled *The Ventriloquist Mummy*. A window washer who could talk to the dead advertised as *Squeegee Board*. An exceptionally large frog with bloodstained horns called *The Horney Toad*. *Lord of the Springs* chronicled the murderous exploits of an escort and her possessed mattress. Then, finally, the pièce de résistance, a B-movie relic displayed on a raised platform—the protagonist's armored wheelchair from the socially reviled *Nursing Home Zombies*.

The buxom blonde who had let him in had disappeared, disinterested in him almost immediately, leaving him milling about for the home's owner. He didn't have to wait long.

Peter Goss—B-movie producer and director, Hollywood mogul, swinging hedonist, amateur cult leader, and minor league magician—appeared at the railing on the landing above him, smiling from ear to ear with perfect, pearly teeth. Despite the hour, he wore a fluffy bathrobe with matching slippers and a pair of designer sunglasses so tight the arms were absorbed into the fleshy temples of his bald head. He came down the stairs with an unexpected spring to his steps, like a bouncing ball.

"My heathen prayers are answered!" he exclaimed, clutching Isaac by the shoulders. "It's great to see you. We've got great work to get done and little time to do it. You look like shit. I'm sure you've been on the road for a while. And up to no good wherever you stop, eh? Set yourself up in one of the guest rooms. Get cleaned up. Trim your beard. You look like a child going for Halloween as a lumberjack. Did you check out the blonde that let you in? She's my new *assistant*." He nudged Isaac several times in the ribs to ensure the double entendre was understood. "She and I are going to be doing some script reviews for my new movie. I'll meet up with you afterward." The producer rapid-fired the sentences and then scurried off before Isaac even returned the greeting.

An hour later Isaac sat in Peter's office, showered, trimmed, and enamored with the plethora of Goss Productions movie paraphernalia that comprised the private collection. He'd swung around the giant spoon from *Cereal Killer* while wearing the pointed hat from *Dunce Slap* until he accidentally knocked over the glass sphere from *Kingdom of the Crystal Balls*. It suffered a slight crack, and he barely got it back on the display shelf before Peter burst in.

Isaac had known Peter for a couple of years. Prior to his Arrangement gig, he'd taught the producer a few minor cantrips: lighting candles without flame, gusting wind to blow curtains, an invisible knock to make noises in unoccupied rooms, et cetera. All easy, safe, and profitable.

Considering Peter's career revolved around low-budget horror movies, these spells enhanced his reputation considerably. That was one reason Isaac liked the man. He understood his limits and never pushed the boundaries. He knew enough about the magical craft to respect that some things should not be delved into.

Once Peter settled into his plush chair and poured two hefty glasses of scotch, he asked, "So, how do we go about summoning a demon?"

The glass froze inches from Isaac's expectant lips as his respect for the man's intelligence flushed away. He almost slammed the glass angrily on the desk, but figured he'd be better off drinking it. He downed it like a cheap shot and held it out for a refill.

"Oh, okay. You know this stuff is like four hundred dollars a bottle." With a sigh, Peter poured.

"To the rim."

"Right," he said. "What's a few expensive ill-mannered moves between friends, eh?"

Cradling his full glass, Isaac asked the producer to repeat his request, hoping that it would change substantially.

"I want to summon a demon." Peter saw the disappointment on the magician's face and moved quickly to push his case. "Hear me out. Just hear me out. I know that's a big request." Isaac waved his hand at the man to proceed. "I have a problem."

"Go on."

"An asshole."

"I don't do that kind of magic."

Peter continued smiling, his years in show business having erased most of his other expressions. "So, you know I've had this whole dark magic sex cult thing going on lately. It started with impressing a few ladies with the tricks you taught me, mixed with some of my own, and just progressed from there."

"I remember seeing a tabloid cover with a headline of 'Horror movie mogul holds Satanic orgies.'"

Beaming with pride, Peter pulled that exact magazine from his desk. *The B-Movie Maniacs* covered all sorts of dirty Hollywood gossip from below the A list. "I got this up-and-coming actor. I've cast him in a few things and his performances have been solid. He's no Oscar winner but he's got the Hollywood image. Rugged good looks, great physique, fabulous hair, and a five o'clock shadow a blowtorch couldn't get rid of. But the guy really thinks he's the next Brad Pitt. All rebellious and cool and play-by-his-own-rules. That kind of attitude doesn't wash in today's market. And get this, his name is Kirkwood Rockwell." Peter scoffed at the nom de plume. "Anyway, he's been coming to all my functions lately. At first, it was fine. The ladies like him. My investors like him. He's about as magnetic as a B-movie actor can get.

"But all this adulation is going to his head. The last few cult events I've held, he's been snickering in the background and telling other guests I fake everything, and all my tricks are just special effects. As if I'd ever pay for decent special effects. Obviously, I can't have one of my main stars damaging my credibility right in front of me. But he's so popular right now I can't just destroy his career and rail him out of town."

Isaac assumed he saw where this drama was heading. "So, you want to summon a demon to kill this guy?"

For the first time ever, Isaac saw Peter look surprised. "What? Kill him? No. Seriously? Have you done that kind of stuff before?"

"Huh. No. Course not. Continue."

The shock was quickly replaced with wide-eyed excitement. "But that's a good pitch. A Hollywood mogul summons a demon to eliminate corporate rivals." He quickly jotted Isaac's faux pas down. "But back to the matter, I need something from you that will really wow the crowd. I want to knock them dead. Something so intense and powerful that he'll shut the hell up and even if he doesn't no one will listen to him anymore. A grand showy ritual with a demonic finale." He leaned forwards. "I'll triple the fee I paid you last time."

Isaac ran a finger around the rim of his glass as he mulled the request over. Sure, it was a terrible idea, but Isaac had never let that stop him before, and a triple fee eased the early guilt just a bit. While he wouldn't call Peter a friend, exactly, the producer had always been an affable acquaintance and helpful business partner. In addition, the man had enough contacts to eventually find someone else to do it should Isaac refuse. What if he hired some callous psychopath or inept half-wit instead? He opted to buy time. "I'm tired from the drive. Give me the night to think about it."

"You can let me know in the morning." Peter kept on smiling as if he already knew Isaac's answer.

"I'm going to hang out in your library. Books help me think." Isaac started towards the door, stopped, went back to the desk, and took the bottle of scotch. Peter's smile dipped a bit at the corners, but he played along. At that moment, Isaac noticed something peculiar. "Weren't you bald when I got here?"

Previously as hirsute as an egg, Peter's artificially tanned dome now sported a wispy comb-over. As Isaac studied it, the strands periodically shimmered as if the light levels in the room were fluctuating. Which they were not.

"Like it?" Peter ran a hand just above the hair, not actually touching it. "It's a glamour spell I've been practicing."

"Who taught you that?"

"You're not the only person I know with skills. In fact, one of my current members knows quite a few of these minor illusions. And charges less than you for lessons, I might add. Once I really grasp them, I'll be rocking a mohawk and six-pack." The producer patted his belly as Isaac left the room.

* * *

Isaac enjoyed visiting Peter's library. The mogul was an avid collector and all-day sucker for any book about magic, occultism, Heaven, Hell, and such, particularly if it had a scary name or disturbing cover. As a result, most of his collection consisted of fakes and forgeries. In fact, he had thirteen versions of *The Necronomicon* alone, each more worthless than the last. Although many more variations existed, he had stopped at thirteen because the number was ominous. "I have all thirteen copies of *The Necronomicon,*" he'd tell people proudly in his best Bela Lugosi imitation. But Isaac found it entertaining to sift through the shelves and occasionally found a nugget of use in one of the many volumes.

There were very few all-powerful grimoires left in the world. Books that contained powerful magic from cover to cover were beyond worth and generally required much bloodletting or soul-selling to obtain. A much less dangerous endeavor was finding tidbits here and there in more commonly circulated books, even some found in chain bookstores. It might be one useful page out of three hundred and it might only contain the wording for a piece of a spell or the designs for part of a magical circle. It could be maddening at times, like assembling a puzzle with pieces never designed to interlock, but useful and worth the effort to someone with the know-how.

He made two separate towers of books on the atrociously tacky but fabulously soft bearskin rug that adorned the library floor. One was the maybe-hopeful pile, which he would go through first, and the other was the good-for-a-laugh stack. Under normal circumstances, this would keep him busy for hours, but the distraction failed to be. His mind returned repeatedly to the pieces of the Bubba skin mask in his everbag.

When Isaac heard the word "fate," he pretended that the definition was a toxic mixture of coincidence, poor choices, and bad luck. Each of those made him feel better than the reality of events and choices being predetermined. The illusion of free will. It felt foolhardy now, pretending the Arrangement assignments were random. The Bubba mask had led to Jughead revealing its secret to his dumb ass, and now he was here. He wasn't sure where the Black Tarot card, the stupid cat, and the shadow powers fit in, but he felt confident that they'd team up to sit on his head and fart at the appropriate time. Or maybe he'd never know their true purpose.

For now, he had a simple choice. A two-pronged fork in the road. He could honor Peter's request, or he could leave, taking the Arrangement artifacts with him. Fleeing was second nature to him, and he excelled at it. But running from both Arrangement and the Faceless Magician would be far different than escaping them. Eventually, they'd chase him to ground.

Fly on, Albatross.

Isaac couldn't begin to fathom Arrangement's motives, but he knew Bizot's character well enough. The path had to be continued as set. He had to bide his time and hope that even these great powers could make a mistake for him to slip by. The only way out was through. That was Bizot's lesson, to fly on course.

Lastly, a thought he was less than proud of: he really wanted to see how this all played out. Any magician who could resist having such secrets dangled in front of them, well, they weren't much of a magician at all. His curiosity would always trump consequences. His own nature couldn't be fought.

Just as he came to a final decision, a voice behind him said, "Hello."

Chapter 32
THE FAUX APPRENTICE

Isaac spun in surprise, knocking over his maybe-hopeful pile in the process. A woman stood just inside the room, leaning against the door. Hadn't he closed it? He couldn't remember. She smiled at him, seemingly as pleased with herself for startling him as he was irritated with himself for being caught unawares.

"Hello back." Isaac found himself staring, not just because of her attractiveness but also because something seemed… not quite right.

"I'm Julia." She brushed her hair, blonde with bold streaks of black, back from her face. She was dressed rather plainly in stark contrast to her colorful hairdo, with a white cropped tee and a loose, billowy black skirt. A scar across her chin caught his attention, as such imperfections didn't play well in Peter's hiring practices.

"Sorry. I didn't mean to startle you."

Isaac doubted the veracity of this statement and smirked as he set about restacking his books. She had snuck up on him because she could. No more, no less. Some kind of power stood there in the doorway. He could feel it.

"Not the talkative type, huh? That's weird for one of Peter's friends. Usually, I can't get them to shut up. They just brag endlessly about their screenwriting or acting or other forms of prowess." She made a *yuck* face and shivered. "You have a name, or can I just call you 'Hey you'?"

"Isaac."

A look of recognition crossed her face. "Peter's demon-summoning expert. He told me about you."

Isaac grumbled inwardly at the breach of secrecy. "Hardly an expert."

"Not from the way Peter raved about you. Whatever the case, you'll be a step up from my skills. I tried to help him with the research, but it's just too complicated to find all the required information."

"Ah. So, you'd be the illusionist he mentioned?"

"Hardly an illusionist," she said, mimicking him. "I know a few tricks." She crossed to the desk and picked up the bottle of scotch. "Peter broke out the good stuff for you. He must be trying to butter you up. You mind?"

"Help yourself."

Julia took a swig and wiped her mouth with the back of her hand. "I already scanned Peter's library. There's nothing here."

"That's not necessarily true. You just have to take your time while looking."

Thirty minutes later Julia sat next to him with her own pile of books, passing the scotch back and forth, and peppering him with questions about every tome she picked up. Now that the small talk had ceased, Isaac warmed to her a bit. There had been no further introductory conversation, no inquiries about personal lives or origins, and no polite social exchange. She simply joined him in drinking, reading, and most importantly, distracting him from weighty decisions.

"The Malleus Maleficarum." She, at the very least, pronounced it correctly. "Sounds sinister."

"The title translates from Latin as *The Hammer of the Witches*," he told her, and she seemed impressed by the ominous title. Isaac frowned like a failed tutor because he knew the book was rubbish. "A medieval tome written to help the Catholic Church catch witches and then... hammer them... I guess. It's complete nonsense from a spellcraft perspective."

She picked up another. *"The Deathronomicon."*

Isaac snorted. "Peter still has that? He's always been desperate to get his hands on a real copy of *The Necronomicon*—which doesn't exist, before you ask—and he ordered one online. That's what showed up instead. It's just page after page of slightly altered heavy metal music lyrics."

Julia giggled drunkenly as she moved on to the next one. *"Satan's Secret Minions."*

"Now, that one's just stupid. It identifies Satan's minions as rock music, drugs, sex, violence, blah blah blah. It doesn't name a single actual servant or agent of Satan. Not one. Not even the popular ones. Or even the little old lady who's actually in charge of the mortal plane." He paused then, realizing he probably said a little too much, with a little too much conviction.

Julia didn't catch his faux pas and looked disappointed as she set the book aside. "I had a weird feeling when I picked it up. Thought maybe I found something real." She stood up, wobbled a bit with a laugh, and smoothed out her skirt. "Well, Isaac, it was certainly fun hanging with you. I've had enough booze and research for one night."

"Likewise."

After she left, Isaac picked up *Satan's Secret Minions.* Nothing jumped out at him from its design, and a quick flip through the pages brought no revelations. Still, Julia's reaction was enough to pique his interest, and he slipped it into his bag before he continued his slog through the rest.

* * *

The next morning came, and Isaac was dragged from his bearskin rug bed by Peter, who was as eager as a kid on Christmas morning. Peter barely gave him time to brush his teeth before leading him to the basement, excited to show the magician the renovations that had transformed what had been a bad-movie-themed hedonistic Hollywood playroom into a cult-themed hedonistic torture dungeon playroom.

Gone were the photos of Peter posing with B- and C-level celebrities, bench-warming professional athletes, disgraced politicians, and porn stars. Gone was the private theater where Isaac had once been treated to an advance screening of Peter's *Nursing Home Zombies*, a film so awful Isaac had telekinetically fouled the movie reel to stop it.

Replacing these items were a plethora of replica torture devices, a rack of sadomasochistic sexual toys, and generic satanic paraphernalia (a stuffed ram's head, crudely painted pentagrams, and other meaningless symbols). At one end of the room stood a raised platform, which had been a dance floor in Peter's younger days. Now it formed the base of a large altar and Isaac assumed it was where Peter performed all his tricks, with his assembled followers lined up in front. The floors, walls, and even the ceiling had been covered with cheap tiles designed to mimic natural stone. Isaac supposed that it did look pretty much like a dungeon, even though he knew if he stomped his foot hard, the "stone" would probably crack.

"What do you think? Pretty cool, huh?" Peter poured coffee at the bar, the only original structure he had left intact.

Isaac examined a fake guillotine with a blade as sharp as a dustpan. He moved on to the iron maiden, flicked one of the spikes, and snickered when it went *sprooong* like a kicked doorstopper. "Well, it's probably good none of these are real. Don't want anyone hurting themselves."

"Exactly. If the maiden were real, you know damn well someone would pass out drunk in it. Imagine when that hits the news the next day."

Isaac nearly said, "You would care?" but bit his tongue.

Ever the businessman, Peter jumped straight to it. "So, where shall we be summoning my horned Hellspawn? I assumed the stage would be the best spot."

"Yes, it would be. But it's not going to be a Hellspawn. Nothing from Hell."

"Aw, come on," Peter whined, a disappointed child. "I hoped I could ask it questions, and it would reply in a deep, scary voice. Ladies love to be scared." He gave Isaac a creepy wink.

"Whatever we summon won't be able to talk. It'll just stand there being incredibly enraged at you for pulling it through dimensions against its will."

Either Peter ignored the part about the unearthly monster being mad at him, or he didn't care. "It won't even be able to talk?"

"This isn't an interview, Peter. You can't call for questions from the audience. If we pull something through that is capable of speech, that means it's more intelligent. That severely increases the threat level. But don't worry, I'm sure it'll make noise. It'll hiss or roar or scream. You'll wish you never heard such sounds."

"Excellent. Sound effects are good." Peter rubbed his hands together, still planning this endeavor like a movie scene. "And it'll look scary? Fearsome? Horrifying? But not be really dangerous, right?"

"Fearsomely horrifying but not dangerous," Isaac repeated, hoping it would sound just as ridiculous the second time it was said out loud. Again, it did not affect the producer. "There's no dimension full of teddy bears out there, Peter. If it looks dangerous it'll be dangerous. Anything strong enough to survive being pulled between dimensions is going to be dangerous." This did cause Peter to balk a bit. "But that's what a protective circle is for. It'll keep it contained as long as no one messes with it."

"This is going to be fan-fucking-tastic," Peter said, and he downed his coffee in one gulp. "So, we're set? You'll do it?"

Isaac sighed. "I'll do it. I'll set the ritualistic circle on the stage. Only you will be allowed near it. I'll write out the summoning spell for you. You'll memorize it word for word. Syllable for syllable. You'll summon in something, let everyone get a good look, then you'll reverse it for the banishment spell and send it back home. That's it."

Peter beamed, gripped Isaac by both shoulders and shook him violently before embracing him in a surprisingly powerful bear hug. And in that genuinely happy moment, Isaac nearly changed his mind. He wanted very badly to tell Peter what a terrible idea this was—warn him again of the incredible cost any mistake could bring, no matter how minor. But in the end, Isaac kept his mouth shut. Peter was a grown man and a knowledgeable dabbler in the Other World. They were occasional business acquaintances, after all, not true friends. He couldn't afford to develop a reputation as a magician who refused magical tasks, not if he wanted to keep working when he eventually got out from under Arrangement and other shadows.

"I want the money up front. In case you get eaten."

Disengaging his hug, Peter nodded, still smiling, still fearless. In his world money and power allowed for anything. He had grown used to life without consequences. "Deal. And I'll throw in a few weeks at my timeshare in Cabo."

"Sounds fine," Isaac said. "I'll need a day to get everything done. And you'll need time to memorize your lines."

"Memorize my lines," Peter said wistfully. "I've never been on the other end of that statement." He started towards the door.

"One more thing," Isaac called after him. "I met your illusionist last night. What's her story?"

"Kind of an odd bird. She showed up at one of my parties a few weeks ago. I figured she was just another small-town girl looking for the ladder to Hollywood. Then every time I saw her there were changes. Different hair. Different eye colors. It took me a bit to catch on to the glamour spells. So, she's joined my crew here for the time being. I get the feeling she'll move on sooner or later. Strikes me as kind of a nomad, like you. But she shows a few tricks at my get-togethers and tells people she's my apprentice. The other members eat that up."

* * *

That afternoon found Isaac setting up the cultist playroom. The stage proved surprisingly perfect for Isaac's needs. Flat, smooth, and easy to paint. Any kind of imperfection, uneven lump or crack, could have created a fatal flaw in his magical design. He took this as a good omen as he started copying the summoning circle from the mask pieces.

He opted to use plain red paint with black outlining. Bold in color, it gave the design a theatrical nudge that would resemble blood to a crowd of amateur cultists. There were certainly more powerful options, such as rare inks, powdered bone, or real blood, but those required considerable time and cost to acquire.

All these considerations were deal breakers for Peter, an impatient frugalist. It was mostly inconsequential. Paint would suffice. The power came from the accuracy of the design. The rarer supplies would just reinforce it.

He had just finished the finer details when he realized he wasn't alone. "You're pretty sneaky," he said to Julia, who was peering over his shoulder.

"I've always been light on my feet. You should see me dance. I can even make high heels silent." Isaac wasn't sure if she was kidding, so he went with an awkward snort rather than a full laugh. "Looks like Peter talked you into it, eh?"

Isaac nodded. "You attending it?"

"Absolutely. I've never actually seen one performed before. Can't pass up the chance. You?"

"I should, but Peter refused. He has a rule about new people attending his ceremonies. He says it helps keep members of the press and people he doesn't trust out. If he lets me in, that'll just be more fuel for his in-house detractors who already hate his rules."

"Seems like a bad idea."

"Of course it's a bad idea. Having a cult is a bad idea. Being a magician is a bad idea. There's nothing about our lives that says, 'good idea.'" He looked up at her. "That said, what the hell are you doing tied up with this silly cult crap?"

Julia glanced around for potential eavesdroppers. "I heard rumors that Peter wasn't just a fake magician, that he actually knew some things. It's hard to find people like us. Joining the cult was the fastest way to gain his trust, and once I taught him a glamour, he let me in pretty quick. Why he wastes his time with these cultists is beyond me."

"Don't care for your fellow members?"

She crossed her arms. "Not remotely. They're a bunch of talentless sheep who desperately crave forbidden knowledge but lack the skill to find it. They need people like Peter to lead them by the nose and make them feel special."

Isaac didn't disagree with anything she said, but silently took umbrage with the term "sheep." Using it in such a manner implied a lofty level of arrogance—a level he had come to distrust. "Yet here we are. I'm setting it up and you're watching with the crowd."

Julia's eyes narrowed, and for a moment he expected a caustic response. Instead, she agreed, albeit begrudgingly. "I suppose you're right. At the end of the day, we all answer to someone." She turned to leave.

"Hey," Isaac called after her. "Some last-minute advice. If anything goes wrong, anything at all, run for the hills, and don't look back."

Chapter 33
PANDEMONIUM

Through all the pre-party arrangements, Isaac kept out of the way and didn't emerge from the library until the soiree rocked in full swing. While the crowd wasn't diverse, it was certainly colorful. There were business suits, evening gowns, black-clad goths, and plenty in the carefree style of look-at-me artists. It reminded Isaac of an amateur version of the Reliquary.

One trait that Isaac had always cherished was his almost total anonymity. Not handsome enough to draw gazes nor ugly enough to turn them, he could usually attend a social gathering and not be remembered at all. This proved the case here and he felt grateful for it. He wandered from one end of the party to the other and drew attention from no one. Peter stayed too busy being host-slash-master of the dark arts to bother with him, and Julia had only given him a curt nod when he passed her.

Eventually, he discovered the jerk that set all this nonsense in motion, Mr. Doucherock Smellgood, or whatever his name was. Rockwell, that was it, Isaac remembered with a finger snap. Isaac didn't possess the ability to see auras, but knew if he could, then the actor's color would be the piss-yellow of ego and arrogance.

He certainly had the look of an A-lister and channeled a privileged vibe as he strutted around the party like royalty allowing commoners to bask in his presence. He shook hands with the suits, smiled slyly at the women, kissed the hands of the most attractive, and whispered things to make them giggle. Peter's rounds of socializing finally brought the two face-to-face for a lifeless greeting with barely concealed mutual contempt. When they parted, Isaac heard Rockwell say to his female sycophants, "Maybe he'll do some card tricks tonight," which elicited a round of laughter.

Isaac decided he disliked every aspect of Rockwell. He scratched his nose, moving two fingers across the tip, left to right. A telekinetic tap flowed across the room and tilted the actor's glass in the same direction, splashing the drink across his chest.

For a split second, the actor's suave persona crumbled, before one of his admirers stepped forwards and, with drunken dramatics, slowly unbuttoned his wet shirt and then threw it aside—much to the delight of the crowd of onlookers. So, with much hooting and hollering, a grinning Rockwell moved his entourage outside to the pool, with many of them losing articles of clothing along the way, and Isaac went to the bar for a refill to drown his defeat.

"I saw that." Julia slid up next to him. When he played dumb, she said, "You somehow made him spill his drink. I don't think it worked out like you wanted. Unless you were trying to make him sexier? Maybe you could cast a spell to make his leather pants bulge more?"

Not seeing a point in pretending anymore, Isaac fessed up with a chuckle. "If I knew such a spell, I'd be a successful B-movie actor instead of a wandering magician."

She crossed her arms. "It was a little too subtle. You should have just aimed for his face. Nothing sexy about a bloody nose."

* * *

Just before the witching hour, Peter began ushering the partygoers to the basement. They dutifully lined up and exchanged cell phones for cheap robes. It would have made an effective B-movie visual, all of them cloaked in black descending to a demonic séance, if not for the occasional drunken giggling or stumbling.

Isaac managed to catch Peter before he descended. "I still think I should be down there with you."

"No. I told you. We never allow first-timers down to the real party. I can't change my own rules. It'll just give the doubters a new conspiracy to hold against me and ruin any awe I achieve tonight."

"Fine. Be careful. Do it exactly as we rehearsed."

The mogul patted Isaac on the cheek several times, downed his drink, and handed him the empty glass. "I got this. You worry too much. I handle Hollywood agents daily. This is small potatoes compared to them."

* * *

Isaac spent the ritual time in Peter's library anxiously flipping through *Satan's Secret Minions* for the umpteenth time. Julia may have been right about the book. He could feel it now, a small tingle of some kind of knowledge, either expertly concealed or of such inconsequential power that it would be akin to finding one grain of sand. He'd even lit an old-fashioned oil lamp and studied the book by its flickering light. Flames sometimes revealed that which electricity wouldn't, but still nothing.

Giving in to frustration, he closed the book and shoved it in his everbag. After pacing the room several times, he pulled out Jughead. While he wasn't in the mood for the vessel's acerbic wit, he needed a distraction from the silence. As usual, the jug came out spewing vulgarities at the rate a swimmer would gulp air after a deep dive. Isaac weathered the storm gratefully.

With the initial outburst completed, the jug asked more civilly, "So what's going on today?"

As if he sat in a confessional, Isaac blabbed every detail from the moment he arrived at Peter's house to now. Jughead absorbed the information, only responding after Isaac fell silent.

"Wow. Let me start by saying how satisfying it is to me that there's a black magic orgy going on and you're the only one in the house that didn't get invited. They know you're here, have laid eyes on you, and still said 'no.' That makes my day. But on to the more chilling news. Are the sex cultists summoning the beast before or after their sexcapades? Or maybe during? During would be the most interesting time to do it. Maybe not the safest, though."

"Before. They should be wrapping up soon if Peter listened to me." He glanced at the clock as if there were a schedule to be followed.

"I'm surprised you took my advice and sold the ritual. Although selling it and then hanging around for the buyer to use it doesn't do much for the whole safety aspect. You can't spend the money if you don't survive."

"I don't really spend money anyway. I'm stashing for retirement."

Jughead scoffed. "You should be so lucky."

Then Isaac felt it. Something shifted in the air as if a giant mouth had expelled a slow, fetid breath. A loud bang came next, like a heavy piece of furniture toppling.

Something had gone wrong.

Then the screams started, echoing up through the vents. Not the rollercoaster screams of the amused, but true cries of terror. Isaac sighed.

Something had gone really wrong.

Jughead sensed it as well and celebrated. "I knew it! You fucked it all up! All those dirty, sexy, naked bastards in the basement will die, and it's at least fifty percent your fault. It won't take long until it comes after you. I can't wait to see this jilted Pandemonium fiend tear you a whole row of new assholes. Turn me towards the door so I can see it coming. And then, if you don't mind, as it's ripping you to pieces, try to use your telekinesis to move me around so I always have a good vantage point of the carnage being wrought upon you."

"You said these things weren't very dangerous."

"I know I said that, but I was always smart enough to not let them run around free. Remember, the quicker you surrender to inevitable fate, the happier I'll be."

"Sorry, Jug, but it's time to go." The spirit's fresh stream of vulgarities cut off when Isaac shoved it back into the everbag and withdrew Wilma in the same motion.

He left the library but paused on the stairs when a new noise began. Like a cicada call in stereo, a deafening chattering noise rose from below and emanated from the very walls. It almost drowned out the screams. Almost. He hurried his way to the basement door and trained the shotgun on it.

The door remained closed. He stood alone on the first floor.

No one had gotten out.

Stunned, Isaac froze, unsure of how to proceed. In the event something like this happened, he'd expected a horde of terrified cultists to stampede out of the basement. That, in turn, would draw the Pandemonium beast out as well. Outside of the basement, he had more room and more options to deal with it. But if no one even made it to the damn door... His thought trailed off to visions of a cramped slaughter being wrought in the darkness under his very feet. He had no clue about the scale of the carnage or even if there was anyone left to save. And if the beast killed that quickly, maybe it was beyond his abilities altogether. His brain scurried through half-baked ideas until fate sped up his decision. The door burst open, and one survivor rushed out.

Julia.

Blood streaked her face, and her robes were tattered as if pulled away from grasping hands. She slammed the door and leaned her weight against it. Isaac noted she was justifiably wired but oddly composed. Hurried, but not panicked. "It's loose. What do we do?" she panted.

"No one else..."

"Even made it to the stairs," she finished.

He winced. "Peter?"

"I don't know. I lost sight of him in the chaos."

Isaac barely had time to process the news before he noticed movement around the door. Thin, pinkish strands, about the size of spaghetti, squirmed through the thin gap between the door and the jamb. They moved fast, subdividing and spreading like ivy across the ceiling and walls, a red ooze dripping from them and leaving oily smear marks as they grew. Not worms. Not snakes. Isaac's stomach twisted when he realized what they were.

"It's human skin, isn't it?" Julia asked, more awed than afraid. The screams from the basement faded as the cicada call intensified.

"Yeah. Yuck." He steadied Wilma. "You should clear out of here. Run now and don't look back."

"You could use me." From within her robes she produced a knife, clicking the blade open. "I'm not helpless."

"These weapons are probably useless. I just need to get its attention when it comes up. If you want to help, at least get out of the house. If it gets by me, then you can show it how not-helpless you are."

Isaac anticipated more argument, but she acquiesced and left. Seconds later she shouted his name. With a curse, Isaac backed across the room until he could see her in the foyer while keeping the basement door in his peripheral.

The skin vines had grown throughout the house by crawling up through the air vents. Contrary to Isaac's first assessment, their movement was not random. The vines were encasing the doors and windows in the fleshy webs of a crafty spider. Much craftier than Isaac anticipated.

"Use your knife. Hack them down."

"I tried." In a demonstration, she made three slashes across the vines, cutting them easily. Each quickly grew back, the severed ends seeking each other out like a magician's rope trick. Exasperated, she reached to tear them, but Isaac shouted a warning not to touch them.

There were no more screams now. The cicada call subsided, and from within the eerie silence came the sound of gnawing, as if an army of mice were working on the basement door. Whiffs of acrid smoke followed, billowing in small plumes with a huffing-puffing rhythm. Dozens of things with tiny mouths were eating and burning their way through the door. Isaac waved Julia to his side and took aim at the door.

Fist-sized insects, spider-like with crustacean shells and wicked pincers, crawled through the splintered wood and scurried along the flesh vines. They had distorted humanoid faces and mouths of needle-sized teeth. From their lips oozed a green fluid that sizzled where it dripped as they scuttled sideways like crabs along the vines.

"That's what was summoned?" he whispered.

"No. There was one big one, but it had those little ones crawling around on it."

Grimacing in disgust, Isaac motioned towards the stairs and the pair slowly inched backwards like hikers slipping away from a sleeping bear. Even these measured movements gave them away, and dozens of tiny eyes swiveled to them.

"Shit." As the word left Isaac's mouth, so did the bile leave theirs. Ejected like jets from water guns, the acidic saliva would have sprayed across him if Julia hadn't yanked him out of the way. The streams fell just short, pitting the floor at his feet with an acid stench. He nodded his thanks to her and raised Wilma to his shoulder.

The range of the shotgun proved superior to that of Pandemonium crab spittle. Adhered to the vines, they were easy targets, and each blast of buckshot brought one or two down in a rain of shells and green ooze. What the crabs did have were numbers, and Isaac quickly found himself reloading as they retreated up the stairs.

The rapid growth of the flesh webs petered out in the stairwell, possibly due to a lack of raw materials left from the basement slaughter. The crabs stopped at the end of the line, like trains out of track. They hissed and spit in frustration, but Isaac and Julia were out of their range when they made it to the library. She went first to the window. "Figures a guy who makes horror movies puts bars on the second floor. We should barricade the door."

"No. Leave it open. We want whatever it is to come through without damaging the wood."

"We do?"

He threw aside the bearskin rug. Underneath it, on the hardwood floor, he'd painted a small circle of protection. "When the demon comes in, step inside. Do not step out or touch any part of it."

"I saw that lesson downstairs. We're just going to wait for it?"

"Trust me. I know what I'm doing."

"Really? A basement full of corpses says otherwise," she snapped.

Isaac started to retort, couldn't, and let her have that one. From the hallway, the crabs watched them like angry guard dogs, chattering and clicking, holding them at bay for their master.

A crash came then, which Isaac assumed to be the remains of the basement door breaking down. Next were heavy footsteps, stumbling up the stairs like a noisy drunk. Finally, it came into view.

It was Rockwell.

Sort of.

Covered in blood, the actor moved stiffly, as if auditioning for a zombie role. His eyes were wide and unblinking, his mouth opening and closing, working to issue a scream that wouldn't come. Riding piggyback on him was the Pandemonium demon.

No. Not riding him, Isaac realized. The thing bristled with centipede legs, some thick as fingers and some thin as hair. Each of these had wrapped around Rockwell's limbs and then wormed into his flesh. The poor sap was more of a puppet than a horse.

The thing reared up over Rockwell's shoulder and locked its insectoid eyes on Isaac and Julia. It had a head reminiscent of a newborn baby's, a mouth full of tiny mandibles, and segmented eyes that glittered. Large mantis claws extended up. As they watched, a gore-slick larva fell from its body and one of the crab things was tearing its way through the skin.

"Damn. That is a lot more horrifying than I thought it would be," Isaac said.

"What did you think it would look like?"

"Like a big teddy bear."

Before Julia could ask if he was kidding, the demon rushed down the hall, limbs flailing clumsily, as if still learning to operate its new host. Instinctively Julia backed up, but Isaac grabbed her and kept her inside the circle.

When it hit the library doorway, Isaac's hidden spell, inspired by the drowning pillar and using inverted symbols from the basement circle, activated. Along the doorframe, the magical runes, done in barely visible pencil, flared to life, flames tracing the markings and arcing across poor Rockwell and his new master.

The actor's skin bubbled and blistered as his blood boiled. While he was unable to scream, the demon did enough for both. Its cicada cries were deafening as steam hissed through its segmented carapace and its limbs sizzled and cracked. Its crab children somehow shared the pain, and along the hallway, they dropped off the ceiling and walls and lay twitching. The vines themselves glowed from the inside as if their cores were red-hot, before shriveling like dried weeds.

"There, see. It is stupid, just like I thought," Isaac said.

Chapter 34
THE GORGON

Dumb though it may have been, it proved much tougher than the magician had anticipated. Although the host appeared fatally damaged, the demon kept the body upright, stumbled into the room, and brought down one of its bladelike claws. The protective circle did its job, and the attack stopped abruptly, as if it had hit an invisible wall.

The claw snapped in twain, and Isaac started to stick out a taunting tongue until he saw the broken end spiral across the room and shatter the oil lamp that he'd left lit on Peter's desk.

"Ah, damn it."

The flaming oil spread quickly across the books and assorted screenplays and then dripped onto the tossed-aside bear rug. Within seconds half of the room blazed.

"Will the circle protect us?" Julia asked, putting a hand over her nose from the smoke.

"Not when the floor burns out from under us."

While Rockwell appeared to be dead, somehow the cicada demon soldiered on. Having a deceased host hampered its coordination and it spun around the room in blind fury, venting its rage on every object in the room with its remaining claw.

"When I step out, run for the hallway, and don't stop until you're outside," Isaac said.

After she nodded, he hopped out of the circle, telekinetically lifted the bearskin rug, and threw it over the insectoid head like a flaming shroud.

Then they were running. Dying crabs littered their path, and shells crunched underfoot. On the first floor, not far from the front door, they found a body. Someone managed to crawl from the basement.

It was Peter, unconscious and covered in blood. Isaac couldn't imagine how the man survived, but then, the producer had always been lucky. His robes had fallen open, revealing several deep gashes to his torso.

Peter proved surprisingly heavy, like an oversized medicine ball with limbs. It took the pair of them, each pulling a leg, to drag the producer. The flesh vines on the front door, now smoldering as their creator burned, snapped like frayed rope, and in short order they were outside, gulping fresh air.

They propped Peter against the side of a parked Mercedes and Isaac took his pulse. Weak but steady, same as the man's breathing.

"Shit. I can't help but feel like this is my fault," Isaac said dourly. Next to him, Julia made a series of faces that suggested she was trying to think of a way to assuage his guilt but never came up with anything worth saying. "So, what happened down there?"

"Rockwell. Peter had him right up by the stage. He really wanted to impress him. When the demon popped into view, Rockwell reached into the circle. I guess he wanted to expose it as a trick, wave a hand through the special effects hologram, but it served as a bridge for the demon to escape. Paid the price, didn't he…"

"They all did. This was a terrible—" Before he could say "idea," the cicada demon came through one of the upstairs walls like a flaming comet.

It landed in the yard, bereft now of its human host, and scuttled towards them, leaving a trail of singed grass. Isaac lined up Wilma, nearly made a crack about how dumb the bug continued to be, and then swore loudly when it went underground. The soil parted for it like water for a fish and it disappeared into the earth.

Seconds stretched out. Nothing moved. They watched the lawn like swimmers waiting for a great white to breach.

The beast burst through the ground behind them in a spray of soil and grass. Isaac spun to aim Wilma, realizing he'd vastly underestimated the creature.

The stint below the earth had rejuvenated it. Its size had increased and already the broken talon had begun to regrow. The blazing carapace had cooled and now looked to be even harder than before, like forged iron. It rose, chittering and hissing with rage, its segmented eyes glittering and its jaws clacking.

Isaac fired. At this range his aim was irrelevant, but so was the buckshot. The pellets pinged off its shell like so much thrown gravel, and it retaliated with a talon swipe that missed taking off his head by mere inches. He stumbled and fell, barely managing to scramble back to avoid the striking talon that impaled deep into the earth between his feet.

The demon leaned in, the baby face elongating out, mouth open, striking like a snake. Isaac brought Wilma up in time to block it and the needle teeth sank into the stock of the weapon, splintering wood. With a twist of its head, the shotgun was ripped from him and sent spinning away. Disarmed, he lay prone before the beast.

Movement caught the corner of his eye. A person materialized next to the battling pair. The beast slithered its head in that direction.

It wasn't a person, Isaac realized. Just a silhouette, an ethereal outline in the air. Dark crimson in color, it glistened as if wet, like a blood-soaked shadow. It stood there, wavering just enough to draw attention.

Neck snapping like an angry cobra, the beast lashed out. When the jaws contacted the figure, it burst apart, blood splashing to the earth like a popped water balloon. The beast tilted its head to and fro in confusion.

Fifteen or so feet away, another of these crimson shapes popped into being. The demon hissed and rushed at it, disregarding the helpless magician in its rage. As it ran, one of its legs stomped his midsection, taking the wind from him. Gasping, he rolled over to watch its path. This time the beast swung its mantis claw in an arc and, just as before, the silhouette came apart in a spray.

Catching on, Isaac scanned the yard for Julia. As he suspected, she stood nearby, arm outstretched, two fingers dripping blood. When the beast destroyed the second figure, she brought her knife to a third finger, opening the tip. She aimed her hand again, this time further away, and yet another popped into view. Again, the insectoid fiend launched itself after this new movement.

By the time Isaac caught his breath and clambered to his feet, Julia was summoning her fourth illusion. Only this time the beast didn't take the bait. It paused, head twitching back and forth, until it spun to face Julia. Maybe it wasn't so dumb, Isaac thought as the beast tore across the grass at the woman.

Julia proved nimble. She ducked and dodged the assaults, hopping back or stepping aside like a matador when it charged. The only flaw in her strategy was that she had no form of counterattack. Eventually, she'd tire. Isaac doubted the beast would.

Maloc's truck sat at the far end of the property, to not visually taint the line of guests' luxury cars. A fair distance, but he might make it at a sprint, and if Julia kept the beast distracted.

Guilt at the thought hit him. Time seemed to slow as he looked from Julia, still dancing with the demon, to Peter's burning mansion. As if to add karmic emphasis, several windows shattered from the heat, and the flames feasted on the new air with a *whoomp*.

He'd grown numb to the catastrophes he routinely left behind. In each situation, he'd been able to convince himself that it was always beyond his control. Everyone who had died had simply been fated to do so.

But this time, this mess was all on him. All the death. Dozens of partygoers. Rockwell. All entirely his fault. None of this would have happened without his cooperation.

He was damn good at walking away from piles of the dead. But he wasn't ready to start leaving behind the living.

This moral epiphany stalled out before it reached steely resolve, as he realized he had nothing that could kill the damn thing. He normally prided himself on planning ahead, but he remained grossly unprepared for this moment.

Across the yard, Julia looked near collapse as she ducked behind an evergreen. The mantis claw tore into it in a spray of pine needles and bark.

Think, he ordered himself. A dozen scenarios shot through his brain. Instantly he knew multiple ways to distract, annoy, tease, or tickle the beast, but not a single method of putting it down permanently before it tore them to bits. There was nothing in his bag of tricks capable of taking down the fiend.

Except he knew that wasn't true at all.

The Gorgon.

The Black Tarot wasn't used in the same manner as its real-world counterpart. There was no spreading them on a table to be interpreted, no insight into the past, present, or future to be gained. The Black Tarot was designed to warp reality, with the effects being subtle or catastrophic depending on how each card was dealt, straight or inverted.

He pulled it from the everbag. On both sides of the card, a ball of snakes undulated. Reptilian eyes glowed and forked tongues flicked. Both were rear views of the famed Medusa head. He knew when he played the card, one of those sides would reveal its true face. He had a fifty-fifty shot.

"Hey!" he shouted.

The Pandemonium fiend turned from Julia to this new challenge, hissed, and made a beeline towards him. He stood his ground and held the card up like a crossing guard's stop sign. Instinctively, he shut his eyes, which he knew to be a mistake. One can't win a coin toss without looking at the results. When he forced his lids open, he saw that the demon had stopped before him, its snakelike neck stretched so that the demented baby face could stare in wonder at the powerful artifact he held. He tore his gaze from the fiend to the card.

A set of eyes on each side. He could think of no other way to play it, other than as a supernatural game of Russian roulette.

Long seconds felt eternal. He waited, convinced that the snakes on his side would part, like hair being combed aside, revealing her face. Would Medusa be beautiful? Savage? Horrifying? Would skin hardening to stone be painful? But the mass of snakes remained. Finally, he looked at the demon and knew Medusa's choice.

The flesh around its segmented eyes darkened as if being dusted by gray powder. It spread around the bulbous cheeks to the jaws, freezing the demonic face in place. The gray continued, through the carapace to its countless legs and finally the upraised talon. Within moments the beast went stiff as stone. A perfectly crafted statue stood before him.

Isaac let out the breath he'd been holding in a long, slow exhale, which ended with a gasp when the Gorgon card twitched in his hand. As if aflame, the edges curled inwards, the card folding repeatedly on itself until it was little more than a wisp. Disintegrated completely, it blew from his fingers with the wind.

Julia retrieved Wilma and walked a circle around the insectoid statue, prodding it with the barrel. Between huffing breaths, she mumbled, "I don't believe it. I just don't believe it."

"Yeah. It wasn't supposed to go that way."

His voice snapped her out of her reverie, and she glanced at the flaming mansion. "Isn't this usually how your jobs end up?"

The question hit him like a load of bricks. He wasn't insulted at the insinuation, more stunned at the accuracy of it. "Excuse me?"

Julia winced. "I guess I just slipped up."

"I'd say so." He sighed. "Where'd you learn that about me?"

"I overheard it at the Athenaeum. People gossiping about the Albatross."

Isaac shook his head. "Arrangement. You work for Arrangement."

"Yeah. The Voice sent me out here a few weeks ago. I've been playing along as a Goss cult member. Peter mentioned your name, so I put two and two together."

"Why are you here? What's the assignment?"

"I was told to stay here until the statue arrived. I didn't understand, so I waited for Peter to buy one or commission one to be carved, but nothing ever happened. Until now." She flicked a finger against the stone demon. "I guess it was all leading up to tonight. Frankly, I'm glad it's over. I've been itching to get out of here. I wish the Voice had sent you earlier."

"It didn't send me." The flames billowed, reflecting red and orange on the statue. "This was freelance."

"Oh. How did it know it'd all work out like this?"

His head swirled at her question and reached no answer worth vocalizing. There was some solace to be had in knowing Julia didn't have any better understanding of Arrangement than he did. He shook the confusion away. Now was not the time to dwell on it.

The burning house glowed like a two-story beacon. It could probably be seen for miles. Some observers would eventually call 911, if they hadn't already.

"Let's check on Peter," he said.

Julia shook her head. "You go ahead. I'm outta here."

"Seriously? I thought you were friends."

She scoffed. "I kept an eye on him because that was the job. The job's over. He's not my problem anymore."

"That's a bit heartless."

"Maybe. This is only my third job. I'm going to go celebrate surviving a team-up with the Albatross. I'm not hanging around to push my luck."

"Whatever. You got a ride?"

"There's a small parking lot here of fancy cars with no owners. I'll take my pick. See you around."

Isaac watched her jog away before heading to Peter. The man lay where they'd left him, eyes closed and unmoving. Isaac checked his pulse and found it steadier than before. Still weak but rhythmic. This struck him as odd. He was no paramedic, but he felt sure that wasn't how deep lacerations and blood loss worked. As he pondered this, one of the producer's eyes cracked open just a slit, before flitting closed again.

"You asshole!" he barked. "I saw you open your eye."

Both now opened just enough to see but not enough to erase the pained wincing on his face. "Yeah. I'm awake. I figured it was best to play dead to avoid the demon killing me or a lecture from you." He looked frantically about. "What happened to our dread beastie?"

Isaac motioned over his shoulder. "I turned it into a stone statue. It's in the yard next to your house…" Several burning beams crashed down behind him. "Where your house used to be."

"A statue? How'd you manage that?"

"Pure skill and intricate planning," Isaac said. "Listen, if anyone comes for it, just let them take it. Don't interfere or negotiate."

Peter nodded. "I didn't listen to you earlier and we see how that worked out."

Faintly, the sounds of sirens could be heard. "Help is on the way. Don't move. You'll be fine."

"Sure. Nothing multiple surgeries, extensive rehabilitation, and lifelong psychological therapy can't fix." He frowned. Isaac had never seen the expression on the man's face before, and it was probably as close to grief as he could get. "Look, I know you thought this was a bad idea. You said it several times. In my defense, you could have done a better job of trying to warn me, and been more assertive, but I digress. I should have listened. So right now, I'm giving you my word, I'm done with magic. No spells. No pretend cult. No demons. Done."

"Well, that's…"

"And I'm done with B movies." The producer ran right over Isaac's sentence. "No more schlock horror or fake exploitive documentaries or edgy-and-cool-but-probably-still-really-offensive films. I'm turning over a new leaf. I'm going to be a better person."

"I see. I think…"

"Oh, shut up. You better get going. I'll come up with a cover story and never mention you were here or that you burned down my house." He patted Isaac on the arm, leaving a bloody handprint. "But thanks for saving me. If you ever need my help, just call. I mean that. Call first. Long-distance. Don't just show up. Don't come anywhere near me without warning. Send me an email from several hundred miles away and I'll do what I can to help."

Isaac nodded and stood to leave but paused to ask a nagging question. "How exactly did you survive down there?"

"It must have thought I was dead after the first attack. When it turned its slice-and-dice rage on my guests, I crawled into the summoning circle. I figured that if the circle was designed to keep it in, it would also keep it out."

Isaac deflated at the news. The producer wasn't wrong, but he missed a key component in his understanding of magical circles. While a summoning circle would serve as protection in the event its occupant escaped, it remained an open portal to the point of origin. Climbing into one could theoretically bring exposure to countless foreign dimensional energies. Isaac studied him for any obvious signs. Maybe it was his imagination combined with the bad lighting, but it almost looked like the chest wounds healed a bit during their conversation. He couldn't be sure. With only conjecture at this point, Isaac could do little else to investigate. He could only hope he was wrong as he said goodbye.

When he got to the truck, Testiculies lay curled in a cozy ball on the passenger seat. The cat never stirred as Isaac clambered in, started the engine, and pulled out of the winding driveway. On he slept until Isaac, annoyed with his comfort, poked him, and said, "There was a big fight. Where were you?" In response, Testiculies rolled over and stretched all four legs in the leisurely satisfying manner that only felines can achieve.

Tired and grumpy, Isaac desperately wanted to pull over but pushed ahead, determined to put distance between himself and the blood-soaked fiasco. Deep down, he knew he could get further away from his latest mess, but there was no running from his real predicament.

Needing to repay what might be an insurmountable debt, he'd taken the position with Arrangement at the behest of his former master. Knowing the character of Bizot, he'd expected to be tasked with something daunting: theft of an artifact, uncovering the source of the Voice, or even destroying Arrangement itself. Instead, he'd been tasked with nothing. No orders. No directions. No targets. He was no different from any other Arrangement operative. Figuring that Bizot would eventually reveal his master plan, this lack of knowledge had merely bothered Isaac.

Until now.

The Voice had, at best, foreseen all the events leading to tonight, or, at worst, engineered them to happen. Even the choices Isaac made with free will had kept him on the path. How could one hope to infiltrate an organization that could see the future or read minds? Even if he knew his objective, how could he hope to succeed?

Ignorance is the point.

Bizot's message on the mirror stuck in his head. His mind couldn't be read if it remained empty of details? A witless spy couldn't be outfoxed? He would have laughed at the absurdity of it if the trail of the dead behind him weren't so long.

He came to an empty intersection. The red traffic light swung on its power lines with the gusty wind. Each road loomed darkly. He had no idea where he was or where he was heading. Did his choice even matter? He pulled Jughead from the everbag.

"Finally! Where's that enraged Pandemonium demon? Ready to flay your flesh, I'm sure." It paused. "Wait. Where are we? Are we driving? Damn it!"

"Sorry to disappoint you."

"This is such bullshit. How did you survive? Is life just continuously unfair? You must be the luckiest mortal I've ever encountered."

Isaac snorted at the statement. "I'll cut you a deal. You do me one favor and I'll leave you out of the bag for the night. I'll even prop you up so you can see out the window as we drive."

"See out the window? Now I'm some kind of dog that enjoys watching the scenery go speeding by? I mean, okay, sure, that's not bad, but still. Piss off."

"Just tell me which way you think I should drive."

"Sure. Drive right into oncoming traffic, dickhead."

Isaac gave up and shoved the jug back into the bag. He sighed and tapped the steering wheel, before turning to the cat. "Okay, which way do you think we should go?"

Testiculies hissed several times before shutting his good eye and curling into a ball on the passenger seat.

"'Allies' my ass." Putting the truck into gear, he turned with the wind, figuring that was the easiest way for an albatross to fly. He had no destination in mind, and for the time being, that was the best he could hope for.

Chapter 35
BOILING BLOOD

In Clarksville, Tennessee, witch-hunter Fergus Unger attempted to drink his grief away as he waited impatiently for his cast-bound arm to heal. He had been prepared to start the hunt for his brother's killer the moment that the anesthesia from the surgery wore off. But once again, his socially inept giant of a brother was the voice of reason. While the best—and only available—course of action, it also resulted in Fergus drinking too much outside of a rented mobile home, while Aldo passed the time reading old copies of gardening magazines.

"This is ridiculous. We could at least be searching for the guy. Even if we don't take him out, we could get some leads," Fergus complained.

"Our people are looking into it. These matters cannot be rushed. Rules cannot be broken if we wish to maintain our professionalism. We must wait for the family heads to decide, and we both know that process takes time. Be patient. Remember, revenge is a dish..."

"Best served cold. I know, I know."

Aldo frowned. "I was going to say, 'best served methodically prepared.' But if you want to go with that nonsensical cliché, go right ahead."

"That's not… It means… Forget it." His arm began to ache, and he reached for his painkillers.

Aldo snatched his hand. Fergus was a strong man, but even he felt helpless in that grip. "Alcohol or opioids. Not both."

"Fine. Fine. Don't break my good wrist." Fergus went back to his bottle of rye. "It's just that waiting here is going to drive me nuts."

"Then do something constructive."

"Like what?"

"Learn something. For instance…" Aldo narrowed his eyes at the current page of his gardening magazine. "Did you know that aspirin was originally made from willow tree bark? I bet you didn't. Now you do, and hence, you've done something constructive with your time."

If Aldo weren't his brother, Fergus would never be able to tolerate the man. Patience was more than a virtue to Aldo—it was almost an autonomic response. He could no more be restless than he could forget to breathe. For a hunter, it proved an enviable trait. But at times like this, when Fergus felt edgy and eager for action, it just endlessly agitated him.

But Aldo was right. A hunt should always be done with quiet patience and cold resolve. Fergus knew the time for revenge would come, and he took some solace in knowing that the wait would just make his blood boil even more.

* * *

In the Reliquary, like a monarch surveying her kingdom, the woman known as Hellebore watched the nightly party in the Great Hall from her private balcony. Her arms, neck, and face—the flesh not covered by her gown—swirled with a kaleidoscope of colors. Periodically, this living ink would merge into forms, painting itself into tattoos that animated across her. Trees appeared on her back. Leaves waved in an unfelt wind. Exotic fish swam up from her wrists to her shoulders, bubbles coming from their mouths that then floated across her neck to disappear into her hairline. All these images would then dissolve, colors melting back together, and the process would begin anew, with different forms.

It was Lucille who came and whispered into her ear that Peter Goss's mansion burned to the ground. Hellebore digested the information without a flinch. On a subliminal cue, her ink twisted into flames, flickering along her forearms, with smoke and cinders ascending to her shoulders and twirling tornado-like around her neck.

Disaster certainly seemed to follow her foolish friend, and it saddened her that someday Isaac would be too slow to outrun it.

But she had no intention of running alongside him.

* * *

Only a few blocks over from the Reliquary, on the top floor of the building referred to in secret as the Iron Embassy, Ambassador Murray had just finished tasking her diviners with delving into the many workings of Arrangement once again. It was a tough veil to pierce, and not without inherent risks. She would love to pass this investigation on to her superiors, those who lurked beyond and wielded much more substantial tools, but like all the great powers of the world, Hell seemed content to let Arrangement call the tunes. Maybe on her last day of service—which would probably be her last day of life—she'd find the highest-ranking devil she could and tell him or her to make Hell grow a pair again.

So, all she could currently do was relinquish her inquisitiveness to her underlings and see what they could uncover. If one of them crossed a forbidden line, it would be a small matter to serve their head up to the offended party. The Embassy had no shortage of staff.

A just-opened beer and a fresh Cuban cigar sat on her desk. Another day, another thirty pieces of silver, she thought as she reached for the intercom to tell security she was clocking out for the night. Before she could tap the button, a knock came out her door. At her beckoning, the guards let in a harried young woman carrying a still-sizzling frying pan.

"Ambassador," the woman panted. "I must speak with you."

"Collect yourself, Cybil, and then explain."

"Signs," Cybil said, and she tilted the pan so the Ambassador could view its contents. Inside, steaming as if just pulled from the stove, was a layer of dark-crimson offal. The blood was still boiling, chunks of organs simmering in the foul broth. Cybil took a finger capped with a metal-hooked thimble and stirred around the contents. The woman was the Embassy's chief haruspex, practitioner of an archaic and foul practice that rarely produced desirable information. But they had wanted to leave no stone unturned.

"I can't read guts. And did you really need to bring the pan with you? My office will reek for hours." To cover the odor, the Ambassador lit up her cigar.

The rebuke only added to Cybil's unease. "I'm sorry, Ambassador. I just wanted to be sure I brought proof."

"Well, you certainly brought something. Now, explain."

"There's been a ripple in the air. A twist. A flap of wings that may spin into a hurricane."

Murray puffed the cigar. "Knock off the theatrics and start yakking about what's happening."

The scryer coughed to clear her throat and started over. "I believe one of the tarot cards you wanted us to watch for has been used."

This caught the Ambassador's attention. "Go on."

"It was a minor effect. I may not have even noticed if you hadn't specified for us to be on the lookout. But that's not why I rushed to you."

Murray tapped ash into her crystal tray. "No?"

She shook her head. "It was what I saw after the card was played that startled me. A premonition. The strongest I've ever had. So many details that I'm sure I missed some. This card was just a key, undoing the first tumbler to a very large lock. But I believe it will set more in motion."

"Like?" The Ambassador restrained a sigh. Talking to these diviners was like conversing with toddlers, one just had to keep leading them.

"I saw a horned demigod awakened with renewed purpose. A prison swamped in a yellow mist, but the doors were blown open and the cells empty. A smiling pestilence that walked like a man unleashed on the earth. I saw unbreakable chains snapping like twigs and bleeding like severed veins, hundreds of eyes going black. And finally, I saw a set of manacles unlocked, falling away into the void. There may have been more. The images flashed too fast for me to absorb them all."

"That's quite a loaded frying pan." The Ambassador blew a cloud of smoke. "What were the manacles securing?"

She stared at her pan. "It's hard to put into words. But I'd have to say it's everything we know. Everything we are." She drew her metal finger through the congealing blood with a shrill screech, one last examination. "Whatever Arrangement is setting in motion will unshackle the world. All chains will fall away." She let out a body-sagging sigh, as if relaying the information had been a massive physical strain.

Ambassador Murray maintained her flat affect. "Ah. Is that it? No lotto numbers or football scores?" The quip visibly rattled Cybil and she began to stutter, fearing she had disappointed her master. Before the young woman could fall to her knees and beg forgiveness (Murray hated when they did that), she reassured the shaken scryer. "Easy, Cybil. I apologize. That's a bad joke on my part. You've done well. Write this up in detail so I can review it later, and then take the rest of the night off. Go out to eat. Catch a movie. Buy some new cookware and just throw that pan away. Then tomorrow, back to the frying-guts grind."

Alone again, the Ambassador puffed the cigar and stared out the window. A Black Tarot card had been played. Unknown things had been set in motion. Perhaps she had been wrong about the albatross' wingspan and now they were all caught up in the wake.

Regardless of the portent of doom, she suddenly felt invigorated, younger than she had in centuries. The Manhattan nightscape sparkled in a manner she hadn't noticed in years. For now, she couldn't guess the meaning of Cybil's vision, but as far as she was concerned, a world unchained would be a more interesting place.

Chapter 36
THE RED WASTES

Long after emergency services arrived to combat the blaze at the Goss Mansion, a pair of eyes continued to watch from a nearby grove. The large albino owl stretched one talon, then the other, before ending its vigil by taking flight with a flap of its massive wings. It sailed through the plume of smoke above the smoldering ruins and then veered into the night.

Ahead of it, a shimmer appeared in the air, a sparkling slash that cut the sky and peeled apart, like a mouth opening, which the owl passed through without pause. Then it soared across a much different landscape. A purple sky dotted with blue stars that didn't twinkle, as if frozen in time. Below it stretched endless red sands, dunes rolled like waves. The bird continued until it reached a ruin of old buildings partially reclaimed by the desert.

A man sat on a flight of stone steps. He was sharpening a row of knives and axes, finishing one and setting each delicately, almost reverently, on the step above him. Nude and covered in scars, he bore the consequences of having scores of body parts replaced over his centuries of life. Upon seeing the owl, he stood up and stretched out his arm. The owl landed, its talons digging in and piercing the skin. Ludworth didn't care. Little blood flowed and the pain barely registered.

The stitch stroked along the feathers, first with his hand, then with his cheek. His nerve endings didn't work well enough to feel the softness, but comfort was not his intention. It was how he read what the bird had witnessed.

"Oh, that fool. Using a powerful artifact without permission. The master will not approve," he said to the owl, to which it simply blinked. It was only an owl, after all.

Or perhaps the master would approve, the stitch thought with annoyance as he ascended the stairs. He could make no predictions on how the Faceless Magician would react to news involving Isaac. The rules applied to the former apprentice until suddenly, *inexplicably*, they didn't. Ludworth despised the scores of apprentices the master took but was always rewarded as each invariably failed and perished, often at his own hand. But somehow Isaac endured, prospered even, and it made the stitch hate his master's favorite student all the more.

Ludworth reached the end of the winding stairs and, with head bowed, slowly entered the simple room at the top of the tower. His hooded master sat cross-legged on the floor, surrounded by stacks of books arranged in perfectly balanced towers.

The only source of light was a figurine centered on the master's desk. Carved from clear crystal, it depicted a robed angel, wings spread wide but head down. Her hands were pressed together, not in prayer, but fist to fist, a length of chain affixing them. From within the statuette glowed an ethereal luminescence. It fluctuated with light-house intensity, alternately blinding Ludworth and leaving him sightless in near darkness.

He hated the figurine. At its peak, the light stung his eyes. And the rhythm of the pulsing had a cadence he detested, almost perfectly matching that of a beating heart. He'd once asked the Faceless Magician about its origin and purpose and the curiosity had cost him a hand for three months. Now he just did his best to ignore it.

"Excuse the interruption, Lord Bizot, but there's news." His master didn't respond, only turned a page of the book in his lap. "Isaac news," Ludworth specified, and he seethed as the name drew a reaction.

Bizot turned to look at him, his skin reflecting the light like a mirror and his eyes ablaze, one red and one blue. "Oh, good," he said.

Ludworth spoke with a malicious grin, an eager snitch ratting out a rival. He relayed everything he'd seen from the owl. The stitch's voice trailed off as he ran out of details meant to rile the Faceless Magician into the rage he'd expected.

"Really stirring the pot, isn't he?" the master replied, his voice still annoyingly even. When the crystal angel light oscillated to darkness, the magician all but disappeared. Only the glowing eyes floated there until the light returned.

"He's violated the rules, yet again. This trespass is worse than his others. He used a powerful artifact simply to save his own hide. Such a prize should have been presented to you immediately. This disrespect cannot be allowed. Now, I beg of you, let me take his head. Then we'll round up all the students he put into hiding and bring them back to where they belong. Enough is enough."

"Is it? Patience, my friend. Certainly, under normal circumstances, I'd agree with you. But the tide is strange. Don't you feel it? No, of course you don't, not with those deadened nerve endings. Change is coming. I can sense it, even from this damnable dimension. And change brings conflict. Do you know how to predict the coming of bloodshed?" he asked, and then he answered himself before the stitch could speak. "The powers that be will start lining up their pawns to endure the first wave. And as you know, thanks to Isaac, I'm currently shorthanded on such pieces. So, for now, we'll wait and see how things play out."

The stitch trembled with impotent anger but knew better than to object. "As you wish."

"Fear not. We'll visit Isaac again soon enough." Bizot closed his book and set it delicately on one of the carefully balanced towers. "It never hurts to remind him that in all matters, great and small, he's damned if he does and damned if he doesn't," he said with a metrical cadence as if singing a nursery rhyme, and he waved a hand to conduct a nonexistent orchestra. "And that is the price and enduring consequence of his freedom." The Faceless Magician then dismissed his servant and returned to his books.

END OF BOOK ONE

ACKNOWLEDGMENTS

First and foremost, thank you, Rebecca, for your unwavering, often taskmaster levels of encouragement. And to Maggie and Fynn, thanks for pretending to be interested when I explained plot lines.

I'd like to express hearty gratitude to my core group of supporters—Shellie, Kim, Stacey, and Paul. I know I said if the book ever made a dozen dollars I'd give you each three. That was a lie.

And a very broad thank you to the countless acquaintances, fellow writers, and book clubbers I've encountered over the years. Isaac Unknown is very different now than from the first draft, so thank you to anyone who took the time to provide feedback. This is the finally finalized final version.

And to MoonQuill, thank you for the opportunity.

ABOUT THE AUTHOR

James McFadden was born in Virginia and raised in northeast Ohio. He graduated from Kent State University with a BA in Psychology and few appreciable job skills. He enjoys collecting fine scotches to save for special occasions and then refuses to celebrate anything. Currently, he resides in Columbus, Ohio, with his wife, two kids, and Milo the Pomsky.

Isaac Unknown is his first novel.

Thank you for reading a MoonQuill original novel. More exciting stories can be found on at www.moonquill.com and on our platform, www.moonquillnovels.com

We would greatly appreciate it if you could take a moment to leave a review. Every review helps the author and supports their ability to continue writing fantastic books for everyone to enjoy!

Want to know when the next release drops? Join our mailing list by scanning the QR code below! You'll get 4 additional e-books for free!